DESCENT

INTO HELL

GEORGE ENCIZO

ISBN-13: 9781548160883
ISBN-10: 1548160881
Library of Congress Control Number: 2017909662
CreateSpace Independent Publishing Platform
North Charleston, South Carolina

Printed in the United States of America

Night falls and the darkness never sleeps

DESCENT

INTO HELL

CHAPTER 1

Tommy Benson leaned back in his chair with his hands behind his head and his alligator boots on the desk—smug in the feeling that his meeting with a prospective client had gone well. He picked up the picture on the credenza of Rhonda sandwiched between him and Eddie holding the framed contract with their first customer. Then he rubbed the top of his head, remembering the hangover the morning after hard partying the night before. Tommy was one of three partners in Benson and Hicks LLC, a design and architectural construction firm.

When his cell phone rang, he set the picture down, sat up, reached for his phone and read the text. *Finished appntmnt. Will meet rest park lot. LUR.*

Tommy felt a rush of warmth. "Love you, too."

The woman who'd texted him was Rhonda Hicks, his partner's wife.

He reached for his Bass Pro Shops ball cap and left his office.

"I'm going to lunch now, Doris." He smiled. "Rhonda may not be back until later this afternoon. If she's not back by the time you have to leave, lock up and go home. I have an appointment after lunch, so I'll see you tomorrow."

Doris smiled. "Thanks, Tommy, I'll see you tomorrow."

Doris had surmised long ago that Tommy and Rhonda were having an affair. But she minded her own business because as a single mother, she needed the job. Doris felt sorry for Eddie Hicks, Rhonda's husband, as she knew what it was like to have a cheating spouse.

In the parking lot of the Fish Tail restaurant in a small shopping center northeast of town, Tommy pulled his pickup truck alongside Rhonda's little blue sedan. She wore a short skirt and sexy blouse, which made her thirty-four-year-old slim figure look quite attractive. Her long hair was tied in a ponytail, which accentuated her long neck and narrow jaw line. Tommy, also thirty-four, wore casual pants and a tight-fitting polo shirt to show off his muscles.

"Damn, Rhonda, you look good." He wrapped his arms around her and caught the familiar scent of the lavender perfume he'd bought for her birthday.

"Not here, Tommy, someone might see us. But thanks for the compliment."

Tommy removed his arms; they went into the restaurant, ordered a light lunch of sushi, and sake to drink.

Tommy put his hand on Rhonda's. "You ready, babe."

She winked and smiled. "Yes, let's go."

After lunch, Rhonda left her car in the parking lot so they could drive to Tommy's house together. He smiled at her as she hopped into the passenger seat and they drove to his house.

Tommy owned a small bungalow in the northeast section of town. He'd done some landscaping in the front yard to make it a comfortable looking home. He pulled into the garage as he always did to avoid the neighbors and closed the garage door. They got out of his truck and went into the house. The only woman Tommy hadn't brought into his house through the garage was Irene, who parked her car in the driveway.

Tommy and Rhonda's affair had started in college. She wasn't just another one of his conquests; she was someone special to him.

Rhonda didn't feel she was cheating on her husband Eddie, who was also Tommy's best friend, since she and Tommy were in love and had plans that included a future together. Both had tried to avoid their feelings for each other long ago. Unfortunately, they were unable to control their desires.

Once inside, they went right to the bedroom and hastily undressed. Tommy took the time to admire her well-tanned, shapely body and her perfectly rounded breasts. While he admired her, Rhonda moved close to him and rubbed her palms over his muscular physique.

She whispered, "Tommy, make me forget that Eddie's coming home tonight."

He kissed her on the lips. "I'll try to make us both forget."

They got in bed; he took her in his arms, kissed her tenderly for several moments, cupped her breasts and fondled them.

"Now, Tommy, take me, please."

The bedroom door was left open because Tommy lived alone and it wasn't necessary for discretion as they were the only ones in the house.

Suddenly Tommy felt an icy chill run down his spine and sensed a presence in the room. He sat up straight.

"Tommy, what's the matter?"

Neither Tommy or Rhonda had heard the front door open, and someone enter the house. That morning when Tommy had retrieved the newspaper from his driveway, he'd been in such a hurry to meet with a prospective client that he'd forgotten to lock the front door.

Tommy turned toward the door, and his face became ashen when he noticed the intruder. "What the hell—how did you get in here?"

"Idiot, your front door wasn't locked. You son of a bitch, how could you do this after being warned and with her of all people?"

When Tommy saw the shotgun, he panicked and immediately got out of bed—fearing the worst for him and Rhonda.

"What the hell are you doing with that shotgun? Are you crazy?"

"Fuck you, Tommy—I'll show you what crazy is, you bastard!"

The blast from the shotgun hit Tommy in the gut and knocked him against the nightstand, knocking over the lamp.

"How's that for crazy? Now this one's for fun."

The second shot also hit him in the stomach causing him to fall back against the wall before he sank to the floor.

Rhonda saw Tommy lying on the floor all bloody and feared that she would end up like him—all their plans would be over, and she'd never see Eddie or her parents ever again.

She backed up against the headboard, saw the evil in the killer's eyes, and held her palms up. "No please don't. I'm…"

"Too late, you should have thought about leaving Tommy alone a long time ago, you bitch!"

The shotgun blast hit Rhonda in the chest. Like Tommy, blood poured from her wound and splattered all over the bed.

"That's what you get for fucking him! What the hell, one more time just for fun. Here we go, ready, aim, fire. Oh hell, once more for old time's sake."

The second and third shots splattered blood like a Jackson Pollock painting.

The killer closed the door and left Tommy and Rhonda alone in their final moments.

"See ya, Tommy. I'm gone." I showed him and that lousy bitch. He'll never get to take advantage of anyone again. I should have done this a long time ago. No one will know I was in town, and they'll never find the shotgun.

CHAPTER 2

Sheriff JD Pickens lived in the Waterford Lakes subdivision, an upscale neighborhood in the northeast section of Creek City, with his wife and daughter. It was a white-collar family friendly neighborhood with a vest pocket park. They lived on Walkabout Circle on a cul-de-sac, in a three-bedroom house. It had a pleasantly landscaped front yard and a spacious back yard, well shaded by an assortment of trees. And the house had central air conditioning.

Pickens walked into the kitchen where the window and sliding glass doors were open letting in fresh air. The aroma of freshly brewed coffee, fried eggs, and bacon permeated his nostrils. Another pleasant morning in the Pickens household.

"Oh man, that smells good," he said with a grin.

"Sit down, and I'll fix a plate for you," said his wife.

He sat and waited for his breakfast.

His wife, Dr. Marge Davids, the county medical examiner, and the little angel with her was their seven-year-old daughter Sarah. Both had just finished breakfast.

JD Pickens was the sheriff of a small rural county in Central Florida with a population of 16,375, and two cities. Creek City, with

12,397 residents, was the largest and located in the northern part of the county. Warfield, the other, with 3,978 inhabitants, was located thirty-five miles to the south. The remainder of the residents lived in several small towns. Both cities had mayors, but the County Commission handled business affairs for the entire county. Warfield had a two-man police force, but the sheriff's office was the primary law enforcement agency.

Marge set Pickens' plate in front of him, winked and smiled.

Bailey, their dog, just came in from his morning ritual, sat at Pickens' feet, and gazed up with his penetrating eyes—he wanted another slice of bacon. Pickens reached across the table, snatched the last slice, and let it slip from his fingers. Bailey caught it in midair and gobbled it up in a New York minute.

Marge shook her head and pursed her lips. "You're spoiling that dog, quarterback." It was her nickname for him since he was once a high school and college quarterback, but JD was the name everyone else called him.

Pickens parents were devoted Christians and turned to the Bible for his birth names. They chose Joshua and Daniel. He hated the names and asked his friends to call him just Josh.

That lasted until he entered high school and played football. The star running back and his close friend nicknamed him JD, and it'd been with him since.

Unfortunately, his circle of friends had dwindled since the running back, Leroy Jones, was black and the son of the local AME Church minister, who Like Pickens father, had worked at MacLeay's Lumber Yard.

Pickens didn't care what others thought. His parents raised him to be respectful of others' differences, and the friendship remains.

Both boys had worked at the Ace Hardware during summers. They shared a love of football, fishing, country rock, and barbecue. Leroy often said someday he would own a barbecue restaurant like

Charlie's Smokehouse on Main Street. Charlie's was a favorite spot for the high school students, especially on Friday nights after football games.

When Pickens was single, he was a lady's man and always flashed his state championship ring to get dates. The girls loved him, but there was one who wouldn't even give him the time of day. An attractive and athletic-looking six-foot brunette named Marge Davids. He met her when called to a horrible accident scene—in which two women were killed when their vehicle went off the road and landed in a ditch. Davids was there as the medical examiner's assistant. She was from Lake Grove and had graduated from Emory University's medical school. She took the position as assistant medical examiner to apprentice under the chief medical examiner, Doctor Winton Torrington, who promised her she'd become the chief medical examiner after he retired.

Pickens tried everything he could to get a date with her almost to the extreme of stalking her. She wasn't impressed by his championship ring as she had her own in volleyball from Suwanee High School in Lake Grove.

When he first approached her, she asked him, "What's a hotshot football player with a law degree doing as a sheriff's deputy?"

"I practiced law for a few years but got the itch to return to my hometown and go into law enforcement," he answered. "What are you doing as an assistant medical examiner with your credentials?"

Marge's ears turned red when she replied. "Well, for your information, forensic science is what I've always been interested in, and I received an offer to work here with the promise of becoming the medical examiner. Satisfied?"

"Hey, you asked me, so I get to ask you. It's only fair. But yes, I'm satisfied."

They both had good reasons for being in the county, but he still hadn't impressed her. After a year of practically pleading for a date, he learned that she enjoyed football, but she was a Georgia Tech fan and he was a Seminole. To find common ground, he wagered her on the outcome of the Georgia, Georgia Tech game. Naturally, he chose Georgia. If they won, she had to go on a date with him. Fortunately, Georgia won, and she honored her bet.

Pickens took her to the Bucket & Boots Country and Western Bar and soon learned that she enjoyed line dancing, could hold her own while drinking Jim Beam shots with beer chasers, and was quite adept at gigging frogs. But being the granddaughter of a veterinarian, Marge drew the line at hunting. Still, she was his kind of woman.

A year later they were married. It was the same year Pickens ran for sheriff. That first year was a sad one as Marge lost their first child when she fell and had a miscarriage. Marge's doctors told her because of the accident she could never conceive. Amy Tucker offered her service as a family counselor and helped them over their grief. Two years later, Dr. Torrington kept his promise and she was named the medical examiner—but kept her maiden name. She used the initials MDP—and included them in her license plate number—MDPME. Sarah was their second child, and they considered her their miracle.

Pickens looked from Marge to the dog and made no attempt to hide his happy face. "It was the last piece. Besides, he deserves to be spoiled just like his momma, wide receiver." His nickname for her was because she was always there for him. "Don't you agree, Sarah?"

"Daddy's right, Mommy." Bailey barked. "Even Bailey agrees."

Marge threw her hands up. "I give up with you three. JD, I have an early meeting this morning. Can you take Sarah to school?"

"Sure, what about Annie, do I have to take her too?"

"No, Daddy, it's just you and me."

"Liana has the day off, and she's taking Annie to school. She'll pick up both girls after school and bring them to her house." Marge removed the apron from her waist. "I have to finish dressing and then leave." While Marge left to dress and freshen up, Pickens and Sarah finished off the remainder of their breakfasts. When Marge returned, she said, "I have to go, so you guys kiss me goodbye. Oh, and don't forget to stop by your parents' house. Your mom thinks you're avoiding them."

"I'm not avoiding them. I've been busy, and I was just there last weekend."

Marge shook her head. "Try three weekends ago, and fishing doesn't count as busy. You could have at least invited your dad."

He raised his palms. "Okay, all ready." Next, he scratched his collarbone and offered his laconic reply. "Shit! Was it really three weeks ago?"

"Yes, and watch your language."

"You better, young man," Sarah added with hands on hips and evil eyes glaring at him.

Pickens and Marge chuckled.

"Whoops, sorry, Sarah, you're getting more and more like your grandmother. I'll be sure to drop by this weekend."

"Can I go with you, Daddy? I want to visit Gramma and Pop-pop, please."

Pickens smiled. "Sure, sweetheart, we'll take Bailey with us."

"That's a splendid idea. Liana and I can do some shopping while you three go visiting. I have to run now." Marge took a last look in her compact mirror.

"You look awesome, wide receiver. Doesn't mommy look awesome, Sarah?"

Dressed in a white blouse and black slacks, and with her auburn shoulder-length hair, she was something to admire at forty-seven— a year younger than Pickens. She always lit up the room when she entered and caused sparks to fly whenever he saw her.

"You do, Mommy."

Marge smiled. "Thanks, both of you." She loved them both, especially Sarah, but never hovered over her like some helicopter moms did. Pickens and Sarah kissed her goodbye. "Let's hope today's another routine day and no major incidents happen. See you guys tonight." She turned, blew them kisses, went to the garage, and left.

"Say goodbye to Bailey and let's roll, sweetheart."

"Bye Bailey." The dog sat down and licked her face.

Pickens closed the sliding glass door, locked it and they left for Sarah's school.

After dropping Sarah off at school, Pickens headed for his office and the weekly briefing of active cases by his deputies. First, he made a quick stop at Lydia's Bakery Shop to get a dozen doughnuts. Lydia had passed some years ago, and her daughter Maddie now ran the shop. Her daughter Paddy, a single mom, owned the Bagel Factory next door.

The doughnuts were his way of showing appreciation for the deputies' loyalty. Pickens hoped that nothing serious would happen to alter the beautiful morning.

CHAPTER 3

Across town in the northwest section was the Highland Park subdivision, a modest working-class neighborhood. There were 111 home sites each with small yards backing up to a greenspace which afforded more privacy. It wasn't a family friendly neighborhood as all the homes were two bedrooms with one and a half baths designed with adult residents in mind and no amenities. In the evenings, there were pickup trucks, SUVs and compact cars parked in the driveways. During the day, there rarely was a vehicle in the neighborhood because the residents were all at work.

Every Wednesday between nine and nine-thirty, Flora Escuella arrived at 4567 Barrington Drive to clean the home of Tommy Benson. She had been cleaning his house for the past eighteen months. Flora and her husband Fernando were legal immigrants having obtained their green cards two years ago. They had four children, all grade school age. Fernando worked as a plumber, and Flora cleaned houses.

Tommy wasn't the neatest person and often left traces of his romantic liaisons. Flora didn't mind because she needed the work, and Tommy paid her well—more than most of her customers.

When Flora arrived, she noticed Tommy hadn't taken in the newspaper. Thinking he might be out of town, she picked up the paper and carried it to the house. She started to unlock the door but it opened without her key. She thought it strange, but knowing Tommy she wasn't the least bit surprised that he might have left the door unlocked for one of his lady friends the night before.

The first time she cleaned his house her husband asked her what it was like. She told him it was a horrible mess and his mother would probably disown him if she ever saw it. Fernando laughed and said they must make sure their boys don't grow up to be like Tommy.

As soon as she entered the house, a sickening smell troubled her. She put the newspaper on a nearby table, set her cleaning buckets on the floor and then went to each room searching for its source. When she came to his bedroom, she opened the door and what she saw terrified her.

She placed her hands on her cheeks and screamed, *"Madre de Dios!"* Then she grabbed her cleaning buckets, ran out of the house and to her car. She sat down, cried and then dialed 911.

Liz Price, the temporary office assistant, answered the call. Price was dubbed the Crisis Center as all calls went through her, except those that went directly to the sheriff's line as well as the deputies. She also answered what few 911 calls that came in and acted as the daytime dispatcher. Pickens had to do the best he could with his limited budget.

Price was thirty–four years old with brown hair and wore glasses. She had been working for the sheriff the past nine months. She'd replaced Stacey Morgan, who was on indefinite maternity leave. The agency that hired Price also trained her and said Price had excellent credentials. She worked from eight-thirty in the morning to five in the afternoon Monday through Friday and was one of four dispatchers who rotated shifts. Price relieved Matt Riley, who worked the midnight to eight-thirty shift.

Price had difficulty understanding Flora because she could barely speak English.

"Ma'am, slow down. I don't understand what you're saying. Is there someone with you who speaks English?"

"No, I by self. You must send someone. They dead."

Price understood the word dead and the seriousness of the call. She signaled for Billy Thompson, her supervisor and the deputy in charge of dispatching.

"Who's dead, ma'am?

"They. You send someone. Hurry please."

"Okay, what's your location?" Price was doing her best to be patient, especially since Flora said they were dead.

"No understand location."

By now Price was frustrated and again signaled for Deputy Thompson.

"Okay, your address then."

The cleaning lady started to tremble. "Not my address. Is Mr. Benson address."

"Tommy Benson's house, is that where you are?"

"Yes, hurry please."

"Okay, ma'am, stay out of the house and wait until a sheriff's car arrives."

"I wait but you hurry."

Price turned to Thompson. "Who should I send, Billy?"

Thompson checked the log. "Send Ritchie Ortiz, he's of Cuban descent and fluent in Spanish."

Price radioed Ortiz who was in the area and sent him.

When Sheriff's Deputy Richie Ortiz arrived, he found Flora in her car sobbing. He knocked on the window and asked her to roll it down.

"Ma'am, what's the problem here? Did you call 911?"

"*Si*, I did. They in bedroom." She made the sign of the cross and said, "*Madre Mia*! I never see anything so horrible."

"Ma'am, *usted Ingles?*"

"*Si*, some."

"*Bueno*, try and speak as much English as you can. Who's in the bedroom?"

"*Senor Tommy y su amiga. Ellos muertos.*"

"They're both dead?"

"*Si, si.*"

"Wait here. *Cūal es su nombre, Senora?*"

"Flora Escuella. I no go anywhere except home. You go look."

"Okay, Flora, my name is Deputy Ortiz. I'll be right back."

Deputy Ortiz wrote her name on his pad, put gloves on, and entered the house. He walked back to the bedroom and stopped when he saw them. Richie had been to several crime scenes when he was a Jacksonville police officer but never anything like this. Tommy Benson and his lady friend were both naked and lying in pools of blood. Blood was splattered everywhere. Deputy Ortiz clenched his abdomen, bolted out of the house, and emptied his stomach.

When Flora saw him get sick, she got out of the car and started toward him.

"You okay, Deputy Ortiz?"

"Yes, but I have to call the sheriff."

"I can go home now?"

"No, you have to wait until the sheriff gets here."

"But I no go back in house?"

"No, you go wait in your car."

Flora went back to her car and called her husband.

Deputy Ortiz knew who Tommy's lady friend was. She was Rhonda Hicks—the wife of Tommy's partner. He immediately called the sheriff's office and asked to speak with Deputy Thompson.

CHAPTER 4

The one-story white stucco building that housed the sheriff's office located in the downtown part of the city was three blocks from Main Street. The front entrance was typical of most rural office buildings with a glass entryway. In the back of the interior was a locker room and a pair of restrooms. The sheriff's personal office was in the rear near the three cells—one for the men, one for the women, and one for juveniles. Toward the front of the building was an interrogation room, a small conference room and a squad room with desks for the deputies.

At six-foot-three, Sheriff Pickens still had the stocky build that he had in high school, but his brown hair was shorter and had the beginnings of a receding hairline. He was a quarterback for the county's only high school located in Creek City and received a scholarship to play at Florida State University. Unfortunately, he played only one year as an injury ended his career.

After law school, Pickens took a job at a small law firm in Tallahassee but soon tired of being hogtied to a desk and missed his hometown. Because his time was taken up in preparing for cases, Pickens hadn't been partying much. One of his colleagues noticed it and mentioned it to him, and that's when he realized he missed his hometown, hunting, fishing, partying and the women, who didn't judge you by the car you drove but by the age of your pickup truck and the older, the better. Pickens was, after all, just a country boy at heart.

He quit his job as a lawyer and moved back home. Pickens moved in with his parents and secured a part-time position as the backfield coach for his old high school. It wasn't as big a deal as being a big-time college coach, but at least he was back on the sideline under the Friday night lights. He then became a sheriff's deputy in his home county.

Pickens patiently waited his time and kept his nose clean. Six years later, he ran for sheriff when the current sheriff retired. The mayor of Warfield, his family, and a fringe element tried everything they could to ensure his failure, but he won regardless. Being the quarterback that succeeded in getting the county its first and only high school state championship won him enough votes to get elected

The first thing he did as the new sheriff was to dismiss some deputies who were known to push the envelope too far when it came to enforcing the law.

There was nothing pretentious about Sheriff Pickens and his office reflected it—just a desk, two chairs, a water cooler, and no pictures, medals or awards.

Amy Tucker, his senior deputy, and the county's first female deputy, had her own desk and none of the deputies dared to use it. She had known Pickens and his wife for many years and was also a licensed family counselor. Before being hired by Pickens, she was a police officer in Orlando for eight years and rose to the rank of sergeant. Amy grew up in Ocala and was the daughter of a police officer who raised her as a single mom. She loved catfish and taters and grew up on them.

Her streaked, dirty-blonde hair was always tied in a ponytail. Although not quite the shape of a fashion model, she had a nice figure and made quite an impression in her uniform. She was the same age as Pickens. Sergeant Tucker was in charge of the bullpen, the area where Billy Thompson and whatever deputy was in house at the time were situated. The other deputies treated her as they would their mother since she was decades older than most of them.

Sheriff Pickens was meeting with his deputies. In attendance besides Amy were Billy Thompson and Zeke Jackson. Sergeant Mia Dunne was on video conference. Sergeant Dunne and Deputy Jackson were both African Americans. Dunne was in charge of the Warfield satellite office. The same fringe element that didn't want him elected vehemently protested her hiring, but he ignored them.

Pickens and his deputies were discussing their current cases— which were mostly routine—but none as severe as the accident years ago, when two women driving North on US 441 went off the road and died when their car rammed into a ditch.

Things were about to change when the telephone rang.

Billy answered and listened as Deputy Richie Ortiz told him about their newest case. Billy said he would tell the sheriff and to wait until he got there.

When he hung up, Pickens gave him an inquisitive look. "What was that about?"

"We got a dilemma, Sheriff."

All eyes turned toward Billy. They knew about his new word a day thing.

Pickens shook his head. "What's the problem?"

"That 911 call I sent Richie on turned out to be a double homicide at the Benson residence."

"Who was killed?" asked Amy.

"Tommy Benson and Rhonda Hicks. They were found in bed together. Damn, I went to high school with them. And Tommy lives in the same subdivision as I do."

"What about Eddie? What happened to him?"

"Don't know where he is, Amy. I went to school with him, too. Maybe we have a pissed-off husband."

"Who's Eddie, Amy?" asked Pickens.

"He's Rhonda's husband and Tommy's business partner."

"Shit, just what we need. Meeting's adjourned. Sergeant Dunne, you stay safe."

"You too, Sheriff."

Pickens stood and pointed at Sergeant Tucker. "Amy, you and I are going to the crime scene. Billy, call the ME and tell her we're on our way. Then do some background on all of them. And find out where Hicks is."

Billy Thompson was known for his computer skills and could get information that others couldn't—sometimes from questionable sources. In addition to a laptop, Billy had a desktop setup that included two sixteen by twenty-four-inch monitors, wireless keyboards, mouse, and a wireless printer. Because of his magic fingers on the keyboard, he was considered the pulse of the office and his area deemed the Nerve Center.

No one ever questioned where he got his information from as long as it was helpful.

"Zeke, be ready. I'm sure I'm going to need you."

"Sure thing. I'll stay here with Billy. Maybe I can help. I knew all three of them, too."

"Zeke, everybody knew all three of them," said Amy.

Pickens stared at them, and they quickly turned and went about their business.

"You know where the house is, Amy?" asked Pickens.

"Everybody knows where Tommy lives," Amy replied.

"Then you drive." Unlike his predecessor, Pickens drove an all-wheel SUV. He tossed her the keys. "And no accidents you hear me?"

"Who me, Sheriff?"

"Yes, you, let's get a move on."

Amy raised her hand, dangled the keys, and drove to the Benson residence. When they arrived, Pickens was pleased to see that Deputy Ortiz had everything under control, the scene taped

off, and a sufficient barrier around the residence. He'd even had
Mrs. Escuella park her car in the street.

"Afternoon, Sheriff. The tech guys are inside. The ME is in
there also. It's not a pretty scene."

"Fill me in on what we know so far."

"Mrs. Escuella, Tommy's cleaning lady, discovered the bodies.
She saw the bodies and left the house. She never entered the bed-
room." Deputy Ortiz shook his head. "Poor woman is all broken up.
She wants to go home."

Pickens looked at Mrs. Escuella. "Did she see anyone go in or
out of the house and does she know if there have been other women
with Benson?"

"I'll ask her." Deputy Ortiz walked over and asked Mrs.
Escuella the sheriff's questions and then walked back. "She says she
saw no one go in or out. But she did say that she knows Tommy
had other women because when she changed the bed there was
always a different perfume smell." He looked toward her car. "Can
she go home now, Sheriff? She's terribly shaken up."

"Did she touch anything?"

"Just the front door and the bedroom door. Forensics already
printed her."

"Okay, send her home. You have her address and phone
number?"

"Yes." The deputy told Mrs. Escuella that she could go home.
She waved to Pickens and left.

"Okay, Richie, now fill me in with what you know."

"Whoever the perpetrator was, he must have surprised the two
victims because they're both naked. From the blood spatter, it looks
like he used a shotgun." Ritchie took a deep breath. "Sheriff, the
bedroom looks like a Jackson Pollock painting. Most likely it was a
crime of passion."

"Where are the victims' vehicles?" asked Pickens.

"Tommy's truck is in the garage. I haven't touched it. I figured
you'd want to. Rhonda's husband, Eddie, could be the killer."

"It's possible he is, but let's wait until we get the crime scene results and the ME's report. Billy's trying to find Hicks. Maybe he's out of town. Amy and I will check his office." Pickens looked up and down the block. "Where are all the neighbors? There should be someone gawking to see what's going on. Damn if it doesn't look like a ghost town."

"It's been like this since I got here. Haven't seen anybody."

"Billy lives in the subdivision. Call him and ask if this is normal."

"I'll do it right now."

"Come on Amy; we got work to do." Pickens paused. "We're gonna do the residence too."

"Sheriff, before you go inside you better put on latex gloves and booties. The ME won't be happy if you mess up her crime scene." Deputy Ortiz nodded toward the street. "That's the nosey reporter's car across the street. He was asking questions, said he suspected a homicide and wanted to know who the victims were. I said no comment and chased him off."

Pickens looked across the street. "Good answer and keep him away. He'll make up a story anyway. Let's go inside, Amy, and thanks for the heads up, Ritchie."

Pickens and Amy put on gloves and booties, entered the house and went to the bedroom.

Benson's bedroom was unlike any that would have suited Pickens and his wife. The color of the walls was a dark gray, the furniture was a dark mahogany, and Benson's pillow shams and bedspread were a pomegranate color. When he entered the bedroom, the horrible sight made him agree with Deputy Ortiz's description of a Pollack painting.

The ME was still taking pictures of the bodies.

"Morning, Marge, what's it look like?"

She couldn't believe he'd asked. "What's it look like?" She saw the look of dismay on his face and decided to be more agreeable.

Dr. Davids was an incredibly attractive woman who turned heads at the annual Grower's Festival dressed in tight-fitting jeans, heels, and a halter top that exposed her back. Pickens was proud to show her off as his eye candy. But you couldn't tell that now because she was dressed in a white coverall due to the nature of the crime scene and wearing glasses.

"Based on the blood spatter and the entry wounds, it appears the weapon was a shotgun." She pointed to the bodies. "My best guess is that this was a crime of passion. One shotgun blast would have killed them, but there were multiple shots." Dr. Davids paused for effect. "Whoever did this was severely pissed off. I'll have more for you after I examine the bodies."

"Thanks, Marge. So much for a routine day, huh? Any shell casings?"

She shook her head. "Yeah, so much. No casings, and my techs are checking the whole house for fingerprints."

"How about TOD?" Pickens asked.

"Best guess, sometime yesterday. I'll have a better idea after I do the autopsy." She smiled. "I'll see you later."

As they left the bedroom, Amy said, "Why don't we go to the offices of Benson and Hicks before we go to the Hicks' residence, maybe their office assistant knows something?"

"Okay, Amy, but first let's check Benson's truck for any evidence."

"Make sure you keep those gloves on," Dr. Davids called out. Then she lowered her glasses. "I don't want any unnecessary fingerprints when my guys go over it." Dr. Davids was also in charge of the crime lab. "Same for the Hicks' residence. And don't remove anything you find." She folded her arms. "Is that clear enough, Sheriff?"

His eyes opened wide. "Clear enough, Doc."

They went to the garage, walked around the truck and opened the doors. The scent of a woman's perfume was prominent. Amy

opened the glove compartment and found the typical contents—
registration, vehicle manual, some unpaid parking tickets plus a
receipt for the Fish Tail Restaurant dated the previous afternoon.
She handed it to Pickens.

He checked the receipt for a date and time. "It looks like they
had lunch there yesterday. Maybe we should go there also after we
see the office."

"I know that restaurant. They serve great sushi."

"Okay, let's go. I suppose you know where Benson and Hicks'
office is too?"

She grinned. "Everybody knows." He shook his head, and they
left.

When they stepped outside, Deputy Ortiz was waiting.

"I talked to Billy, and he said it's not unusual to see none of the
neighbors during the day since they all work. He also said the best
time to interview neighbors would be in the evening when most are
home."

"Shit. Thanks, Richie," Pickens replied with his usual expletive.
"We're heading to their office now."

CHAPTER 5

The offices of Benson and Hicks, an architectural construction firm, were located in a light business district in the northern part of the city. They occupied two store fronts, one for the architectural firm and the other for the construction company. Amy told Pickens that from what she knew Benson ran the construction business while Hicks oversaw the architecture business.

When Pickens and Amy arrived, he asked Amy who the woman locking the door was.

"Maybe she's their assistant, let's ask her."

The attractive woman in casual attire, who appeared to be in her late thirties with shoulder-length brown hair and brown-rimmed eyeglasses, hesitated when she saw the sheriff's vehicle. She reached into her purse and gripped the gun she hid in it—concerned that the sheriff was there for her. She glanced at her car and wondered if she could pull the weapon from her purse in time to shoot her way out of the situation. But that wouldn't fare well for her and her children. She gripped the gun so tight that her knuckles turned white.

"Sheriff Pickens. I was just closing up." The woman attempted to remain calm, hoping Pickens' purpose there was for something other than her.

Both Pickens and Amy had noticed her apprehension. Being law enforcement officers, their instincts caused them to step in her path automatically.

The woman held tight to the gun in her purse and feigned a smile. "What brings you here today?"

Pickens raised his eyebrows while Amy focused on the woman's purse.

"Mind if I ask your name?" Pickens asked.

"It's Doris Young. We've never met. Probably a good thing, but I'm curious as to why you're here."

"Let's go inside, and I'll explain. I also have some questions to ask you."

"Sure." Doris considered making her escape but worried if she failed, who'd get custody of her children. She removed her hand from her purse. "Please, come in. Should I make a pot of coffee?"

"No thanks, but I appreciate the offer. Are any of your bosses around, Ms. Young?"

"Please, call me Doris." In situations like this, she was advised to remain calm and be friendly. "No, neither is here. Mr. Hicks is out of town on business. Mr. Benson went home early yesterday and hasn't been in today. Neither has Mrs. Hicks."

"How long has Mr. Hicks been out of town?"

Doris felt relieved that it wasn't about her but Eddie. "He's been out of town a lot recently because he's working with a new client. He likes to do that in person, with the plans in front of him, rather than over the phone. Is there a problem with Mrs. Hicks?"

"Tell me, when was the last time you spoke with either Mr. Hicks or Mr. Benson?"

"Mr. Hicks called around lunchtime yesterday to talk to Mr. Benson, but he had already left. He often leaves early when Mr. Hicks is out of town. Mrs. Hicks left early too."

"Is that unusual, the two of them leaving early?"

Concerned again, Doris looked away. "I don't want to get in trouble, Sheriff. I need this job. I have two kids to feed."

"I understand. Just tell me what you know. It's important."

"Sheriff, is there something you're not telling me?" Doris felt agitated and wondered why it was important.

"Ms. Young, I'm afraid we have bad news. Mr. Benson and Mrs. Hicks are both dead. Anything you can tell me will help us find out what happened." Pickens suspected that from the look on her face, Doris was distraught.

"Oh my, that's awful. Were they together?"

Pickens wasn't about to reveal critical information, and since Doris seemed upset he decided to let Amy take over because of her background. He gave Amy the nod indicating to do so.

"Ms. Young..." Amy started to ask but was interrupted.

"Please call me Doris, Deputy."

"Okay, Doris, tell me about Mr. Benson and Mrs. Hicks. You seem to be implying that they often left early when Mr. Hicks was out of town. Were they having an affair?"

Doris rubbed her wrist, nervously deciding what to do. Her concern was that an investigation into the affairs of The Hickses and Benson might lead to one of her. She reconsidered the gun in her purse and if she could get it in time to shoot her way out of the situation.

Both Pickens and Amy wondered if Doris' apprehension might have had a nefarious meaning.

Doris checked her watch. "Is this going to take long? Because I have to pick my children up at school." Suddenly there was fear in her eyes.

"Is there a reason you're hesitating to answer me, Doris?" asked Amy.

"No, it's just that I'm in a hurry."

"Just tell us what you know, and we'll be on our way," said Pickens.

"Yes, they were having an affair and didn't think I suspected anything, but it was evident that something was going on. I believe that it's been going on for quite some time. The three have known each other since high school and college. When Mr. Hicks called looking for Mr. Benson, he seemed annoyed when I told him he'd left early. He then asked if Mrs. Hicks had also left early.

"I didn't want to get anyone in trouble, but I like Mr. Hicks. I felt I should be honest, so I told him they both left early. He said 'Thanks,' then hung up. Mrs. Hicks wasn't the only woman with whom Mr. Benson was having an affair. There were others."

Pickens looked at Amy, and she seemed as surprised as he was. "Did Mr. Hicks know what they were doing?"

"I don't think so."

"Can you tell us where Mr. Hicks is staying, what city he's in?" Amy asked. "Do you have a number for him?"

"He's in Jacksonville at the Park Plus Inn. Here is the number for the hotel and his cell phone number. You can try him at both. I don't know the clients' phone number. He prefers I leave a message at his hotel or call his cell when he is out of town." Doris was gravely concerned for Eddie. "This is awful. He is not going to take the news well. All three of them have been best friends since high school." Once again, she checked her watch. "Do you need me anymore because I really need to go pick up my kids and go home?"

Amy took Doris' information from her. She and Pickens left, but before getting in the SUV Amy asked him if he still wanted to go to the Hicks residence.

"Yes. Let's see if Hicks owns any guns. He probably suspected his partner and wife were having an affair and may also have known about the other women."

"Jacksonville is a long way from Creek City."

"Yes," Pickens replied. "Providing he was there when he called the office."

Doris waited inside until they left and before locking the office, she used several Handi Wipes to wipe down everything she touched, including the doorknob and then left.

Pickens drove by the Hicks residence. He saw no signs of Hicks' car, but decided under the pretense that he was a suspect and on the guise of exigent circumstances, to park and enter the house to look around. Amy used her key kit and unlocked the front door. Hicks' home was well decorated, and there were plenty of pictures of the couple and some with Benson in them.

"See the picture on that shelf of the three of them holding rifles." Pickens pointed to it. "Guess they're hunters, but it doesn't look like they're holding shotguns. Let's make this quick."

"What are we looking for?" Amy asked.

"Obviously not Hicks, but maybe a shotgun. Let's check his office." Hicks had a spare room that he used when working from home. Pickens pointed to a cabinet. "That looks like a gun cabinet. Let's check it."

"What if there is one, what do we do then?"

"We come back with a warrant."

Amy didn't bother to open the glass door. "That empty spot might be where a shotgun should be. Now what?"

Pickens scratched his chin and replied, "We'll have Billy check if there's a shotgun registered to Hicks. Amy, this makes the husband number one on the suspect list and most likely the shooter. We've got to find him somehow."

"Where do we start?"

"With Billy's magic fingers." He laughed. "Billy said he went to high school with all three of them, and Doris stated that they knew each other since high school and college. Maybe the affair started back then."

Amy ran her fingers through her hair. "Maybe, but we can ask Billy."

They closed the residence and headed back to the sheriff's office. Billy hadn't located the whereabouts of Eddie Hicks but said he would keep trying. The ME was scheduled to perform the autopsies in the morning.

"Amy, there's no sense hanging around, so I'm going home. Call me if anything comes up. Otherwise, that's it for today."

"You take care. Say, did you know that Benson and Hicks have been a threesome since high school?"

"Are you serious, a threesome?" Pickens asked.

She shook her head. "Not that way, I mean practically joined at the hips."

Pickens' eyebrows hiked. "Oh. So, how did they end up in business together?"

"Billy said they went to the same college and after graduation, pooled their talents and formed what's now known as Benson and Hicks LLC."

"Interesting to know. Say, how are we doing with next of kin?"

"Billy said that Benson's parents are both dead. Hicks' mother used to live in town, but he can't find an address for her."

"What about Rhonda's?" Pickens inquired.

"I've tried calling her parents and have left several messages. They may be out of town."

"Okay, keep trying. We need to come up with something before the mayor gets on my ass."

CHAPTER 6

Pickens had arrived at the office a little earlier than usual the next day. He was eager to see if there was anything new on the double murder case. Marge was dropping Sarah off at school and then going to the Medical Examiner's office to perform the autopsies as required—even though the cause of death was apparent. All his deputies had arrived early as well, and Pickens had bought fresh doughnuts for all. It didn't hurt that he liked a fresh jelly doughnut with his coffee in the morning.

"The doughnut man arrives.... Welcome Mr. Doughnut Man," shouted Billy.

"You guys keep that up, and I'll eat these doughnuts myself. Amy, you and Billy got anything for me?"

Anxious to tell him, Billy uttered, "I called that hotel where Hicks was supposedly staying, and he was registered there. He checked out at noon Tuesday. It's almost a three-hour drive from Jacksonville to here. I don't see how he could have got here and done the shooting."

"Makes sense, but we still don't know where he is. If he checked out, where did he go? We're aware that he made a call to his office and know he owned a shotgun that's missing from his home, so we got ourselves a quandary. Call that hotel back. Get the exact time he checked out and if he listed an automobile. Amy, put out an APB on Hicks. When Billy knows the make and model of his vehicle, include it."

"On it. Doris Young should know what kind of vehicle he drives. I'll call and ask her."

"Good, and maybe we should go back to their office and see if we can get the names of some clients. We might find out if there were any complaints. For now, Hicks is our prime suspect. We need the ME's report and a more accurate time of death. I'll go see how she's doing."

"Didn't have enough last night, huh? Need another excuse to see her?"

"Careful, Amy, I don't need an excuse to see my wife for your information, and yes, I did get enough last night!"

She blushed. "Way too much information for me."

"Hey, you asked the question."

Marge was just finishing up the autopsy on Rhonda Benson when Pickens walked in. Just as in the accident case, she discovered that Rhonda was approximately six weeks pregnant.

"JD isn't going to like this, Tom," she told her assistant Tom Morgan.

"What am I not going to like? Don't say you've got bad news for me?" Pickens asked.

"I'm afraid we have a dilemma."

"Not you too, Marge?" She gave him a confused look. "What's the problem now?"

"Rhonda was six weeks pregnant."

"Shit! Not again! Now it's a triple homicide. Do you have an exact TOD yet?"

"The best I can do for now is around three Tuesday afternoon. There's no evidence of another COD. The shotgun did it."

"What about Benson?" he inquired.

"We've almost finished with him, but it looks like the results are the same except for the pregnancy."

"You reasonably confident about the TOD?"

"As certain as I can be. Why? Is there a problem with that?"

"Not sure yet, but the husband is our prime suspect. He may have been on his way back from Jacksonville around that time, so I'm not sure. Did you run a tox screen?"

"We did, on both victims, but it will be a few days before we get the results."

"How about fingerprints? Any luck there?"

"The victims and the cleaning lady. Whoever did this was careful."

"Okay. Thanks, Marge. You up for ribs tonight?"

"Of course, it will be great to see Leroy and family."

"I'll pick you and Sarah up at the house. Love you." Pickens paused a moment and watched her. "You okay, wide receiver?"

Marge smiled. "I'm fine, how about you?"

"I'm fine too. You go do your ME thing."

Pickens was worried that the death of the unborn child might have had an effect on her, but the way she said she's fine assured him she was. He left and headed back to his office.

"You two have an update for me?" Pickens asked when he walked up to Amy's desk. "I need something because this case is getting to be like that horrible accident case."

"What do you mean by that?" Amy asked.

"Rhonda Hicks was six weeks pregnant."

Amy had a look of surprise and shock on her face, and she wondered how Marge had reacted to the death of the child. The last time there was a homicide involving a pregnant woman, it had a dramatic effect on her.

"That's awful. Do we know who the father was?"

"No," Pickens replied. "The DNA test hasn't come back. Neither have the tox reports. It will be a week at least, probably more."

"Well, I hope if it turns out to be Hicks' child, he wasn't the shooter."

"So do I," Pickens said. "You get anywhere with Doris Young?"

"No. We don't have a number for her, and there's no listing for a Doris Young. I also tried the office, but there was no answer," Amy answered.

Disappointed, Pickens replied, "I was hoping we could get a vehicle description from her."

Billy took that as his cue to jump in. "Sheriff, I heard back from the hotel where Hicks was staying. He officially checked out at noon. I did get a make, model and license plate number, and I put an APB on the vehicle."

"Good work, Billy. I still want to talk to Doris Young. Maybe she's at the office. We can get some information on the clients while we're there and maybe even a telephone number for Doris.

Pickens and Amy left and drove to the offices of Benson and Hicks. While they were in his SUV, Amy asked, "How are you and Marge, especially after the autopsy?"

"I'm fine, and so is she. There doesn't seem to be any problem. Maybe Sarah changed everything."

"I'm glad."

When they arrived at Benson and Hicks' office, it was closed. They walked up to the door and knocked but no one answered, and there also were no cars in the parking lot.

"What do we do now?"

"Exigent circumstances, Amy. You have your kit with you?"

"I always do. Give me a minute and I'll have the door open." Two minutes later, she had the door unlocked and open.

The place looked neat and tidy.

"Amy, you look for an appointment book. I'll check the file cabinet for employment records. Maybe we'll get lucky and find some information we can use."

The appointment book on Doris' desk listed some meetings including Hicks' trip to Jacksonville. Pickens checked the file cabinet and found a folder marked Doris Young, which contained a home address and telephone number. He tried the number but got no answer.

"At this hour, maybe she's picking up her kids from school. You want to go by her residence?" Amy asked.

"Let's make a quick run there, but if she's not at home it will have to wait. Tonight's rib night at Leroy's, and I have to pick up my girls."

"Good for you. You've got your priorities straight."

"Sarah keeps me in line."

They closed the office and left for Young's address.

Doris Young's neighborhood was a typical suburban one with modest homes and numerous for-rent signs. There was no car in her driveway.

They rang the bell, but no one answered.

"Either no one's home or they're not answering. What do you want to do?"

"Let's go. We can try again on Monday," he replied. "Have someone watch the Hicks' residence and the office in case he comes home. I don't want to be late picking up Marge and Sarah. Call Billy and tell him to put someone on it. Any luck with Rhonda's parents?"

"Not yet. I'll try over the weekend."

"Thanks, Amy. I'm worried the mayor may talk to the commissioners and then they'll be on my back." Pickens shook his head. "That newspaper story didn't help. The mayor wants to know both victims' names."

"What did you tell him?"

"What do you think I told him? I wasn't about to give him Rhonda's name and have it known before we talk to her parents. He thinks that I'm a miracle worker. A murder case isn't solved overnight; it takes time. I understand his concern that the citizens of Creek City might not feel safe with a killer on the loose, but this isn't television." Pickens slammed his hand on the SUV's roof. "Damn it."

CHAPTER 7

Irene Noristan worried about the death of Tommy Benson. She wasn't sure what to do since she'd been having sex with him and could be considered a jealous lover. Her assistant, Alice Parker, also knew about the affair. Irene thought of it as a mutual liaison since both were consenting adults and neither was married or in a committed relationship. For her, it was a sexual release, and she'd had many of those. Tommy was just another knot in her string of boy toys.

Alice hadn't been in for several days, and Irene was concerned. The two of them had previously discussed the relationship between Tommy and Irene. She seemed to think that Alice didn't approve of the relationship. She suspected that Alice might also have been seeing Tommy.

Irene decided she would do nothing for the present and wait until approached by someone from the sheriff's office. Until then, she wouldn't do anything that would call attention to herself. Irene had enough to concern herself with, since without an assistant she was lost. With no one to answer the telephone, it meant she would have to use an outside answering service or spend more time in the office—which wasn't her style.

She had tried several times to reach Alice by telephone with no luck. Since it was already lunchtime, she decided to close the office and drive by Alice's house. She got the address from the personnel file, wiped her hands with a Handy Wipe, and left.

Alice lived in a nice neighborhood, but it was apparent the homes were all rentals. Her car wasn't in the driveway, so Irene got out of hers and walked to the front door. She rang the bell and knocked, but no one answered. She tried looking in the front windows but couldn't see in because the blinds were all closed.

"Damn, this is the strangest thing. Where the hell could she be?" Then she realized that Alice's neighborhood wasn't far from Tommy's and wondered even more if Alice also saw Tommy romantically. She wouldn't put it past Tommy to have several women since she figured him for a player.

"I would never have suspected it," Irene thought to herself. "But now I'm thinking that maybe the way Alice's eyes lit up whenever Tommy came to the office and the way she looked at him makes, me wonder if she was a lovesick puppy. I hope she's not the jealous type."

Irene decided to drive by Tommy's house to determine just how close Alice lived to him. Since it was only a few blocks away, she was now confident that Alice and Tommy were doing it together. As Irene drove by, she noticed the sheriff's SUV in the driveway. Not wanting to look conspicuous, she drove on by without slowing or glancing at the house.

Irene had hoped the sheriff didn't find out about her relationship with Tommy. She was sure he'd think of her as a suspect. With Alice not home and not coming into the office, Irene began to suspect that something was wrong.

"Maybe I should talk to the sheriff about her?" Irene asked herself. "But if I do, he'll suspect me." Then she decided that she'd just mind her own business for now. "I have enough problems of my own."

Irene drove back to her office. When she got there, she had an afterthought. Why not do a little more background check on Alice? When Irene hired Alice, she only did a cursory check. She went to her computer and searched for Alice Parker. Irene found nothing for an Alice Parker in Creek City and was now even more suspicious. She knew she should have been more careful when she first hired her. Realizing her mistake, Irene thought again about talking to Pickens but decided once again to wait awhile. She reached into her desk drawer, took out a Handi Wipe, and used it on her hands.

CHAPTER 8

Pickens and Marge were having a leisurely dinner while discussing the day's events. Sarah was playing with her food and seemed preoccupied. Marge noticed that Pickens looked the same way.

"JD, is something bothering you? Is it this case?" When he didn't respond, Marge became concerned and asked again. "JD, what's bothering you?"

"It's this case. I feel like I'm doing something wrong."

"I have an idea. Think of it as a football game. You called a pass play, your receivers are all covered, the blocking broke down, and you're scrambling for your life."

"A quarterback's worst nightmare."

She pointed a finger. "Exactly, so what do you do?"

He rubbed his chin. "Throw the ball away and avoid the sack."

She pointed her finger again. "Right, quarterback, and then what?"

"Where is this going?"

"Just play along with me. So, what next?"

"Punt, then regroup on the sideline and decide what to do on the next series of downs."

Marge raised her palms. "And?"

"Go to the ground game and grind out each yard."

"Right you are, quarterback, and slowly but surely you reach the end zone without a Hail Mary play."

Her analogy finally hit him. "So, I do what works and stick to a game plan. Damn, you're good, wide receiver."

She winked. "You bet I am."

"I need to visit the crime scene again and talk to Benson's neighbors as well as Hicks." It was as though a light bulb lit up. "And I need to find out more about their secretary and who else Benson dated besides Rhonda. Maybe I need to do a little more investigating on Eddie. He might have been having an affair. After all, his wife was."

"Now you're talking like a quarterback."

"We've been so focused on the husband we missed the simple things. That won't happen again. First thing in the morning I'm setting up a murder board, and I'm taking Amy with me to the crime scene."

"That a boy, Sheriff. You get em!"

They both laughed. Marge had a way of lightening the mood when it was necessary, and he always appreciated her for doing it. She'd been doing it for quite some time, and he knew he was one lucky man.

First thing in the morning when Pickens arrived at his office, he motioned for Amy and Billy to come to his office. He poured himself a cup of coffee then told them to get one for themselves. When they were all seated, he went over his game plan.

"Look, we've been going about this case all wrong. We're so focused on Eddie that we haven't been paying attention to basics. Starting this morning, we're going to begin knocking on doors. Amy, we're taking another ride through Benson's neighborhood. Maybe we'll get lucky today." Amy nodded agreement. "We're also going to try Doris Young's residence again. If she's not there, then we go in. We don't need a search warrant since she's now a suspect. Another visit to Benson and Hicks' residences might help." Pickens shouted for Zeke and Ritchie to come into his office.

"Yes, Sheriff," Ritchie asked when he entered.

"You and Zeke go to Benson and Hicks' office. See if you can find an appointment book and get me some names for the past two weeks. Better yet, check the past month. If Doris Young is there, you call me. Keep her there until I arrive. Get me something, damn it."

"We're on it, Sheriff. Come on, Zeke, let's get rolling."

Pickens then turned toward Billy. "Billy, you set up a murder board with the names we have so far. We'll add more later. There's got to be something we're missing." He addressed everyone. "Anybody got any questions? If not, then let's get going."

Now that everyone had their instructions, Pickens felt better. He and Amy left and drove to the Benson home first. When they arrived, they noticed a neighbor a few doors down pulling into his driveway.

"Amy, we may have gotten lucky. Let's ask that neighbor if he saw anything." They walked over and introduced themselves. "Excuse me, sir! I'm Sheriff JD Pickens, and this is Sergeant Amy Tucker. Mind if we ask you a few questions?"

The man looked to be in his sixty's and might be someone who took notice of things in the neighborhood. Pickens surmised he might even be the Neighborhood Watch.

"I know who you are, Sheriff. You investigating the Benson murder?"

Very alert Pickens thought to himself. He might prove to be helpful.

"Yes, sir, I am. You see anything suspicious in the past few days?"

"Name's Roger Farmer, call me Roger. Can't say that I did, and I notice pretty much everything that goes on in the neighborhood.

But I've been away the past few days, so I wasn't here to see anything. One thing I can tell you, though, I've noticed a red sports car parked in the driveway on several occasions. Saw a good-looking woman going in and out of the house when it was parked there. Don't know who she was."

"That's a lot of help, Roger. Notice anything in particular about her or the vehicle?"

"Only that she was a real good looker. Don't know if it means anything, but I could swear that car went by a few minutes ago. Didn't see the license plate, but there definitely was a woman driving. Hope that's helpful? That Benson kid had a lot of women come to his house."

"Thanks again, Roger."

"No problem. Glad to help. Say, how's that pretty wife of yours and that cute little girl. I'm a retired principal, and I volunteer at the elementary school where she goes. I often see your wife dropping her off. That little girl has a special gift, Sheriff."

"They're both fine, sir. Thanks for asking. You take care."

They left Mr. Farmer to his business, then walked back to Benson's residence. He told Amy to open the door. She opened it, and they proceeded to enter.

"What do you think? Think that red sports car has anything to do with our case?"

"Don't know, Amy, but it's a strange coincidence that it drove by as we got here. We need to find out who the woman was. Maybe she was a jealous lover. I don't believe in coincidences."

"It would make things a lot easier for us if she was."

"Don't I know it? I'm going to have Billy do a search of registered red sports cars. Maybe we'll get the name of the owner. Let's look around and see if there's anything that would tell us something. It seems Benson was a player."

"Why, Sheriff, you devil you! Where did that expression come from?"

"Hey, I'm no prude. I can be hip."

"Okay, now I'm sorry I said anything. Let's look around."

They proceeded to walk through the house checking cabinets and closets. There didn't seem to be a lot of furniture in the house. Tommy Benson lived like a bachelor with the barest of essentials. The last room they checked was the bedroom. It still had the bloodstains from the crime.

"Sure looks like a horrible incident took place here even with the bodies gone. Someone really didn't like those two," commented Amy.

"You're right, but did you notice the front door didn't look like a forced entry, and there are no broken windows. Whoever did this had a key or was let in. Could this have been a love triangle gone wrong?"

She thought about his question and had another thought. "It's possible, but if so, who was the third party? Maybe it was the husband? Or it could have been the woman driving the red sports car?"

"Or maybe it was Doris Young? We need to find both women and Eddie. Come on, let's try Young's residence."

Amy locked the door and both left for Doris Young's house. Amy knocked several times, but no one answered.

"Since she's a person of interest, we'll use probable cause as a reason to open the door. You have a problem with that? Because I don't."

"I do," Amy replied. "But, like you said we need something so I'll open it." She was about to unlock the door when a blue Honda SUV pulled into the driveway.

"Hold on, Amy."

A couple in their early fifties got out of the vehicle and walked toward them.

"What the hell's going on here? Why are you trying to get in my home?"

Pickens and Amy exchanged confused looks. Something wasn't right here.

"I'm Sheriff Pickens, and this is Sergeant Tucker. We're conducting an investigation of a crime and looking for Doris Young. We understand this was her residence. Who are you, sir?"

The woman turned to the man, and it was evident by her expression that she was as confused as Pickens was.

"My name's Lester Monroe this is my wife, Margaret. We've been away on vacation. Don't know any Doris Young, and she sure doesn't live here. We've owned this house for ten years, and there's never been a Doris Young in this neighborhood. We know most of the neighbors even though most of them rent. Somebody gave you wrong information, Sheriff."

Pickens was both confused and surprised. Doris Young had just become a very suspicious suspect.

"Obviously, Mr. Monroe, but just to be certain who I'm talking to, do you mind showing me some identification? You can tell by the SUV that we're indeed from the sheriff's office so that shouldn't be a problem."

Monroe didn't seem to appreciate Pickens's request for identification and hesitated. He looked at his wife, the sheriff's SUV, and the badge on Pickens's belt and then decided to cooperate. He carefully reached into his pocket, pulled out his wallet and showed Pickens his driver's license.

"You can see I'm telling you the truth about who I am, Sheriff, but that still doesn't answer the question who Doris Young is and why she gave this as her address?"

"I can't answer that, Mr. Monroe, but now I have a problem. We'll leave you folks alone, and I apologize for the inconvenience."

"Before you go, Sheriff, mind if I ask you what the crime is you're investigating?"

Pickens hesitated before answering. He didn't want these folks to be overly concerned about a murder.

"I'm not at liberty to say, but it's nothing that should concern you. We'll be on our way now. Good day, folks!"

The Monroes looked at each other with astonished looks and watched as Pickens and Amy got into the SUV and drove off. Mrs. Monroe handed her husband a Handi Wipe to use.

"What the hell was that all about? Is there another Doris Young that we don't know about?" Amy asked.

"Don't ask me," he replied. "I'm just as confused as you are. We've got ourselves a real conundrum now. Let's hope Billy and Ritchie have some answers for us. We might as well go back to the office."

Amy's eyes lit up. "Where did that word conundrum come from?"

"I'm a father now. I have to improve my vocabulary, so I've been practicing using big words. I am a college graduate, you know, and Billy isn't the only one who can try a new word a day."

"But that's not today's word."

"So, litigate me," Pickens said. "Now let's get back to the case."

Amy rolled her eyes. "Okay, I surrender, you're right."

"Of course, I'm right. I'm the sheriff."

Amy rolled her eyes again.

They drove back to the office. Richie and Zeke had already arrived, and Richie seemed as though he had something important to say because he was smiling when he saw Pickens and Amy.

"You have something for us, Richie?"

"I've got something, Amy. Don't know if it's important, but it's something."

"Well spit it out, Richie," said Pickens.

"Okay, Sheriff. Zeke and I went through the files at Benson and Hicks' office, and we found some records of past jobs. We looked at the most recent, within six months. Nothing stood out except for one."

"Why?" asked Pickens.

"Because, Tommy and Rhonda did a job for an Irene Noristan. By itself it doesn't seem unusual, but it seems Tommy closed the contract and was extensively involved in the work. There's no mention of Rhonda's involvement. If it was their contract, why wasn't she involved?" Pickens looked at Amy. Both raised their eyelids. "It's not my place, but I'm going way out on a limb here. What if Tommy was having an affair with her? Noristan has a reputation for..."

"For what, Ritchie?"

"You know, Sheriff, for..." Billy and Amy were smiling as they knew Ritchie had put himself under the gun with his comment.

Out of the corner of his eye, Pickens could see Billy and Amy's smiles and understood.

"And you know this how?" Ritchie started to sweat. "Never mind," said Pickens with a smile. Ritchie relaxed.

"You may not be too far out on that limb, Ritchie," Amy said. "We talked to a neighbor, and he said a red sports car was often parked in Tommy's driveway. Maybe it belonged to Noristan."

Pickens addressed Billy. "Check DMV to see if this Irene Noristan drives a red sports car. And add her name to the murder board."

Billy checked DMV for red sports cars. It took a while, but he found three registered in the county. Irene Noristan was one of the owners. Billy wrote down her address and then checked the telephone book for a business listing. Billy handed the information to Pickens.

"Amy and I will check the addresses starting with the business. Billy, check the DMV records again and see if there's anything for a Doris Young. Also, check the elementary school for any of her children. You may have to go to the school and ask the principal, but keep it on an information request only. We don't want to start a panic at the school. Also, add her name to the board."

"Got it, I'll be discreet," Billy said. "I just happen to know the principal, so I think I can handle it."

"Anybody you don't know, Billy?"

"Nope, no one comes to mind. Say, Sheriff, you mind if I ask you something?"

Billy's comment got a laugh out of everyone and was a welcome respite, albeit only temporarily.

"No, I don't. What's up?"

"You asked me to check on several women, and I was wondering if they had anything to do with Tommy Benson. Tommy was known to be a player and had relationships with many women. You think these were some of his lady friends?"

"Maybe so, we'll find out soon, anything else?"

"Not now, but who knows?"

"Yeah, who knows?"

CHAPTER 9

As Marge placed the breakfast dishes into the sink, she looked out the large picture window and watched her daughter playing in the backyard. She had taken the day off because it was a school holiday, and Sarah was home for the day. Usually, she would have gotten a sitter but she decided to spend the day with her. JD would have liked to take the day off, too, but he had an obligation to solve a double-murder investigation.

Sarah had been out in the backyard for over an hour and seemed to be playing nicely by herself with Bailey at her side. Marge couldn't tell what game she was playing, but it appeared to require Sarah's intense involvement. Curious, Marge decided to see what she was doing.

When she got closer to the child, Marge saw that Sarah had something in her hand and was rubbing it. Bailey watched her every move and was mesmerized by her actions.

Sarah suddenly realized her mother was there. "Shh, Mommy," she whispered.

Marge carefully stepped closer and noticed Sarah had a bird in her hand.

Sarah was gently petting a female cardinal, and Marge also noticed a splint on one of its tiny legs. She wondered how the splint got there since Sarah was alone except for Bailey.

On a tree limb, well above them, three Cardinals intensely watched Sarah. Two beautiful reddish-orange males and one female stood guard over the bird in Sarah's hand, making sure it was safe. They seemed comfortable with Sarah's attention to the bird as well as Marge and Bailey's presence.

What Marge witnessed with Sarah and the bird was astonishing. Her grandmother had a special gift with animals as well as birds, and she wondered if her daughter might have inherited that same gift. Watching Sarah brought back memories of her grandmother, Sarah. She was an amazing woman, and the gift she had with animals was memorable to everyone who came in contact with her.

Marge sat and watched as Sarah calmly talked to the bird. She couldn't hear what Sarah said but kept very still not wanting to do anything that would break the magic. Sarah gently stroked the bird while talking in a soft, soothing voice.

Finally, the bird stood up in Sarah's hand. Chirping came from the trees above as the female cardinal flew off with the splint attached to her leg. Sarah sat watching the bird in flight. What happened next stunned Marge. Four birds flew down to Sarah, chirped at her and then flew off into the trees.

Marge felt a tear run down her cheek. She had heard some wonderful stories about her grandmother, but seeing her little Sarah cure an injured bird was something she would never forget. She couldn't wait to tell JD.

Sarah got up. "Did you see that, Mommy?"

Marge took a deep breath and answered, "Yes, Sarah, I did. It was unbelievable. Where did you learn to do that?"

"I don't know, Mommy. It just came to me."

Marge grabbed her daughter and gave her a big hug and a kiss. "You are an amazing little girl, Sarah. I think you have a gift just like your great grandmother did."

"Was she special too, Mommy?"

"Yes, she was, and her name was Sarah, just like you."

"Mommy, I like being special. Would you tell me about her?"

"Okay, sweetheart."

Marge recounted the story about her grandmother, Sarah Riddling, as her grandfather, Josh Farber, told her and how she had the uncanny ability to talk to creatures.

When Marge finished, Sarah's eyes lit up, and her smile brightened her face.

"So, honey, just like you, your great-grandmother could talk to the creatures." Marge smiled. "She used her ability to become a veterinarian. Maybe one day you'll be one too."

"That was a beautiful story, Mommy. Great Gramma was like Doctor Dee on Animal Planet, wasn't she?"

"Yes, she was, and your great grandmother could converse with the animals too."

"So, I'm like Great Grandma Sarah and Doctor Dee?"

"Yes, you are, and she would be proud of you." Marge was beaming with pride.

"Can I tell Daddy about the bird?"

Marge grinned. "Yes, sweetheart, it's okay. I'm sure he'll enjoy hearing about it."

When Pickens arrived home, Marge and Sarah were waiting and Sarah was anxious to tell him about the bird. She was so excited that she left a few things out. He listened patiently but wasn't sure of what he heard. Pickens gazed at Marge, and she nodded agreement with Sarah.

After Sarah had finished her story, she said she was hungry and was going to get a cookie.

"Just one, Sarah, you don't want to spoil your appetite for dinner."

"Okay, Mommy, just one. I promise."

Pickens and Marge smiled.

"That was some story. She sure has some imagination for her age."

"It's not her imagination, JD. It actually happened. I couldn't believe my eyes. It was incredible. When those other birds came down, I thought they were going to attack her, but it was as though they were thanking her. I think she may have the same gift my grandmother had. JD, I witnessed a miracle today; so did Bailey."

"Well, if it is a gift, we best keep it to ourselves. Otherwise, it will become a curse. People will want her to demonstrate, and we want to spare her all that attention."

"I agree, but this will be our secret. And hers, of course!"

After dinner, they all went for a walk with Bailey. Later, he brought Marge up to date on the case.

When he mentioned Hicks and Benson, Marge said, "Everyone knows them. They've been together since high school."

"How come everyone knows them except me?"

"You just don't get around enough, that's why."

"Maybe after I solve this case I'll get around more, starting with you."

CHAPTER 10

Four days into the case and Pickens still didn't have a viable lead, an actual suspect or a bona fide person of interest. As far as he was concerned, what they had so far was zilch. But it was the weekend, and the case would have to wait until Monday because he promised to take Sarah and Bailey to visit his parents.

Before leaving, Marge noticed a look of concern on Pickens' face and asked, "JD, is something bothering you? Are you concerned about taking the weekend off?"

"Yes, I feel guilty about it."

Marge placed her hand on his cheek. "Well don't, there's nothing you could do. You've got Billy, Amy and other deputies working the case. You'd only get in their way. Let them do their jobs."

Pickens considered her suggestion. "Maybe you're right. It's just that..."

"JD, look at it this way. You have to maintain balance or else you'll lose your perspective." Marge smiled and added, "Besides, I'd strangle you myself if you go back on your word, and Sarah and Bailey probably wouldn't speak to you for days. Go visit your parents."

Pickens shook his head. "Just what I need another murder to investigate and complaints from the mayor and the county commissioners. And you can forget about me getting reelected next year."

"There you go, Sheriff, now you have reasons to visit your parents."

They both laughed and then Marge left to pick up Liana—Pickens' friend Leroy Jones' wife—so that they could spend the day shopping.

Pickens remembered how he always laughed when Leroy would say, "Someday that brown sugar's gonna marry me."

And she did after Leroy had retired from professional football and returned to his hometown. After retiring from the Tampa Bay Bucs, Leroy purchased Charlie's Smokehouse. He remodeled the restaurant and renamed it Leroy's Bar-B-Que Pit. Leroy was also the minister of The Shady Grove AME Church.

Liana still lived in her grandmother's house with her ten-year-old son, William. Her grandmother had passed and left her the house. She continued to waitress at the restaurant after Leroy purchased it. They started dating and eventually got married, sold her grandmother's house and bought their own in a charming subdivision. The house they bought had central air conditioning, unlike Liana's grandmother's house. Leroy later adopted William and then they had Annie.

Sarah and Bailey sat in Pickens' truck waiting impatiently for him. "Daddy, sure is slow right, Bailey?" Bailey barked.

Pickens was inside struggling to get his boots on but finally succeeded, grabbed the keys, left the house, and climb in the front seat.

Sarah squinched up her eyes, crossed her arms, and said, "It's about time, young man." Bailey barked his agreement.

Pickens shook his head. "You're just like your grandma. Got your seatbelt fastened?" He checked to be sure. "Okay, here we go." And they left, with Sarah's nose peered out the window.

Pickens parents still lived in the same house on Houghton Street. When Pickens lived there as a boy, it didn't have central air conditioning, just a window unit in the living room. But his father only turned it on during hot and humid summer nights—which meant evenings spent on the screened porch. Pickens high school friend, Leroy, also didn't have air conditioning at his house, so Leroy welcomed the times when JD invited him to his house. In their senior year of high school, both boys' parents installed window units in all the bedrooms. What a relief from those hot summer days and nights. It also helped when recruiters came to town to interview both boys and their parents.

Little had changed in the old neighborhood, except a couple of neighbors had moved to Sarasota to be near the Gulf. Young families had purchased their homes. Mr. Pewarski—next door to his parents—had suffered a stroke and now spent his days in a wheelchair. Pickens' mother took Mrs. Pewarski shopping since she didn't drive anymore.

When he pulled into his parent's driveway, his dad was mowing the Pewarski's lawn. His mother was sitting on the porch.

Sarah leaped out of the truck and ran up to greet her with Bailey running beside her.

"Morning, Gramma," she shouted.

"Well, good morning, my little darling. It's been a while since you visited."

"That's Daddy's fault, not mine," she answered and shook her head at her father.

"Hey, wait a minute. I've been busy," he retorted.

"Too busy to visit your mother and father? That's a poor excuse, young man." Jeanette Pickens was in her early seventies with graying hair and still dressed in loose-fitting jeans. Mrs. Pickens could still put a fright in JD, same as she did when he was a boy.

Pickens raised his hands in surrender; he knew he'd never win when it came to his mother.

"Okay, already, I give up. Sorry, Mom, I should have come sooner."

"Well, don't keep your mother waiting, JD, you know better," said his father as he walked up behind Pickens.

"Sorry, Dad. See you've finished Mr. Pewarski's lawn. That's awfully kind of you. How's he doing?"

Russell Pickens was in his mid-seventies, what little hair he still had was gray, and at six-foot-two, he was a burly man, and his hands were the size of ham hocks. He laid a hand on Pickens' shoulder and nodded his head.

"He's getting by, and so is she." JD winced at his father's inference that he should have asked about both the Pewarskis. "Their daughter was here last week for a visit. She came by herself."

"Your lawn looks good, too."

"Yup, it does." Mr. Pickens grinned. "You could come by more often and do it for me."

"Or I can have my gardener do both yards."

Mr. Pickens slapped him on the back. "You're getting too soft, JD, you need the exercise. Let's go inside so I can cleanup. We can talk after."

"Okay, besides it's starting to warm up."

"You know kid you're getting soft. It's not that warm yet."

"If you say so." Pickens followed his parents, Sarah, and Bailey into the house.

Mrs. Pickens walked around the house closing the windows in the living room, dining room, and the spare bedroom. Then she turned the air conditioner units on and opened the slider in the kitchen.

"Okay, Sarah, you and Bailey ready to bake some cookies?"

"Chocolate chip, Gramma? And some special ones for Bailey?"

"You betcha, now come on."

"Come on; Bailey let's go."

Pickens walked around the living room in search of something. Then he noticed what he was looking for on the mantel.

"Ball looks great up there, doesn't it?" said Mr. Pickens.

"Sure does, I was..."

"Forget it; it stays there," his father replied. "So, hotshot Sheriff, how's the case going?" Pickens froze in his tracks. "Nowhere, huh? Well, like I always told you, one down at a time, don't hurry things. You'll get there eventually."

His face lit up. "Thanks, Dad, as always you're right."

Mr. Pickens grinned back. "Of course, I am. Let's go see what the girls are up to."

Mrs. Pickens, Sarah, and Bailey had gathered around the kitchen table. Bailey sat attentively watching the two as they put a tray of cookies into the oven. Chocolate chip for Sarah and two special cookies for Bailey.

"Where are you going," asked Mr. Pickens.

"Outside," replied Sarah.

"Well, I want a hug and kiss before you go outside."

"Sure, but you have to give Bailey a kiss, too, Pop-pop."

Mr. Pickens picked up Sarah, hugged and then kissed her. He set her down, bent over, and let Bailey kiss him. "Now you two can go outside."

Sarah and Bailey left the kitchen and went outside through the screened porch.

Mrs. Pickens checked the oven timer. "So, what's new, JD?"

He frowned. "It's this case, but I'd rather not discuss it. I'm here to visit you guys."

The oven timer beeped. "Good for you. Now go get Sarah and Bailey. Dad, you make coffee, and I'll get some sweet tea for Sarah and me."

Pickens called Sarah and Bailey in and then they sat at the kitchen table. Mr. Pickens poured JD and himself a cup of coffee. Mrs. Pickens poured her and Sarah each a glass of sweet tea.

Sarah scooped up several cookies and the two for Bailey. She shoved one into her mouth and dropped one onto the floor for Bailey. Then she took a sip of her sweet tea. The Pickens adults smiled.

"Gramma, guess what?"

"What, child?"

"I'm gonna be like Doctor Dee on Animal Planet when I grow up. Mom said…"

Her father interrupted her before she could continue. "Sarah, have another cookie." Pickens was concerned that Sarah might reveal her secret. "It's her favorite television show."

After two hours of visiting, Pickens said that it was time he took Sarah and Bailey home.

"So, how long will it be until we see you again, JD?"

"Two weeks, I promise, Dad."

"Sarah, you make sure he keeps his word."

"Don't worry, Gramma, I will. If he knows what's good for him, he'll be here." She scowled at him. "Won't you, Dad.?"

Pickens shook his head. "Yes, Mother." He didn't want to tell them that he hoped to go fishing next Sunday with Leroy. "We better get going. Mom, Dad, thanks for being patient with me."

"You know we're always here for you," replied Mr. Pickens.

"Thanks, Dad. Okay, Sarah let's hit the road."

Mr. and Mrs. Pickens laughed. Then Pickens, Sarah, and Bailey left. Sarah waved to her grandparents as they drove off.

Although grateful for the respite, Pickens felt guilty for not working the case and it nagged at him the entire weekend.

CHAPTER 11

Doris Young knew she couldn't stay in Creek City any longer. The deaths of Tommy Benson and Rhonda Hicks might call attention to her or make her a suspect. Her life and that of her children had become close to ordinary, but now for their sake she had to move on. If they found her, there would be repercussions and she couldn't take the chance of losing her children. With the help of some very special people she'd been able to settle in Creek City, but now she had to call on another favor from those same individuals. Doris made the call and was told to get her children and drive to the designated location where someone would meet her. She and her children would spend a couple of days there while plans were in the making.

Doris' children were unhappy that they would be moving again. Both had come to like the elementary school they were attending and had made some friends. Doris explained that it was necessary, and someday they would understand the reason why they had to make so many moves. Doris would like to find somewhere permanent to settle down, but she knew it wasn't possible.

The location where they would be staying for a few days was a serene setting with a lovely building that had a cottage-like interior. The children had plenty of grounds to play on, and they could enjoy watching the squirrels and rabbits that freely roamed the grounds. There were ample trees, and many species of birds made use of the plethora of bird feeders set out for them.

The children did the best they could to enjoy themselves, but it was evident to those at the sanctuary they were sad. Doris tried to play games with them, but their excitement just wasn't there. Fortunately, after a few days, their time was up and Doris was given instructions to a new location. She packed their belongings in the trunk of her car, and they said goodbye to everyone before leaving on their journey.

Several days later Mrs. Preston, Sarah's teacher, obtained permission to take her second-grade class on a field trip. She chose to take them to the church she attended as they had a beautiful campus with lots of activities for the children. All the children were excited; especially Annie Jones since it was the same church her family attended. Mrs. Preston had also obtained permission to use the church bus to make the trip because it came with a special driver—Leroy Jones, the church's pastor.

When the children arrived at the church, they were so excited they couldn't wait to get off the bus. Mrs. Preston had them exit the bus in a single file then line up once they were off. Knowing how excited they were, she told them to take off and have fun but stay within eyesight.

Sarah Pickens and Annie Jones wandered off by themselves until they found a spot where there were some critters. Two squirrels and a rabbit came close to the little girls. Sarah started talking to them, and Annie just watched fascinated. Soon several birds came and landed on the girls' shoulders. Annie was so delighted watching as Sarah continued to talk to all the creatures.

"What are they saying, Sarah?"

"They said we don't seem sad like the children who were here days ago. They weren't here long, but the kids didn't seem like they wanted to travel and their mother took them away."

"Do they know where they went?"

"No, just that they had to leave, and their mother didn't seem too happy, either."

"Should we keep this a secret, Sarah?"

"I'm not sure. I'll ask the squirrels."

Sarah talked to the squirrels and also the birds. "Annie, they said this was a secret place, and we should keep it our secret."

"Okay, Sarah."

At lunchtime, Mrs. Preston told the children that she had a surprise for them. The church folk had fixed a nice lunch for them and would serve it in the pavilion. Mrs. Preston made sure beforehand that no child would receive anything that might cause an allergic reaction. After lunch, the school kids played a while longer before boarding the bus and going back to school.

As the children were getting off the bus, Annie whispered to her father, "The creatures said the children who left there weren't happy, Daddy."

Leroy was surprised by her remark so before leaving he mentioned it to Mrs. Preston. Her face took on a look of surprise.

"What do you think, Leroy? Do we have a problem concerning Doris Young and her children?"

"I'm not sure. I know we took the necessary precautions. I'll have a talk with Pickens. Maybe he can explain."

Marge decided to leave a little early so that she could get Sarah and spend some time with her. She drove to the elementary school to pick up Sarah. Mrs. Preston waved to her and watched Sarah get in Marge's car—which was odd because usually Mrs. Preston would come over and engage Marge in conversation. Marge shrugged her shoulders and made sure Sarah had buckled up.

"How was your day, honey? Did anything interesting happen?"

Sarah's eyes lit up. "We went on a field trip today, Mommy. Mrs. Preston took us to Uncle Leroy's church."

"That's wonderful. Did you enjoy it?"

"Yes, it was so much fun. Annie and I talked to some of the creatures. They said the children that were there before us were very sad."

"Why were they sad, sweetheart?"

"They said the children didn't want to leave, and their mother also didn't want to, but they had to. They got into their car and drove away. Uncle Leroy was there and waved goodbye to them."

"Did the creatures know the children's names?"

"No, Mommy they didn't say. Should I have asked?"

"No, honey, it's okay. I'm glad you told me this. You're special, Sarah, and I love you a lot."

"I love you too. Mommy, the creatures said I must keep it a secret about the children, but I guess it was okay to tell you. Oh, I forgot, Annie told her daddy."

Oh, no, Marge thought. Now both Annie and Leroy know about Sarah's gift and maybe Mrs. Preston too.

After her conversation with Sarah, Marge decided to call JD at his office and tell him about Sarah's field trip, wondering if it had anything to do with his case.

Pickens was getting a little frustrated and stressed over the case. So far, the only suspect was Eddie Hicks but he believed there might be another or possibly other suspects. There's the mystery woman who drives the red car, and there was the secretary who hasn't been seen or heard from since the day they were at Hicks' office. He needed a break in the case, something to help break up the bottleneck.

Pickens's phone rang, he answered it and recognized Marge's voice instantly.

"What's up, wide receiver?" Marge hesitated. "Hey, is something wrong?"

"JD, Sarah went on a field trip today."

"So, she's been on them before. Why are you concerned about this one? Did something happen?"

"Yes, she and Annie were talking to the birds and..."

"Wait, what do you mean she and Annie? Does Annie know?"

"She does now, but that's not why I called you. Sarah said the birds told her that a family that was staying at Leroy's church had to leave and the children weren't happy."

"So?"

"I thought I heard you say you were looking for a woman and her family."

Pickens couldn't remember if he had mentioned it to Marge or not, but he was looking for Doris Young. Maybe it was her, he considered.

"Okay, I am, but what does that have to do with Sarah and Annie?"

"Annie told Leroy, and Mrs. Preston might know also. You should talk to Leroy."

Pickens rubbed the back of his head and decided Marge was right.

"All right, I'll call him. Thanks, wide receiver. Love you, and I'll see you tonight."

"Same here."

After talking to Marge, Pickens called Leroy.

Afternoons at Leroy's were slow, so when Pickens called, he was able to get through to Leroy right away.

"Leroy here, what can I do for you?"

"Hey, buddy, it's JD."

"Hey, old buddy, I was going to call you. It's about Sarah's field trip today."

"I was calling you about the same thing. Why don't you go first?"

Leroy hoped his friend would understand what he had to tell him.

"I have a special request of you, buddy."

"Anything. You know you're my best friend. Ask away."

"I got to talk to you, JD, in private. Can you meet me here at the restaurant? It's paramount that I talk to you."

Leroy's request seemed odd, but Leroy was his best friend. He was also the minister of The Shady Grove AME Church, so Pickens decided to honor his friend's request.

"Sure, Leroy, I can do that. Is it something we can discuss over the phone?"

"I'd rather not, JD."

"Okay, I'll see you at six-fifteen."

"See you then."

After Pickens had hung up, he became even more concerned about Leroy's request. He wondered if it had anything to do with the case as Marge had implied. Anything was possible Pickens told himself and hoped to find out later. At 5:45, Pickens finished what he was doing, said goodnight to Amy and left to go to the restaurant. Leroy was waiting for him and climbed into Pickens's SUV.

"What's so important that we have to talk in private? You've never made a request like this before."

Leroy wasn't sure how to go about having the conversation, but he knew it was important to them both. He decided just to be up front with Pickens.

"JD, this may have something to do with your case. I'm not certain, but I need to tell you something."

Pickens had hoped whatever Leroy wanted to say to him wouldn't have anything to do with the case, but now that Leroy brought it up Pickens became gravely concerned.

"I was hoping to forget about my case at least for one night, but now you've got my interest. What do you know about it?"

"I know you're looking for a woman named Doris Young. She was Eddie Hicks and Tommy Benson's secretary, wasn't she?"

Pickens was very interested in what Leroy knew especially about Doris Young, one of his possible suspects. However; he wondered how Leroy knew she was their secretary.

"Yes, she was, and we can't seem to locate her. The address on her job application doesn't belong to her. Someone else lives there, and the owner never heard of Doris Young. According to him, she doesn't even live in the neighborhood. I find it strange that she suddenly disappeared right after we talked to her." Pickens' eyes narrowed. "You know something I should be aware of, Leroy?"

Leroy pursed his mouth. "JD, there's no such person as Doris Young. It's a fictitious name she was given to protect her and her children."

Pickens was startled by Leroy's information. Now he knew why they couldn't locate her and was even more curious about whom Doris Young actually was.

"What do you mean a fictitious name to protect her children? What's this all about and how come you're telling me this?"

"You have to trust me on this, JD. Doris, for lack of another name, is fleeing from an abusive husband with powerful connections. They're so powerful that she can't go to the authorities. You have a suspicion about what my church and I do. Your suspicion is correct. We help women in trouble. I put Doris in touch with a group I work with to help her. We got her a false identification and the job with Hicks. Unfortunately, what happened resulted in your inquiring about her background.

"I knew you would do some serious investigating on her so that's why I did what I had to. We had to get her away from here, for her safety and her children's. Had it not been for Sarah talking with the creatures at my church and Annie asking about her kids, I could have kept this information to myself. I'm sorry, JD, but it was necessary."

Pickens understood what Leroy was talking about and agreed with his actions to protect Doris and her children. It was similar to what happened years ago when a woman from South Florida suddenly went missing, and her abusive husband never heard from her again.

Now that he knew about what had happened to Doris and her children, Pickens considered crossing her off as a potential suspect. But he would have to be delicate when he told Amy and Billy to forget about looking for Doris Young or whatever her name was. Pickens decided he would wait until Monday morning to give them the news. It's not likely anything would change before then.

"Okay, Leroy, I understand. I know what you do is a good thing, so we'll just forget about it. I appreciate you telling me everything, but what does it have to do with Sarah?"

"After what happened today, I suspect that I'm not the only one who knows about her secret. Mrs. Preston might, too. Don't worry about her; she won't say anything. The creatures Sarah was talking with told her about Doris and her children. How sad they were to have to go away. Once you heard about Sarah's conversation, I figured you would be suspicious since it happened at my church. We all square now, buddy?"

Pickens gently punched Leroy's arm and replied, "We're all square, pal. Hold on, what's William doing now that basketball season is over?"

"He's concentrating on his studies, but still gets some playtime at the practice facility with his teammates. He knows where his priorities are."

"Good for him. You take care, pal."

"You too."

Pickens held his hand up. "Wait, one more thing. Are we going fishing Sunday?

"I wouldn't miss it. See you bright and early."

Now that Pickens was satisfied with the information, and Leroy glad he got things off his back, Leroy went back into the restaurant and Pickens went home.

Marge was waiting in the kitchen when Pickens arrived. She turned the oven off, retrieved two beers and sat down at the counter with him.

"Did you talk to Leroy?"

"Yes, I'll tell you about it later after Sarah's in bed."

After Sarah was tucked into her bed, Pickens and Marge discussed what he learned from Leroy.

"So, are you satisfied with what Leroy told you?"

"Yes, I am and glad he did. Now I have one less person to suspect. You know, wide receiver, that's one amazing child we have."

"Yes, she is, and she's very special. We can look forward to some amazing events in her future; of that I am certain."

"Me too, wide receiver; what say we go play some football?"

"Game on, quarterback..."

"Damn, I love this woman..."

"You damn well better..."

CHAPTER 12

When Pickens arrived at his office Monday morning, he immediately told Billy to drop his investigation of Doris Young and to cross her name off the murder board. The only explanation he gave him was that she was no longer considered a person of interest. Billy was quite surprised but knew better than to ask questions. Amy overheard him and inquired as to why.

Impatiently, Pickens answered, "Because I said she isn't, that's why. Now let's get busy finding the woman driving the red car. She's more of a person of interest. Billy, any update on her?"

Billy gave Amy a look that said, "Drop it." He had some information and was glad Amy let the Doris thing go.

"I've got that business address for her. Her company is called Noristan Industries, LLC. I know that name. Someone from that company contacted me a while back and asked if I was interested in an IT job with the state. It wasn't this Noristan woman, and I can't remember the name of the person who contacted me. You want me to check it out?"

"No, Amy and I will. Let's hope we get a good lead. We need one. Still nothing on Eddie Hicks?"

"Not yet, but I'm still searching."

"Keep doing it. We need to find Eddie. What about their phones?

"I'm still trying to get their passwords." Billy pushed his shoulders back and thrust his chin out. "If they're anything like me—which I'm sure they are—they change them often and make them complicated..."

"Or simple," commented Amy.

Billy sneered. "Or that. It might take a while, but I'll get them."

Pickens shook his head. "Anything with Rhonda's parents yet, Amy?"

"No, I've left several messages and no call backs."

"Keep at it, I don't want them to find out about their daughter before we talk to them. Okay, let's go, Amy, and no questions, understand me..."

Pickens's comment surprised Amy, but she knew not to argue with him when he's in a bad mood.

"No problem, Sheriff," Amy sniped, addressing him by his title and not his name. "I'm right behind you."

Pickens ignored her and they drove to Noristan's office in silence. When they arrived, they noticed the little red sports car in its designated parking space. The name on the door said, Noristan Industries LLC, just like Billy said. As soon as they entered, they noticed how well designed the place was. It was like entering someone's home. It didn't take long for Ms. Noristan to greet them; apparently, she was expecting them.

Irene Noristan looked to be in her mid-forties and very attractive. She dressed in business attire and had two buttons opened on her blouse. When she spoke, there was a bit of seductiveness in her voice.

"Sheriff Pickens, it's so good to see you, although not under pleasant circumstances. I suspect you're here to talk to me about Tommy Benson and Rhonda Hicks."

Pickens and Amy exchanged surprised glances.

"Ms. Noristan, it's a pleasure to meet you. Meet Sergeant Amy Tucker. Yes, we are," Pickens replied. "Is there anything you would like to tell us about your relationship with them?"

Irene hesitated. At first, she presumed he meant business but suspected he was also implying otherwise and decided to tell him everything. It's not like she killed Tommy and Rhonda.

"I had a business relationship with them. Benson and Hicks did most of the design and construction work for my offices as you can see. I am very glad I hired them."

"What kind of business is Noristan Industries?" Pickens was curious because she was the only one there.

"We're an information technology search firm. We find IT personnel for municipalities and state governments. Our role is to find qualified people, vet them and submit their qualifications to the public entity via an RFP. That stands for request for proposal. If they're selected, we make a commission, and the person gets a contracted job. It works for all involved. That's as best I can explain."

Pickens was satisfied but still wondered why she was the only one in the office.

"Thanks for the explanation. You do this all by yourself?"

Before she could answer, Amy interrupted her. "Do you often visit your contractors at their homes, Ms. Noristan?"

Pickens was surprised at Amy's question. He wasn't ready to ask her about her visits to Benson's home. But the question was asked.

"You're quite direct, aren't you, Deputy?" Irene pushed her chair back and opened another button on her blouse. "Yes, I was seeing Tommy, if that's what you're asking. It started after I first met both Tommy and Rhonda here in my office to discuss the remodeling job. I liked their proposal, and we agreed in principal to have them do the work. They were both smiling when they left."

Irene smiled and unbuttoned another button. "Tommy came by the next day with the contract for me to sign and to collect the deposit." She reached for another button and continued. "I signed the contract, gave him a check and then offered him a bonus." Both Pickens and Amy's eyes narrowed. "Tommy liked what he saw and we consummated our relationship here..." Irene pushed her seat forward and ran her hand over the desk. "We did it other times after I made payments on the contract. Then we started having lunch and dinner together with dessert afterward at his house." Irene crossed her arms and looked at Amy. "Does that answer your question, Deputy?" Irene searched both Amy and Pickens' face expecting a look of condemnation. Seeing none, she wondered if they were quite adept at masking their feelings or was there something between them and they were players like her.

Amy rolled her eyes. "Yes, thank you."

"I'm glad, and before you ask, I wasn't the only one seeing Tommy. He wasn't a one-woman man, not in the least. Besides me, I knew there was Rhonda. The way my assistant, Alice Parker, lit up whenever he came to my office, I wouldn't be surprised if she was doing him too." Her eyes glowed. "I slept with Tommy, but I didn't kill him, Deputy. I'm not the jealous type. I'm a big girl. I knew about his appetite for women.

"And to answer your question, Sheriff, I used to have another employee who was superb at doing what we do. Unfortunately, she qualified for a position with the state and got the job. I hated to lose her, but I didn't want to stand in her way plus I couldn't match the salary. I'm looking for her replacement."

Her comments about Benson caused Pickens to consider that if Tommy was sleeping around, then maybe Eddie Hicks wasn't the only jealous husband. It also raised the possibility that a jealous lover could be the perpetrator. Alice Parker was worth looking into as a person of interest.

"Is your assistant here today?" Pickens asked.

"No, she isn't. She hasn't been here for several days. I've tried calling her and even went to her house, but there was no answer there or on the telephone. I'm worried about her and where she could be. She didn't show up the day after Tommy and Rhonda's murder."

Alice Parker had just moved to the top of the list along with Eddie Hicks as the perpetrator.

"You went to her house and there was no answer? When was this?"

"Just the other day. I was apprehensive."

Pickens' eyebrows furrowed and then released. "Would that be the same day you went by Tommy Benson's house?"

"How do you know that?"

"Because we saw your car," replied Pickens.

"Yes, it was the same day. Alice lives a few blocks from Tommy so after going to her house, I thought I'd drive by his place. I saw you and your deputy there and thought about coming to see you. Honestly, I was worried you'd suspect me, and now you probably do."

Pickens saw her worried expression, the concerned intonation in her voice, and started to wonder if she was lying.

He crossed his arms and replied, "You're right about that, Ms. Noristan. Can you tell me more about Alice Parker?"

Noristan's demeanor changed, and she became defensive.

"Well, when I hired her I only did a cursory background check. Her resume seemed excellent, so I didn't do much of a check on it. I knew some of the firms she listed as references, so I felt if she worked at any of them, I was sure to get a good response. That was my mistake. After I had returned from visiting her house, I did a more extensive background check. What I found or rather didn't find, was nothing for an Alice Parker. It's as though she doesn't exist."

Pickens looked at Amy and could tell she was thinking the same way he was, more complications.

"I was hoping you'd found something useful. Instead, you've made my job more difficult. You're on my list of suspects, so you know what I'm about to say. Don't leave town."

"Don't worry, I won't. Would you like my file on Alice?"

"That would be helpful. Give it to my deputy. Mind if I look through Alice's desk?"

"Help yourself. With Tommy gone, now I have to find a replacement. Mind if I ask if you're married, Sheriff?"

"Not at all, and the answer is yes."

"What about you, Deputy, are you spoken for?"

"Sorry, I'm spoken for too."

"Damn, the good ones always are, just my luck."

Amy and Pickens ignored her comment and then Pickens thoroughly went through Parker's desk. It was apparent the woman had cleaned it out except for a package of Handi Wipes. He found nothing that would help with the case. Just as a precaution, he asked Amy to take another look.

Amy looked from the desk she was searching and said, "I don't know if this is important, but it's worth a look. It's just a piece of paper, but there appear to be initials scribbled on it. It says MB. Take a look."

He looked at the initials. "Do these mean anything to you, Ms. Noristan?"

She looked closely at the initials. "No, nothing. I haven't the faintest idea why that piece of paper is there."

"We're all done here. You've been very helpful. I just wish you'd come forward when you knew Tommy was killed. Give us Alice Parker's address. We're going to her residence."

Irene gave them the address and said goodbye. Outside of Noristan's office, Amy asked, "What did you think of her?"

"Excuse my language, but that's one horny lady and she stays on the murder board."

"Horny without a doubt; however, she sure ain't no lady. I wonder how many other horny fillies Tommy kept in his corral." Amy shook her shoulders. "I feel like I need a shower after listening to her."

"You're not the only one." Pickens shook his head. "Can you believe she propositioned both of us?" They both laughed.

"Now we know of at least two maybe even four of Tommy's fillies," said Amy. I guess we'll eventually find out how many others there were."

"Yeah, eventually," said Pickens and then they got in his SUV.

Irene Noristan felt a little more confident that the sheriff might not believe she was the killer; however, she wasn't going to take anything for granted. She decided to take matters into her hands. Irene wanted to know just who Alice Parker was and where she was. It was something she just couldn't get out of her head. She knew of a private investigator who had done some work for her in the past and he'd always wanted to get in her bed. Irene decided this may be the time to make his wish come true, so she called him.

Bobby Ellison had been a private investigator for the past ten years. Before that, he was a police officer in Jacksonville. When Irene called him, he was delighted to hear from her and eager to help her, especially since she offered to make his wish come true and satisfy his lust for her. Irene asked him to track down Alice Parker and told him what her search revealed, what little there was.

"Can I come to your office and see if I can get any fingerprints and maybe some DNA?"

"Yes, and maybe you could go to her house but be careful not to alert the sheriff. I'll give you a down payment when you get here." That made Bobby happy. Irene was a woman on a mission to track down Alice Parker.

When Pickens and Amy arrived at Alice Parker's residence, they noticed the neighborhood was comprised mostly of rentals just like where Doris Young supposedly lived. They walked up to the front door and as a precaution knocked several times, but there was no answer.

"What do we do now, JD?"

Pickens rubbed his hand down the back of his head and replied, "Since we don't have probable cause, we'll have to get a warrant and come back. Shit, I was hoping we might find some tangible evidence. Let's go to the office and see if Billy has anything for us."

When they arrived at the sheriff's office, Billy was waiting for them. As soon as Pickens entered, Billy told him that he had visitors.

"Sheriff, Mr. and Mrs. Marsden are here to see you. They're Rhonda Hicks' parents."

"Shit, where have they been all this time?"

"They've been traveling and just got home yesterday. Mr. and Mrs. Marsden heard about the murders last night and came in this morning. I told them you were out working the case, but they wouldn't leave until they got to see you."

"Okay, put them in the conference room. Amy and I will be right there. And thanks, Billy."

"No problem. How did things go at Noristan's office?"

"It was productive in a way. Noristan's assistant Alice Parker may have been having an affair with Benson, and Noristan hasn't seen her since the day after his death. We went to her residence, unfortunately, no one was at home. Add her name to the board under Benson along with Noristan. She did some background checking on Parker and got nothing, so it's time for you to work those magic fingers on the computer. Here's her file."

"I'll get right on it."

Pickens and Amy went to the conference room to meet with the Marsdens. They were in their fifties. Mrs. Marsden wore red-rimmed glasses and perfectly coiffed hair. Her eyes looked sad, as though she was in mourning. Mr. Marsden's hair was gray with a receding hairline, and his eyes seemed like those of an extremely concerned parent.

By their expressions, Pickens sensed they were upset about their daughter's murder. He wasn't going to let Amy take the lead on this; it was time for him to ask the questions.

"Mr. and Mrs. Marsden, I'm Sheriff Pickens and this is Sergeant Amy Tucker. We're sorry for your loss. Can I get you anything, coffee, soft drink, anything?"

"No thank you. We're okay, but thanks for offering. Can you tell us anything about what happened? Not the details of the murder, but about the case. Is Eddie a suspect?" asked Mr. Marsden.

Pickens wasn't sure how much he wanted to tell them but was glad they didn't want the gruesome details. He also wasn't sure if they could help with finding Eddie Hicks, but he planned on asking, anyway.

"We're still working on our investigation, Mr. Marsden, and there isn't much I can tell you yet. Eddie is a suspect, but we can't seem to locate him. You have any idea where we might find him? Also, do you know of anyone who might want to hurt your daughter?"

"No, I don't," Mr. Marsden replied. "And I don't understand what you mean by not being able to locate Eddie. Hasn't he been home since the tragedy occurred?"

Pickens was surprised at his comment about Eddie, especially about not being home.

"No, he hasn't. He was out of town when it happened, at least from what we can surmise, but we still can't locate him. I have to ask you a sensitive question, and I hope you folks won't take offense."

Before Pickens could ask his question, Mrs. Marsden interrupted him.

"You want to know if we knew about Rhonda and Tommy's affair. Is that what you want to ask us? The answer is yes, and Eddie also knows. Rhonda and Tommy have been doing it ever since college. Rhonda and Eddie should never have gotten married." She paused and Mr. Marsden placed his hand on her arm. "Once they decided to, things just spiraled out of control. At first, they thought they were in love with each other, but it soon became apparent they weren't."

"Excuse me for asking Mrs. Marsden, but did you know Rhonda was pregnant?"

Amy was surprised that Pickens came right out and asked that question. He had forgotten about sympathy for these grieving parents and was concerned only with solving the case. She thought of saying something but decided against it.

"Yes, we did, so did Eddie. Tommy would have been the father if this awful tragedy hadn't happened. Rhonda told us that she was pregnant and that Tommy was the father. We asked her to please tell Eddie. We even suggested she ask Eddie for a divorce. She said she couldn't do that to Eddie." Mrs. Marsden rubbed her eye with the back of her hand. "We told her she wasn't being fair to him, and he should know the truth. Eventually, she did tell him, and they agreed to get a divorce. Eddie was having an affair of his own. We believe the woman lives in Warfield. That's where Eddie's mother lives. Have you talked to her yet?"

As soon as Pickens looked at Amy, she knew what he wanted. Amy excused herself and went to find Billy. He was working the Alice Parker matter, but she told him to hold off on that and instead see if he could find a woman by the last name of Hicks in Warfield. Billy ran a quick search but came up with zilch. He tried Creek City and came up with one name, a Jacqueline Hicks with a last known address on Brackston Street. Amy thanked him then went back in to join Pickens and whispered in his ear what Billy found.

"We ran a search on the last name Hicks, and we found one name, a Jacqueline Hicks with a last known address on Brackston Street. Is she Eddie's mother?"

Mr. Marsden looked at his wife and decided to answer Pickens.

"Yes, that's his mother, but she changed her name when she married Tommy's father quite a few years ago. They both lost their spouses a long time ago. They started dating when Eddie and Tommy were in college. After Tommy's dad had died, she moved to Warfield. We thought Jackie changed her name to Benson. Maybe she changed it back to Hicks, we're not sure which. It could even be her maiden name. Don't know what that would be. We've always called her Jackie.

"Last we heard from Eddie was that she was working part time as a waitress at a restaurant in Warfield. I think it's called The Outer Café. It's easy to find. You may want to talk to her. Maybe she knows where Eddie is and maybe the name of his girlfriend. I hope you can solve this, but we don't believe Eddie killed Rhonda and Tommy."

The information shed a whole new light on the case and added more to the confusion. They had to find Eddie, his girlfriend, his mother and Alice Parker; whoever she was. Pickens thanked Mr. and Mrs. Marsden and said goodbye.

Before leaving, Mrs. Marsden asked when they could see Rhonda and when they could arrange for her burial. She also asked the same for Tommy since he had no family.

"I'm very sorry but it may take some more time, Mrs. Marsden. I'll check with the medical examiner and let you know. Leave a number with my deputy. Once again, I am so sorry for your loss. I promise you we are doing all we can to resolve this matter."

"Thank you, Sheriff. We're sure you are as we know about your reputation as a good man. One more thing, please don't judge our daughter. She really was a decent person; she just made a mistake and now she's paid for it."

Pickens felt sorry for Mrs. Marsden as he would for any grieving mother. He understood her loss of a child just like when he and Marge lost theirs.

"I'm not judging your daughter at all, Mrs. Marsden. Everyone makes a mistake sooner or later in their life. I've made some myself. As far as I'm concerned, your daughter was a decent person."

"Thank you, we appreciate that."

Amy took their number, gave them her condolences, said goodbye and then went to join Pickens and Billy.

"What do you think about what we just learned from Mr. and Mrs. Marsden?" asked Amy.

"It sure sheds a whole new light on Eddie as the perpetrator and makes me wonder about Alice Parker. We know about The Outer Café and its owners. I think it's time to pay a visit to Warfield. First, I'm going to make a call to Richard Logan, the owner of the café, and ask if he knows this Jacqueline or Jackie Hicks, Benson or whatever."

"I wouldn't do that," said Amy. "You may be alerting Logan and he might tell Eddie's mother."

"You think they would do that?"

"No, but I believe we should be cautious," Amy replied. "We have enough problems with this case."

"I guess you're right. We'll be cautious and surprise them."

"I'm always right. You just don't realize it."

"Smart ass!"

"By the way, have you noticed what time it is? I don't think this is a good time of day to go to Warfield. In the morning would be better and before lunch. We may get lucky and catch Eddie's mother then."

"Okay I give up, Amy, you're right again. What the heck what's another day and besides it's not too far from dinnertime. Let's all go home early today. Except for you, Billy; you find Alice Parker for me."

Billy felt slighted that everyone but him was going home early. He knew the importance of finding Alice Parker, so he didn't gripe about it.

"Gosh, Sheriff, I always get the dirty work and miss out on going home early."

"Yeah but when you come through, you're the hero."

Everyone laughed and left for the day except Billy.

CHAPTER 13

Early the next day, Pickens arrived at the office. Waiting patiently for him was Amy. They greeted each other, entered through the front entrance and then went to find Billy. As usual, Billy was at his desk with his fingers working the computer earnestly trying to find Alice Parker. Unfortunately, he hadn't accomplished his mission and hoped Pickens would understand. He was there all night and was still unsuccessful.

"Morning, Sheriff. Morning, Amy... You folks have a good night because I didn't." He rubbed his forehead. "I was here the whole night and haven't been able to find anything on this Alice Parker, but I'll keep trying. She's a conundrum."

Everyone stopped what they were doing and looked at Billy.

"Man, you sure got today's word in, Billy."

Billy hunched his shoulders. "What can I say, Zeke. When you got it, you got it."

Pickens thought about giving Billy a hard time about his lack of progress but since he had been there all night and the shadows under his eyes and unshaven face made it obvious that he was, Pickens decided to go easy on him.

"Well, I can't say you didn't go the extra mile, Billy, but flowery words won't help solve this case. We need to find Parker, and I appreciate your effort." Amy was about to say something but

Pickens continued. "Why don't you go on home and take a nap, shower, and shave. Come back after lunch. Maybe you'll get lucky. Go ahead, go on home."

Billy was relieved Pickens was giving him a break. He needed a nap and a shower, so he was going to leave before Pickens changed his mind. Amy was also pleased that Pickens gave Billy the time off.

"Thanks, Sheriff, I'll be back right after lunch. Y'all still going to Warfield this morning?"

"Yes, just as soon as we do some paperwork. Amy was right; we don't want to get there too early. We'll probably leave around ten."

"Okay, then I'll see you later."

Billy gathered his things and left for home. As he was leaving, Pickens and especially Amy gave him a smile and a wink. Billy was pleased with himself.

Pickens and Amy drove to Warfield to meet with the Logans and hopefully Eddie Hicks' mother.

"You have a plan for when we get there?" asked Amy.

Pickens took a while to respond as he hadn't given it much thought, but he knew that they couldn't just go there without a plan.

"I really don't. I'm not sure what to expect. Hicks' mother may not be working today, and if we alert the Logans, they might alert her. We're gonna have to play this carefully and keep all options available. You got any suggestions?"

Amy was surprised he was deferring to her, and now she had to come up with something however meager it might be.

"I agree, but we need something to at least set the tone," she replied. "How about we say we were in the area and decided to stop for lunch? We can ask to speak with one of the Logans while we're there. That way it won't look suspicious. While chatting with whichever one is there, we can casually ask about their waitresses. If Hicks' mother is there, we can inquire about her. What do you think?"

"I like it. Good thinking. We'll do it just as you laid it out. We make a good team, don't we?"

His comment surprised her. Pickens didn't usually come right out and give her credit for anything.

"Wow! I can't believe you said that. Yes, we make a good team and don't you ever forget it."

"Okay, but you're pushing it now. Let's get to Warfield."

On the way to Warfield, they passed a sprawling horse ranch with several horses grazing and a work crew from the Department of Corrections juvenile detention center. Pickens waved to the officer in charge.

When they arrived in the city, they drove to the Outer Café and found a place to park. It was early enough before the lunch hour, and there were plenty of empty spaces.

The Outer Café had changed some since they were last there. The restaurant's outside seating area had more tables, and its interior appeared larger. It appeared as though the restaurant was profitable, and the Logans were enjoying its success. And with Richard Logan as the mayor of Warfield, it probably helped bring in more customers. Pickens and Amy walked into the restaurant and were immediately greeted by Randy.

"Sheriff Pickens and Sergeant Tucker, what brings you to our café?"

Since Randy didn't seem suspicious about their visit, Pickens looked at Amy to see what she thought he should do. Amy nodded, indicating he should go ahead with their plan.

"It's good to see you, Randy, especially under more pleasant circumstances. We were in the area and decided to stop for lunch. Are we too early?" Pickens asked.

"We're not quite ready for lunch yet, but we can certainly accommodate you two. How about a seat outside under the awning? That way you can enjoy the ambiance, and I can join you for a chat so we can catch up."

Pickens was glad Randy had suggested a table outside since it was a lovely day, the temperature hadn't heated up yet, and because they were the only customers. Also, that Randy wanted to chat. So far, their plan was working.

Randy escorted them to their table, gave them menus, poured them each a glass of water and said he would be right back. While they were waiting, the waitress looked their way, and Amy noticed she seemed a little concerned. Amy glanced at Pickens then toward the waitress. Pickens glanced at the waitress then nodded his head at Amy signaling he understood.

"Miss, excuse me, but could you help us here?" asked Pickens.

The waitress hesitated as though she didn't hear him, then decided to walk over and see what they wanted.

Amy looked at Pickens. He hunched his shoulders and whispered, "Think it's her?"

"Could be," Amy whispered. "Let's wait and see. And don't confront her yet." Pickens nodded in agreement.

"Yes, Sheriff, what can I do for you? I overheard Mr. Logan call you sheriff that's how I knew who you were," commented the waitress.

"You're very observant, the sign of an excellent waitress. We've looked at the menu, but could you tell us the special or what you would recommend?" asked Pickens.

The waitress seemed to relax—which pleased them both.

"I recommend the eggplant lasagna. It's delicious. Mind if I ask you something?"

Pickens and Amy glanced at each other, relaxed, hoping her question had to do with why they were there, and maybe she wouldn't take off on them if she was Hicks' mother.

"Not at all, go ahead and ask," answered Pickens and then looked at Amy. Her expression suggested she was as curious as he was as to what the question was. Had their little ruse worked or failed?

"I'm Eddie Hicks' mother, and I suspect you're looking for him and want to talk to me. You probably want to know if I know where he is. Am I right?"

Neither Pickens nor Amy expected this, and he wondered if the Marsdens had contacted her.

"Were we that obvious, Mrs. Hicks?"

"I expected you sooner or later. Why don't I take your order, then I'll sit with you? I'm sure Randy won't mind. He knows I've been expecting you."

"Sounds like a good idea. We'll each have the eggplant lasagna."

She left to place their orders and then she and Randy Logan returned to join them—which surprised Pickens.

Logan sensed that Pickens and Amy were surprised he was with her.

"You two are probably wondering why Jackie asked me to be with her while she talked to you. Jackie has been a loyal employee here for several years, and she's like family. She told us about what happened to her daughter-in-law and Tommy Benson. We know you're looking for her son Eddie and expect Jackie might know where he is. I'm going to leave that information up to her, but I can assure you Eddie didn't murder his wife. I'll let Jackie explain, and you can decide what you believe. We already have an attorney on call if necessary. Jackie, why don't you take it from here?"

Pickens looked at Amy, and both knew they had made the right decision by not calling the Logans ahead of their visit.

"Before you start, Jackie, may I call you by your first name since I'm not sure what your last name is now?" asked Pickens. "I know about your marriage to Tommy's father. What I'm really interested in is why neither of you hadn't bothered to contact us, and why we had to come find you?"

Logan gave Pickens a daunting look and replied, "I take umbrage to your remark, Sheriff!"

Pickens didn't hesitate to respond and followed with, "Take whatever you want, Randy, but you should have known better after the support I gave your brother Richard for his election."

Jackie hesitated before responding. Logan sat back in his chair with a dejected look on his face realizing Pickens was right and said nothing.

"I'm sorry, Sheriff, I know I should have, but I'm a mother and was protecting my son. If I knew he was guilty, I would have asked him to turn himself over to you." She was hoping for his understanding. "Eddie is worried that his life may also be at risk and that of his girlfriend."

Pickens was baffled by her comment about protecting her son. What did Eddie need protection from besides the murder of his wife and best friend? That was for an attorney, not the sheriff.

"I'm not sure what you mean by protecting him, Jackie. From whom or what does he need protection?"

Jackie hesitated again. "When Tommy was in college, he dated a woman. When they broke up, she didn't take it well and Tommy started receiving threatening calls. Eddie wants to talk to you. He just doesn't know how to prove his innocence. If I get him to talk to you, will you protect him?"

Pickens and Amy both thought of Alice Parker.

"We'll do our best. Can you tell me if that caller was a female or a male?"

"I don't know, Sheriff. You'd have to ask Eddie."

Pickens decided it was time for her to tell them where Eddie was. If he was innocent as she says he was, then there was no reason for him to hide anymore.

"Jackie, I need to talk to Eddie. Can you call him and ask him to meet with us or at least speak to us?"

Jackie looked at Logan, and he nodded.

"I'll call and ask him. Just so you know, my last name is Morison. It's my maiden name, and I use it now that both my husbands are deceased."

Amy made a note of it as Jackie Morison dialed her son. Amy's phone buzzed, and she glanced at it. It was a text from Billy.

She showed it to Pickens, and he mouthed, "What's that?"

She leaned over and said Billy got her maiden name from social security records.

Pickens whispered, "Oh."

Jackie Morison stepped away from the table so she couldn't be overheard and placed a call on her cell phone to Eddie. The call was made to her home phone in case Pickens was monitoring Eddie's telephone.

When Eddie's girlfriend, Mitzi, answered, Jackie told her she wanted to talk to Eddie. Mitzi said he was right next to her and she would give him the phone.

"Mom, what's up?" Eddie asked. "I didn't expect to hear from you this morning." Jackie hesitated before responding. "Mom, did the sheriff find you?"

"Yes, Eddie, he did, and he's here at the restaurant. We've had a lengthy conversation, and he wants to talk to you. I think you should speak to him. He's trying to solve Rhonda and Tommy's murder, and if you don't talk to him I may be in trouble for hiding you. It's your decision, but I really think you should speak to him."

Eddie hesitated before responding then spoke to Mitzi and told her what Jackie said. Mitzi agreed with Jackie.

"Okay, Mom. I will. If he's there now, I can do it over the phone."

"No, I think you should come here. It would be better, and I don't want them going to my house."

"Okay, tell him I'll be there in fifteen minutes. Thanks, Mom."

"I love you, and I believe everything will be okay."

"I hope you're right. See you in a bit."

CHAPTER 14

While they waited for Eddie Hicks to arrive, Pickens and Amy ate their lunch. Jackie said he would be there in fifteen minutes but already forty-five had passed. Pickens started to worry that Eddie might have taken off and the conversation between Jackie and him was a ruse to give him a head start.

Customers were starting to arrive at the restaurant, so Logan and Jackie excused themselves to wait on them.

Amy gave Pickens a suspicious look. "Think he's not going to show?"

Pickens was thinking the same thing. "I've got that feeling."

Just then, a couple entered the restaurant and looked their way. The man raised his hand as a gesture of recollection, and the two walked over. Pickens recognized Eddie from the pictures in Hicks' home office, but he didn't recognize the attractive woman.

Hicks looked directly at Pickens and said, "Sheriff. I'm Eddie Hicks. I believe you're looking for me. Sorry for the delay, but we had to do something before coming."

Pickens got up from his seat and extended his hand. At first, Eddie thought he had a pistol in it, but when he saw the open hand he reached out and shook it.

"Thanks for meeting with us, Eddie," Pickens added with sincerity in his voice.

"I appreciate your willingness to hear me out, Sheriff," Eddie said cautiously, still not knowing if he was about to be arrested.

Amy glanced at her watch—her signal that she wanted him to move on. Pickens narrowed his eyes and calmly said, "Why don't you sit down and tell us your story. First off, how did you and Benson become partners?"

Eddie and his companion sat down. "Sheriff, this is my girlfriend, Mitzi. She's here because she's an important person in my life, and I don't keep secrets from her."

Just as Hicks was about to continue, the Warfield police car drove by. The officer rolled down the window and gave Pickens a two-fingered salute. Pickens returned it but wasn't pleased by the distraction. The officer was one of several Pickens dismissed when he became sheriff. Since the Warfield City Council had gone through a drastic change, the mayor now had the authority to terminate both police officers when their contracts expired—which meant the guy would be out of a job again.

But that wasn't Pickens' concern. Hicks' story was, and the unwelcome intrusion was an annoying distraction.

Before Eddie could continue, Pickens turned to Logan, who had just returned from waiting on customers, and asked, "Randy is there someplace we can talk that's more private?"

Randy looked around and replied, "We have a private room that's not in use. It has bi-fold doors that you can close for more privacy. Follow me."

He led them to a section in the rear of the restaurant furnished with a large table and eight chairs. Logan closed the bi-fold doors.

Everyone sat and then Pickens said, "Thanks, Randy this will work. Okay, Eddie, continue."

"Sheriff, I didn't kill Rhonda and Tommy. I would never do such a thing. Rhonda was my wife, and Tommy was my best friend and we were all business partners. I've known about their affair for a long time. It's been going on since we were in college. Rhonda and I should never have gotten married, but we thought we were really in love and it would last forever.

"When Rhonda said that she wanted a divorce and that she was pregnant, I was glad to grant the divorce but I was surprised about the pregnancy. Rhonda and I didn't want children, and she was more against it than I was so it was a lot to digest.

"After I finished my business in Jacksonville, I decided to take some time off to decide what I was going to do. I called Rhonda to tell her I wouldn't be home for a few days but got her voicemail. I left a message for her. I then called Tommy and got his voicemail. I didn't want to leave him a message about my plans, so I called the office in the event he was there. Doris said they both went to lunch, so I told her I would be out for several days and she should tell Tommy and Rhonda. I figured they were probably at Tommy's house and their phones were off for reasons you can surmise." He paused, and Mitzi placed her hand on his. Grateful for the reassurance, he continued.

"I drove straight here from Jacksonville to be with Mitzi. I called my mom and told her I would be here in Warfield. On the drive here, I decided to propose to Mitzi so we could get married after finalizing the divorce. Mitzi said yes, and before coming here we went to the jewelers and picked out a ring."

Mitzi raised her left hand and flashed a ring.

Jackie had just joined them and when she saw the ring, she shouted, "You're engaged!" And then walked over and hugged them.

"Yes, Mom, we are."

Again, Amy glanced at her watch.

Pickens coughed and said, "I hate to break up the celebration but you were saying."

Jackie sat down. "Sorry about that. Mom gets excited sometimes." Eddie glanced at Mitzi, smiled and then asked, "Have you spoken with Doris yet?"

Mitzi's face lit up with a smile. Both Pickens and Amy could see that she was happy. Eddie's mom beamed with joy at them both.

"Eddie, Doris is no longer available. It's a long story, and you don't need the details but she knows what happened. When we spoke with her, she didn't mention you telling her you wouldn't be coming back to the office or staying away for a few days. Do you have any reason as to why she didn't?"

Silence, then Eddie spoke up. "She probably forgot, Sheriff, or was trying to protect me. Doris suspected what was going on between Tommy and Rhonda. I'd say she forgot."

Although he was suspicious, Pickens chose not to reply but instead looked at Amy and she gave him a critical eye.

Eddie continued with his story. "When I heard about the murders I called my mom, then I called Mr. and Mrs. Marsden to tell them what happened. They were on vacation, but I have their cell phone number. Mr. Marsden asked if I had done it, and I assured him I didn't. I told him about Mitzi and me, and he understood and believed me."

Pickens and Amy glanced at each other both thinking; why didn't Mr. Marsden mentioned Eddie's call? Was there a conspiracy going on here?

"Eddie, is there some reason why Mr. Marsden didn't tell us about your call when we talked to him?"

"He knew you would suspect me right away, so he asked me to stay here until the time was right. Maybe you would solve the case and then I could come to Creek City. He didn't mean to deceive you; he was just trying to protect me. Mr. Marsden's been like a father to me ever since high school."

Pickens and Amy looked at each other skeptically.

"How did the three of you meet and become partners?" asked Pickens.

Eddie looked at his mother. She smiled and then he answered Pickens' question.

"Tommy and I were friends in high school. That's when we met Rhonda. Tommy's father was a member at a hunting and fishing camp. Rhonda's dad was also a member. At a hunting outing, she recognized us as we rode the same school bus together. She knew our first names only. One time when we were at the hunting lodge, we introduced ourselves and struck up a conversation.

"Rhonda thought I was the quiet shy type. I was and a little self-conscious too. But with some egging on from Tommy, I asked her out." Eddie grinned. "She brushed me off and said she had to check us both out with her dad. After her dad gave her permission, we went on a date. Tommy later asked her out and she said yes. We both started dating her, and the three of us became inseparable best friends. Eventually, she started dating just me."

"Tell him what happened after high school and during college, Eddie. And that woman," interrupted Jackie.

"I will, Mom," Eddie replied. "Don't you have customers to attend to?"

Jackie turned to Randy. He waved the back of his hand. "I suppose so," she sniped, then got up and walked off.

"Sorry again, Sheriff, she doesn't need to hear anymore. After graduation from high school in 2000, the three of us went off to Langston College and roomed together." Pickens raised his eyes. "Mr. and Mrs. Marsden gave their permission as long as she had her own room."

"What about that woman and Tommy?" asked Amy.

Eddie shook his head. "Oh her. Tommy met her during spring break 2004, when Rhonda and I went to the Keyes to sort out our relationship. Tommy stayed at school. He told me he met her at her sorority house. They went to a party and then he took her home with him." Eddie glanced at Mitzi. She mouthed, 'It's okay.'

"Tommy called her a sex feign and couldn't get enough of him. They had this little Bret and Scarlett thing. He let her move in with him during the rest of Spring break. After that, she returned to her sorority house and they continued dating. When graduation

came, Tommy had to distance himself from her as she wasn't going
to be part of his life after college.

"Sheriff, the breakup didn't go well. Tommy said the last words
she said to him were, 'You'll be sorry, Tommy Benson.' That's all I
know about her. There's something else. While in college, Tommy
and Rhonda were intimate and again after Rhonda and I got married. I'm not faulting him. Rhonda never really made up her mind
about which one of us she wanted to be with."

Eddie's explanation of Tommy's relationship with Rhonda
agreed with what the Marsdens had said, but Pickens was interested
in the woman with whom Tommy had an affair. He'd get to that
after he talked with Amy.

"How did you all end up in business together?"

"At Langston, the three of us enrolled in the School of Visual
Arts Design. I enrolled in the architectural program, which helped
me get a part-time job. It also got me a paid internship during the
summers. Tommy signed up for the construction engineering program, and Rhonda enrolled in the school of design. We all graduated with honors.

"We each found jobs at different companies. After two years
working apart, Tommy suggested we go into business for ourselves.
He had his contractor's license and had taken on a few small jobs.
Rhonda thought Tommy's idea made sense and that we should
do it. I considered it and then agreed. We formed a corporation,
obtained an SBA loan from the local bank in Creek City and rented
an office.

"At first, Rhonda acted as the secretary. Years later, when her
design services were more in demand, we hired Doris Young as the
office assistant. She was the perfect candidate, a single mom with
two children plus she had a good resume. Doris occasionally had to
leave early to get her children from school. We didn't mind. Before
long, the business was doing incredible, and we were reaping huge
rewards.

"I was often out of town working with clients several times a month. That left Tommy and Rhonda alone at the office, except for Doris. I guess that's when their relationship began and later Rhonda became pregnant." Mitzi placed her hand on his arm. "And now my best friends are gone."

CHAPTER 15

Pickens and Amy glanced at each other. Pickens decided it was time for a consultation with her.

"Can you excuse us a minute, Eddie? I need to discuss something with my sergeant." Pickens tilted his head, stood, and Amy followed him.

When they were out of hearing range, Amy asked, "What's up?"

"Nothing, I wanted your opinion. What do you think about his story so far?"

Amy crossed an arm over chest, raised the opposite arm, and rubbed her chin. "He seems sincere, but getting engaged soon after your wife was murdered? That's harsh, or I could be wrong. He still hasn't proven his alibi to me. Doris could help establish his timeline, but…"

"Forget about Doris. What about that woman Tommy had the affair with in college?"

Amy shook her head. "Okay, I'll forget about Doris for now. And now we have that woman. We could use a name. It would be great if Billy could get into Rhonda's phone and check her messages."

Just then Pickens' phone chirped. He checked the caller ID and saw who was calling. Leroy's message said it was urgent that Pickens call him.

"I have to take this call, Amy."

Amy gave him a daunting look—which he ignored—walked away and called Leroy.

"Leroy, this better be important because I'm in the middle of something."

On the other end, Leroy responded with, "I'm holding an envelope in my hand that says Sheriff Pickens on it. It's from Doris. She must have written it before leaving. The woman who cleaned up after Doris left had it in her pocket but forgot to give it to me. She realized it when she got home and just brought it to me."

"Any idea what's in the envelope?"

Leroy hesitated at first but then replied, "I have no idea, JD, but I'm worried if I give it to you, you'll check for fingerprints. If you do that, you may be putting Doris and her kids in harm's way. I can't let that happen."

Pickens didn't like where this was going. Leroy was his friend, but the envelope was evidence. He needed to make a leap of faith here.

"We may be good friends, and I understand what you're saying but that envelope is evidence. I have to know what's inside."

There was a silence before Leroy responded. "Let me open it and tell you what's in it. If it's important enough, I'll give it to you but you have to promise me no fingerprint check."

Pickens decided it was a fair compromise. "Okay, open it and tell me what's inside. I promise no fingerprint check."

Leroy trusted his friend and opened the envelope. Inside was a handwritten note from Doris.

"It's a note from Doris. Want me to read it?"

Now extremely curious Pickens replied, "Go ahead and read it."

Leroy put his phone on speaker and read the note.

Sheriff Pickens
I apologize for not telling you this when you talked to me.
It wasn't intentional. I just forgot on that fateful day.
Mr. Hicks called me and said he wouldn't be coming to the
office. He said he was taking a few days off and left a mes-
sage on Mrs. Hicks' phone.
Doris Young

"That's all there is. Is it helpful?"

"Maybe, we'll see," Pickens replied suspiciously. "I have to think
about it. Keep the note and the envelope. If I need them, I'll come
get them."

Still concerned, Leroy asked, "We okay, JD?"

"Yeah, we're okay, Leroy." Both hung up, and Pickens went to
join Amy and the others.

Pickens walked back over to Amy. "What was that about?" she
asked.

"That was Leroy. There was a note from Doris that helps with
Eddie's timeline." Amy eyed him suspiciously. "Don't ask. Just trust
me. Let's go finish our talk with Eddie." Amy clenched her jaw and
followed Pickens.

When they rejoined Eddie and Mitzi, Pickens said, "Eddie, I
just got a call that proves what you told Doris, but not Rhonda."
Amy's face took on a surprised look. "Obviously, your mother and
fiancé are your alibis and no doubt Randy is too. But I still need
more proof that you called Rhonda."

Eddie gave it some thought before replying. "Check Rhonda's
messages. My call should be on her phone."

Amy spoke before Pickens could. "Eddie, her phone may be
password protected. Any idea what the password is?"

"That's easy. It's Eddie."

"Sheriff, you want me to call Billy and have him check Rhonda's phone now that we have her password?" asked Amy.

"Sure, and have him do that text thing you two do when he has an answer."

Eddie's girlfriend Mitzi asked, "Sheriff, don't take offense, but don't you text?"

He turned to her and curtly replied, "I do, and no need to apologize as there was no offense." Pickens grinned, and Mitzi smiled. Then Pickens asked the inevitable question, "Eddie, do you have any idea who would want to kill your wife and business partner?"

Eddie thought for a while before answering. "I'm not sure, but maybe that woman that Tommy had his fling with in college meant something more serious when she said, 'You'll be sorry, Tommy Benson.'

CHAPTER 16

Pickens thought about Irene Noristan's missing assistant and wondered if there was a connection. He thought about the piece of paper with the initials on it that they had found in Alice's desk.

"Eddie, do the initials MB mean anything to you?" he asked.

Eddie thought for a while and replied, "No." Eddie then pointed a finger in the air. "Hold on; now I remember Tommy once said the girls' name was Melissa. Does that help any?"

Pickens and Amy exchanged glances. Pickens felt they might have a possible first name.

"It might; I'm not sure. For now, I'm going to accept your story, but don't go any farther than Warfield and you should come to my office and give a statement. Do we have an understanding?"

Eddie's face registered concern and decided that what he hadn't yet told Pickens might make him seem guilty of Rhonda and Tommy's murder. He figured Pickens would find out eventually, so he decided to tell him.

"Sheriff, there's something else. You'll find out anyhow, so I might as well tell you now."

Pickens and Amy froze, wondering what was coming next.

"Let's have it."

"Besides the divorce, the three of us were splitting up the company. Tommy and Rhonda were going to buy me out. I'm opening my own firm with Mitzi. There's a buy-sell agreement in place that's funded by life insurance. We each had key man life insurance policies. All paid for by the company. Now that Tommy and Rhonda are gone, there's no need for the buy-sell but I'm probably beneficiary on both their policies. That probably makes me a suspect again but I had nothing to do with their deaths, especially not for the insurance. If I killed them, I can't collect anyway."

"You should've told us that in the beginning, Eddie. We'll let it go for now, but because of it you're still considered a suspect. Make sure you're in my office first thing in the morning."

"Thanks," Eddie nervously replied and then asked, "I'll be there, but is it possible I could give my statement here in Warfield? I'm not ready to be seen in Creek City yet."

Pickens considered his request. "Sure, I'll alert Sergeant Dunne that you'll be there in the morning."

"Thanks, can we go now? Mitzi and I have a lot to talk about."

"Sure, and thanks for talking to us. It was pleasant to meet you, Mitzi. Next time be honest with me, Eddie, understand?"

Pickens gave them both a stern look and then as he and Amy got up to leave, he gave Eddie a look of concern.

Before leaving, Pickens turned to Mitzi.

"I can't help noticing, but you seem familiar. Have we met before?"

Mitzi smiled. "No, we haven't, but you've met my sister, Betsy. We look similar. She worked for Mayor Larson, but now she works for Mayor Logan."

Pickens laughed, and thought about Larson's secretary and the help she provided when he investigated Larson's wife's disappearance some years ago.

"Tell your sister hello. I owe her thanks."

Mitzi said she would and then they all left the restaurant. On the way out, Pickens said goodbye to Logan and Jackie.

When they were in the SUV, Amy's phone buzzed. "That must be Billy. Let's see what he has for us." She showed the text to Pickens. As far as he could tell, it was just gibberish.

Pickens' eyes narrowed. "What's it say?"

"Billy was able to get into Rhonda's mailbox. Eddie's message was there, sent at one o'clock the day of the killings. His story checks," she replied.

"Good, it makes it easier. Now we have to find out who MB is. Tell Billy to add Melissa to the board under Benson. That meeting with Eddie was exhausting. At least we can cross him off as the perpetrator for now. He's someone who fell in love with the wrong woman, lost her to his best friend, lost them both to a murderer, then got lucky and fell in love with somebody else. It's a real tragedy. What do you think?"

She glanced at him, and her first thought was is he spouting Shakespeare with the tragedy comment or is he still working on increasing his vocabulary.

"I don't know about a tragedy, but I agree with you—Eddie isn't our shooter. At least we got a possible name for the initials. Now if we can get the last name to go with Melissa, we may have our killer and maybe Tommy's stalker." She followed her comment with, "But, I'm not so sure our killer was a woman. A shotgun isn't the choice of weapon for a woman. A man, yes, but poison is usually a woman's selection of weapons."

He contemplated her comment. "What about you? If you had a husband or boyfriend who dumped you or cheated, what would be your weapon of choice?"

She pointed her finger at him. "I wouldn't hesitate to shoot him between the legs."

Pickens's eyebrows lifted. "Well, if ever I find one of your male friends shot, I'll know you did it."

"What about Marge? What do you think would be her choice of weapons if she found out you cheated on her? Not that you ever would."

He ran his finger down his chest and abdomen. "Marge wouldn't hesitate to slice me open with a scalpel."

They both grinned.

"Are you going to tell me about Leroy's call?"

"No," he answered curtly.

She glanced at him with anger in her eyes, but decided to drop it and said, "Maybe Billy can research Langston's records and get a name to match Melissa."

"I like that, let's get him working on it. Not bad for a day's work. We uncovered some evidence, hopefully. I'm thinking of going home after I drop you off and take a nap. The stress of this case is starting to get to me."

Concerned, Amy asked, "You okay?"

"Yeah, like I said it's the stress of this case. Every lead is ending up a dead end. Eddie and Noristan were our best suspects, but not anymore. Now we have Melissa, the mystery woman. And I'm getting calls from the mayor. I wouldn't be surprised if he calls the county commissioners and convinces them to call me and suggest I turn the case over to the State or the Feds."

"Would you do that, JD?"

"Hell no, this is my case, and we'll solve it without outside help messing it up." Pickens glanced in the rearview mirror. "Shit, is that that damn reporter following us?"

Amy turned in her seat. "Looks like him. Think he followed us to Warfield and saw us talking to Eddie?"

"I hope not. Otherwise, he'll write one of his bullshit stories."

"What say we stop at Bartley's and get some homemade ice cream and see if he follows us?"

"Good idea, Amy."

"Can we sit on the porch or do we have to eat in the car?"

He glanced out the window. "It looks like rain. If it does, we'll wait it out on the porch."

"What if that reporter stops, too?"

Pickens grinned. "We get out of the SUV, stand firm with our hands on our weapons and see what he does."

Amy smiled. "Love it. If any one's sitting in the rockers, should we show our badges and make them move?"

"No, that wouldn't be right. We just say it's a beautiful day to be sitting on the porch with ice cream and see what happens."

"That's better, JD."

Pickens parked, and they stepped out of the SUV, stood their ground, and watched the reporter's car as it drove on down the highway.

They walked up onto the porch of Bartley's Country Store, a popular lunch place for farm and ranch hands and Department of Transportation work crews. Bartley's was a fixture in the county since the early 1930s, and its compound consisted of the retail store with a wooden porch with four rockers on it, a farmhouse, a shed for logs, a rarely used outhouse and what they called the factory. The factory was where they butchered the pigs into cuts for sale.

"Did you know that Leroy gets his meat here," asked Pickens.

"No, I didn't," Amy replied.

Just as they entered the store, it started to rain. They went inside and ordered triple scoop cones and then sat in the rockers listening to the rain as it pounded on the tin roof.

"This is the life, ain't it?"

"Yep, it sure is." Amy looked up. "JD, what are those clear balloons up there for."

"They're not balloons; they're plastic bags filled with water to catch flies. Didn't your folks ever use them?"

Amy scratched her forehead. "Not that I remember. Must be an old wives' tale." She licked her cone savoring the taste of butter pecan ice cream. "Being here, JD sure makes you forget about the case."

Pickens put his feet up on the porch rail, crossed his legs, licked his cone of French vanilla ice cream, and smiled. "Yep, it sure does."

"What if the mayor or a commissioner, calls?"

"They can go to hell. I'm off duty."

CHAPTER 17

That evening, Marge asked Pickens if he would take Bailey to the groomer for his quarterly bath and grooming because she had an early meeting at the examiner's office.

"I can take him, no problem. He's much calmer when I take him." He looked over at their daughter. "What about Sarah? Want me to take her to school?"

Sarah stopped drawing and smiled. "Yes, Daddy, and we can pick up Annie on the way. She'd love to go with us."

The corners of Marge's mouth went up. "Okay, sweetheart. I'm sure Daddy doesn't mind. Do you, Daddy?"

Pickens's palms turned up. "What can I say? I'm just here to please my women."

Marge put her arms around him and kissed him. "I'll make it up to you, quarterback." Both grinned.

In the morning, Marge left for her office and Pickens, Sarah and Bailey piled into his SUV and then he drove to Leroy's house. Annie was waiting anxiously by the door with her mother. Pickens rolled the window down.

"JD Pickens, are you the designated driver today?"

"I sure am, Liana. Marge had an early morning meeting. I can get Annie after school if you'd like. I have to take Bailey to the groomer. Sarah and I are picking him up after school when he's ready."

"That's okay; I'll get her. She's going to the restaurant with me."

Annie bolted for the car. "See you later, Mommy."

"You too, honey."

Annie got in the backseat with Sarah and Bailey. The two girls said hello.

"See ya, Liana."

"Take care of those girls, JD."

Pickens nodded, checked to make sure the girls had their seatbelts fastened, waved to Liana and left. Annie said hello to Bailey and let him lick her face. Pickens dropped the girls off at their school, drove to the vet to drop Bailey off and then to the office.

Billy waited to tell him what he found on a Melissa at Langston College.

"I found several women named Melissa at Langston College, but one looks interesting. Her last name was Nolan, and she left school shortly after Tommy graduated. I got her home address."

Pickens raised his hands. "I don't want to know how you managed that. Just tell me."

Eddie grinned. "If she's the right one, she lives in Davie." He smiled. "Did you know that Davie was once a big stop on the rodeo circuit? I had an uncle who lived in Plantation Acres not far from there. My cousins and I used to horseback ride on his property. And we went to the rodeo. They did it up big with a parade, cowgirls on horses and a rodeo clown. They had high school rodeo contests."

"What does that have to do with our case?"

"Just digressing, Sheriff. I got a phone number for a Nolan there. You want me to call it or do you want to?"

"Amy and I will handle it. Good work, Billy."

"Thanks, Sheriff."

"So, what do we do?" asked Amy. "Call or make a trip to Davie? It's like five hours to there. Or, we can have the Broward County Sheriff's office check it out."

Pickens scratched his head. "If she's our killer and we call, she may rabbit. If we asked Broward to investigate, she may make up a story and still run." He rubbed his chin. "I got a better idea." He looked at Billy. "See if you can find anything about this Melissa Nolan in Broward records. There has to be something there. Check the local paper, too. But keep it low key for now. And add her name to the board. She's just a person of interest for now."

"Got it, Sheriff."

Later in the afternoon, Pickens picked up Sarah and they went to get Bailey. While they waited for the assistant to get him, another man was there with his dog waiting to pay. Sarah asked if it was okay to pet his dog.

"Sure, he's harmless and older than me in dog years."

Sarah smiled, bent down and rubbed the dog's head. "What's his name?"

"Romeo, and he loves children."

"Hello, Romeo, my name is Sarah." Romeo licked her face.

"Sheriff, are you investigating that thing at the Benson house?"

Pickens raised his eyebrows. "Yes, sir, I am. Why, did you see something?"

"My name's Andy Brodson. I live across the street, but I'm at work during the day. His house was dark the night before, and I didn't hear anything." He looked down at his dog. "Romeo may have, but he can't tell you anything."

"Too bad, Andy, because I could use all the help I can get."

Sarah rubbed Romeo's head, took his paw, and thanked him.

When the assistant brought Bailey out, Pickens and Sarah said goodbye to Brodson and Romeo. Bailey hopped onto the back seat, and Sarah joined him. Before leaving the parking lot, Pickens called Amy.

"What's up, JD? I thought you were going home."

"I am, but I wanted to let you know that I met Benson's neighbor who lives across the street. He works during the day, and he said the night before the murder Benson's house was dark and all seemed quiet." He looked back at Sarah and Bailey. "We almost had a witness. His name's Romeo, but he's a dog so he can't help. Just wanted to let you know."

Sarah tapped him on the shoulder. "Daddy, Romeo saw someone come out of the house across the street."

Pickens's eyes squinted. "Hold on, Amy." He turned his head. "Sarah, what do you mean Romeo saw someone? How do you know?" Then it dawned on him. "He talked to you, didn't he?"

"Yes, he said he saw someone come out of the house in the afternoon and get in a dark truck like yours. He also heard several loud bangs."

"Are you sure, sweetheart?"

"Yes, but he didn't know if the person was a man or a woman. That's all he told me."

"Okay, that was very helpful." Now he had to tell Amy.

"You still there, JD?"

He scratched his forehead. "Yes, Amy, but you're not going to believe this but we have a witness who saw someone leave Benson's house the afternoon of the murder and he heard several loud bangs coming from the house."

"That's good news but who's this witness?"

"I'll tell you when I see you tomorrow. It's gonna sound weird, but you'll have to trust me."

"Okay, if you say so. I'll see you tomorrow." Amy scratched her chin.

"Thanks, and tell Billy to add an unknown male or female to the board." They ended their call, and Pickens started his truck. "Okay, Sarah, let's go home."

When they arrived home, Marge was already there fixing dinner.

"We're home, Mommy and Bailey's spotless. I helped Daddy with his case. I'm gonna let Bailey out."

Marge stopped chopping vegetables and looked at Pickens.

He mouthed, "Wait until she leaves."

After Sarah and Bailey had gone outside, Pickens told Marge what had happened at the Vet's office.

"Now I have to explain to Amy how I learned about the person of interest. Any ideas on what I should say?"

Marge rubbed her neck. "Well, she is a good friend and knows a lot about us already so you might as well be honest. I'm sure she'll keep our secret." He reached for a vegetable but stopped when she held the knife up. "You'll spoil your dinner."

"It's just a vegetable, come on."

"No."

"Okay, damn, you're not nice. You're right about Amy. I'll tell her the truth. What's for dinner?"

"Tripe soup."

"What the hell, I'm going to Leroy's."

"Just kidding. We're having beef stew for a change."

"That's better." He turned his head. "Here come Sarah and Bailey."

Pickens, Sarah, and Bailey went to watch television while Marge fixed dinner. Later they ate together, watched television, and retired for the night.

CHAPTER 18

The next morning, Pickens called Amy into his office. He closed the door and told her about Sarah and Romeo. She was quite surprised with what he said.

"Are you sure she didn't imagine it? Kids her age can make up things, especially to please their parents."

"I'm sure. It's not the first time, and I expect it won't be the last."

Amy touched his arm. "Do you want me to have a talk with her or do you prefer someone else?"

He brushed her arm away. "No, and it's not like that. She doesn't need psychoanalysis or whatever it is you do." She raised her eyebrows, astonished that he might be doing the word a day thing again. "Listen, I'm asking you as my senior deputy and as a friend to trust me on this. Marge thinks we can trust you, and she said I should be up front with you." He scratched the back of his head. "Marge believes she may have inherited it from her grandmother. Can we trust you to keep our secret? It's imperative for Sarah's sake."

Amy considered his request but wondered if she was doing the right thing for Sarah's sake. "Okay, but I'm not sure I'm making the right decision. But if you and Marge are satisfied, I'll go out on a limb and honor your request." She nodded her head. "You know this is really weird, don't you?"

He turned his palms up. "Believe me; I felt the same way when Marge told me. Thanks, Amy." He reached out to shake her hand.

She took it and smiled. "Okay, now let's see what Billy has for us."

They left his office and walked over to Billy's desk. Pickens turned and checked the murder board.

"Before you update us, Billy, I want to review what we have on the board." He grabbed the marker and pointed to Benson. "So far we have three women we know slept with Benson." He turned toward Billy. "There may be more, but these are the best we have so far. They're all considered persons of interest until we rule them out." He drew a line under Rhonda. "She's definitely ruled out. This Melissa Nolan looks good to me and so does Noristan's assistant, Alice Parker. She could also have slept with Benson, so she's a person of interest." He had previously erased Doris Young's name and didn't bring her up.

Billy interrupted him. "I Googled Melissa Nolan and found several articles. There's one in particular you'll want to see. I'll print a copy so you can read it." He pulled up the article and printed it. "It's in a Broward County newspaper about a Melissa Nolan who committed suicide on June 17, 2004. It says she was twenty when she took her life." The copy came out of the printer. "Here it is."

Pickens took the copy and read it out loud.

WOMAN'S DEATH RULED SUICIDE
By Michael Abado

The Broward County Medical Examiner's Office has ruled the death of Melissa Nolan, age twenty, a suicide. Her

body was found in the barn on her parent's ranch in Davie,
Florida on June 17, 2004. Sources say the lead investigator
has also concluded that it was a suicide.

Ms. Nolan attended Langston College, and friends said she
was distraught over a relationship that ended badly.

She was a rodeo queen as a teenager and often participated
in youth rodeo contests. Ms. Nolan will be laid to rest at
Forest Grove Memorial Gardens.

"Guess we can cross her name off as a person of interest," remarked
Amy.

"Yes, and I bet the boyfriend was Tommy Benson. She would
have had motive if she was alive." Pickens rubbed his forehead. "I
wonder if she had any friends who might have sought retribution
against Benson."

"Is that today's word, retribution?"

Pickens evil-eyed Amy.

"Forget I said that. It's possible, but who and how do we find
Nolan's friends from back then unless we talk to the parents?"

"I could try to see if she was in a sorority at Langston College
and maybe locate a sister or roommate," said Billy.

"That's a good idea. See what you can find. Meanwhile, let's
focus on Alice Parker for now."

"I already Googled her and, unfortunately, found nothing in
Florida. I even checked Georgia and Alabama, just to be safe. It's
like she doesn't even exist."

"How about a driver's license?"

Billy shook his head. "Nope, nothing."

"Shit, this case is getting weirder the more we investigate." He
pointed to the board. "Parker moves up the list. We need to find
out who she really is. You have any ideas, Billy?"

"I've tried everything, but I'll keep at it."

"I've got an idea."

Pickens glanced at Amy. "Well, let's have it."

"What about the reporter? Maybe he has some info that might help."

Pickens looked at the article again. "On Alice Parker or Melissa Nolan?"

"Nolan. It's worth a try." Amy walked over to the board and pointed to both women's names. "We may get lucky. We have to do something."

"Amy," Billy interjected. "Talking to a reporter is like telling the whole world we're investigating. You know how they are."

"He's right," said Pickens. "Let's not start there. Besides, he's liable to talk to the local authorities, and they might not like us digging into their case."

Amy turned her palms up. "Okay, then how about Googling the reporter and see what he's about?"

"Go ahead, Billy."

Billy swiveled in his chair, pulled up Google and entered the reporter's name. He pursed his lips. "It won't make a difference if we try to contact him, Amy."

"Why?"

"He died of pancreatic cancer in 2011." Billy scratched the top of his head. "Now what?"

"What about a death certificate?" asked Zeke. It may have some useful info. Who knows?"

Pickens's eyes squinted. "Of the reporter? Why?"

"No, of Melissa Nolan."

Impressed, Pickens replied, "Good idea. Do it, Billy."

Billy tapped into the Broward County Vital Statistics website and entered death certificates and then entered Nolan's name.

"You have to order a copy, and it may take days. You want me to order one?"

"Might as well. Keep searching for something, and I don't want to know how you do it." Pickens checked his watch. "It's lunchtime, so I'm going to Leroy's." He hesitated and said, "Better yet, Billy, wait till I get back from lunch." He turned, started to leave but stopped. "You all do what you have to do. Hopefully, you'll have something when I get back." He waved his hand and left.

"I'm going to the Fishtail restaurant where Benson and Hicks ate their last meal. Anyone care to join me?" asked Amy.

"I'll go," replied Zeke.

"Bring me back a double cheeseburger, fries, and a milkshake from Burger Shack."

"Eating healthy, are we, Billy? Gotcha covered." Amy motioned toward the door. "Let's go, Zeke."

When Pickens exited the building, Jimmy Noseby, the local newspaper reporter was standing there with a pen in one hand, pad in the other; his ball cap turned backward, and a shit-eating grin on his face.

"What do you want, Nosey?"

"It's Noseby, Sheriff. You got a suspect in that homicide yet?"

"No comment. You know the drill, Nosey. The case is an active investigation. When we have something to tell the press, you'll get it like everyone else." The creases between Pickens's brows deepened. "I won't have you making something else up just to look good. You've caused me enough problems." Noseby's jaw dropped. "And don't bother any of my deputies." He waved his hand, turned, and walked off leaving Noseby standing there with a look of disappointment.

Five minutes later, Amy and Zeke exited the building.

"Sergeant Tucker, can you comment on the investigation?"

Amy shook her head. "No comment."

Noseby turned his hands up. "Come on, Amy, give me something."

"What part of no comment don't you understand?" Amy replied and gave him a dismissive wave. "Come on, Zeke, let's go to lunch."

Noseby turned his ball cap around, slumped his head and shoulders and walked away.

When Pickens arrived at Leroy's, most of the lunch crowd had already left. He took a seat at the counter and picked up a menu. The waitress walked over and greeted him.

"Good afternoon, Sheriff, anything particular you want to order?"

"Afternoon, Wanda, I'll have a pulled pork sandwich and a Coke."

She wrote the order down and placed it in the window on the rack.

Leroy grabbed the order, made his sandwich and then brought it out to him.

"Here ya go, JD, enjoy it." Wanda brought his Coke and set it down in front of him. "How's the case going?" Leroy asked.

Pickens shook his head. "It's not. We're not having any luck on finding who the killer was."

"You'll solve it, don't worry." Leroy reached under the counter and pulled out an iPad. "I got something I want to show you." He hit the keys and then turned the iPad so that Pickens could see it. "This is my new website. What do you think?"

Pickens grabbed the iPad and scrolled down the info. "Man, this is great. When did you do this?"

"William did it for me. Kid's a computer whiz. He even gave me a Facebook page." Leroy smiled. "I could friend you if you want."

Pickens scratched his head. "Friend me? What's that mean?"

"It's social media. You can hook up with friends and family, or you can post your thoughts." Leroy took the iPad back. "You need to get with the twenty-first century."

Pickens rubbed his chin. "You mean I could look up old friends, classmates or sorority sisters?"

"Sorority sisters? You don't have any but Marge might."

"Yeah, but one of our persons of interest might. Thanks, Leroy you just may have helped."

Leroy hunched his shoulders. "I'm not sure what I did but if it helped, great. How's the sandwich?"

Pickens had a mouth full, but mumbled, "Great!" He wiped his mouth. "Hold on; I want to call Marge." He dialed her number, and she answered on the second ring.

"Hey, quarterback, what are you up to and how's the case going?"

"I'm having lunch at Leroy's." Pickens rubbed the back of his head. "We're at a crossroad and grasping for straws."

"What does that mean?"

"It means we haven't got a clue as to who the killer was. Our first suspect committed suicide in 2004, so we're back to square one. Billy's requesting her death certificate from Broward County. Her name was Melissa Nolan." He swallowed a bite of sandwich. "It's gonna take a while."

"You could save time and look it up online. What do you want the DC for?"

"I told you we're grasping at straws. Every time we come up with a possibility we end up at a dead end." He realized what he said. "I mean that literally and figuratively as with this latest one. Maybe it will tell us something. I don't know."

He was aware that she would question his decision because he was crossing into her territory. Early in their marriage, they agreed to respect each other's profession. She wouldn't discuss the legality of his cases, and he wasn't to get involved in forensics. But being as how they were married and lived together, he couldn't help taking an interest. Plus, he had read her latest book *Forensics Made Easy,* a collection of gaffes, spoofs by colleagues and fellow employees on special occasions, and other interesting tidbits compiled during interviews at conventions and video conferences. It was the number one seller among the forensics community and was gaining popularity with the public.

She was often asked to speak at several different medical schools where her lectures were popular and well attended. She used simple layman's language, such as corpse instead of a cadaver, and when describing certain body parts she used ridges and peaks as large as Mt. Everest. She also described the cutting open of the body as unzipping its outer layer of covering. Her comments always brought laughter to her audience and Pickens. Although recognized as an authority in her field, she wasn't smug and didn't act like a know-it-all as some others did.

"You got any suggestions, wide receiver?" He knew she would—which was why he told Billy to wait until he returned from lunch.

She deliberated a moment. "Let me call the Broward Medical Examiner. Maybe I can get some info from the autopsy. I'll have them fax me the DC as a courtesy." She knew it was what he had hoped from her.

"Thanks, Doc."

"You're welcome, Sheriff."

He ran his hand down the back of his head. "Say, are we on social media?"

"You mean like Facebook?"

"Yeah, tell me we're not."

Marge's face lit up. "No, but I'm on a site for forensic scientists. It helps us stay in touch with each other. We share what's new and sometimes help each other with a difficult question." She took a drink from her water bottle. "Why, you want to join one?"

"Absolutely not because then I'd have to listen to everyone sharing their life stories and those of people I don't even know or care about."

She laughed. "I feel the same way, so don't worry we'll keep our privacy."

"Thanks, I'll tell your husband you were very helpful." This time both their faces lit up with a smile.

"You're welcome, and I'll tell your wife you were a good boy. See you tonight."

They hung up; she went back to writing her autopsy report while he finished lunch.

"I gotta go. Thanks for lunch."

Leroy's eyebrows shot up. "Hey wait a minute, you gotta pay."

Pickens smiled. "Just kidding. Here's ten, that should cover it."

"What about my tip?"

Pickens grinned. "Don't trust the sheriff when it comes to money." He tossed a five next to the ten. "See ya." Then he left as he knew the tip would go to the waitress, as always.

CHAPTER 19

When Pickens returned to the office, he immediately sought out Billy. He was at his desk eating lunch and playing solitaire on the computer. When Pickens approached him, Billy was surprised and almost choked on his roast beef sandwich.

"Geez, Sheriff, you scared the hell out of me. I didn't expect you back so soon." Billy quickly placed the sandwich in the paper bag and exited solitaire.

Pickens shook his head and smiled. "It's okay this time because of this case. But next time use the lunchroom." He didn't mention the solitaire because he sometimes did it himself.

"Sorry, it won't happen again. What can I do for you?"

"Can you see if the Nolan woman was on social media? Like Facebook or whatever?"

Billy immediately pulled up his Facebook account and searched for Melissa Nolan. The other deputies walked over to see what he found.

"She was on Facebook but hasn't posted anything since 2004, before she died. She had a lot of friends, though, mostly sorority sisters."

"Damn, Billy you're good," said Amy.

"Hey, I'm not just a pretty face who can play the keyboard. I'm good at a lot of other things." He winked at Amy.

"Okay, that's enough," said Pickens. "See if any of her sorority sisters have posted anything recently."

"On it."

Pickens turned to Amy and asked her where she ate lunch. Amy nodded at Zeke.

"We went to that sushi restaurant where Benson and Hicks ate their last meal."

The lines between Pickens's eyes deepened as he asked, "They may have gone out for dinner somewhere, so what makes you think that was their last meal?"

"Remember the ME gave us a time of death sometime in the afternoon, so they didn't go for dinner."

"Right. So, what did you learn?"

Amy checked her notes. "Benson and Hicks were frequent diners there, mostly for lunch, but occasionally for dinner. He also had dinner with other women." The corners of her mouth rose. "Seems he was a famous customer always leaving generous tips."

"Any chance they could describe the other women?"

"One was definitely Noristan."

"How about Parker?"

"There was a brunette, but that's all they remembered of her. And before you ask, they don't have security cameras. Hicks' car was in the parking lot. I had it towed to McCann's for impounding."

McCann's was a salvage yard on the outskirts of the city. The county didn't have the necessary property, and Pickens didn't have enough manpower to operate an impound yard, so McCann's Salvage suited the purpose.

Marge called the Broward County Medical Examiner. Her assistant said she would call Marge back and asked if she was available for a Skype call. Marge gave the assistant her information and waited for the call. She suspected the medical examiner was taking precaution to be certain who Marge was.

Dr. Isabelle Montero Skyped Marge. She was familiar with Marge's background and her books. When Marge's image appeared on the screen, Montero greeted her.

"Dr. Davids, how can I help you?" Dr. Montero was in her fifties, a brunette, wore glasses, and had been the BME for the past ten years. "I read your latest book and thoroughly enjoyed it."

"Thank you, it's good to hear that." Marge wasn't exactly sure what she wanted from Dr. Montero, but since she was doing Pickens a favor she decided to be direct. "My husband is the county sheriff, and he's working on a case that involves a double homicide."

"What does that have to do with us here?"

"During their investigation, a name came up as a person of interest. When they researched this person, they discovered that she committed suicide in 2004 in Davie. They were going to request the DC, but I offered to contact your office to see if it was worth the effort."

"What was the person's name?"

"Melissa Nolan."

Dr. Montero removed her glasses and put the tip of the frame in her mouth, and then removed it. "I remember that particular case even thought it was more than ten years ago."

"Was there something about the case that makes it stand out?" Marge asked.

"Yes, but I'm not sure I can tell you. It's privileged information." Marge blinked. "You understand, don't you?"

Marge kept a straight face. "I guess so."

"Good. I did the autopsy. Hold on, let me pull up my report." She turned to her laptop, brought up her reports and typed in Nolan's name. When the report came up, she browsed through it. "There was nothing out of the ordinary." She took a deep breath and exhaled. "Such a heartbreaking loss for her parents. You have children, Dr. Davids?"

Marge smiled, thinking of Sarah. "Yes, a daughter; she's eight years old. If anything happened to her, I'd be devastated."

"So would I. I'm sure it's heartbreaking to lose a child." Marge's complexion whitened. "Did I say something wrong because you look like you just saw a ghost."

Suddenly, there was silence and Dr. Montero wondered if they had lost the sound.

"Are you still there, Doctor?"

Marge was trying to decide if she should mention the miscarriage.

"Yes, I'm still here. I lost my first child because of a miscarriage. My husband and I were devastated and had to go through counseling. We did, and we got through it, but my doctors said I would never be able to conceive again."

"I'm so sorry for you."

"Thank you. I was okay until there was an accident here and two women died. I had to do the autopsy and discovered one of the victims was pregnant. I took it hard, but my husband consoled me and nine months later we received a miracle when our daughter was born." She swallowed hard before continuing. "One of the victims in this case was pregnant, which is why I'm trying to help my husband."

"Dr. Davids, I'm going to go out on a limb here and tell you something that is extremely confidential." The crease between Marge's eyes deepened. "There was something that I left out of my report at the request of the investigating officer and her parents."

Marge's eyebrows lifted. "If you don't think you should, you don't have to. I don't want you doing anything that's unethical."

Dr. Montero pursed her lips deliberating whether she should. "It's rather delicate." She put her glasses back on and fingered her pen. She was trying to decide between helping a colleague and breaching a trust that someone placed in her. "Maybe you should have your husband talk to the original investigator. He's retired and may be willing to share." She decided to keep her trust. "There was something kept secret because of the nosey press, especially one reporter in particular."

Marge nodded her head. "I know what that's like. We have one of those here. We call him Nosey."

Dr. Montero grinned. "That's funny." Montero's eyes made strong contact with Marge's, and said, "You know what? I'm going to take a chance and tell you something else that I left out of my report. Ms. Nolan had an abortion."

Marge's eyebrows hiked. "Oh my, that may have had an emotional impact on her and influenced her to take her life."

"I thought the same thing." Dr. Montero took another look at her report. "When did you say that homicide happened?"

Marge referred to her report. "Not too long ago. In fact, it was the thirtieth of March. Why?"

"Ms. Nolan would have turned thirty-two on that date. Don't know if it means anything, and it may just be a coincidence."

"Could be, or the killer may have known Ms. Nolan and was acting out of revenge. One of the victims was intimate with Nolan in college in 2004. He might have been the father."

"Could be, but at least you've got something to tell your husband and maybe he should call that investigator." She again referred to her report. "His name is Frank Rinaldo. He's a bit of a character, but he was a good detective. You still want a copy of the DC?"

"Couldn't hurt. Will the sheriff need a case number?"

"All he needs is a name. Rinaldo has every case name in his head." She looked at her report. "Here's his number." She read it to Marge. "Anything else I can help you with?"

Marge wrote Rinaldo's name and number on her pad. "You've been quite helpful already, and rest assured I'll keep our conversation confidential. Mind if I call you Isabelle? You can call me Marge."

"Please do. We're colleagues, so why not." She smiled. "My husband calls me Izzy."

Marge smiled back. "I'll call you Isabelle. Thanks a lot."

"You're welcome. Tell your husband good luck." She held up her hand. "Wait, what's your husband's name in case Rinaldo calls me?"

"JD Pickens." Montero's forehead furrowed in confusion. "I still use my maiden name for professional reasons."

"Good for you, so do I."

They both logged off, and now Marge had to decide how much she should share with Pickens.

Billy again checked Nolan's Facebook page for any posts that may have been from sorority sisters. He found several, some mentioning her death and offering condolences. One in particular seemed like the person wasn't happy with what happened and sounded like she wanted revenge. Billy focused on her and searched her Facebook page.

Barbara Williams had posted some pictures of herself and comments about Nolan.

Marge called Pickens and told him what she learned from Dr. Montero but not about the abortion.

"That's interesting and real helpful, wide receiver. Now we can forget about the DC."

"Yes, and she gave me the name of the investigator on Nolan's case. She said you should call him." Marge gave him Rinaldo's name and number.

"I'll call him and see what he can tell me."

"One more thing. Nolan would have been thirty-two on the date of your homicide. Don't know if it means anything but you should consider it." As soon as she said it, she knew she was treading on his turf.

"So, are you now an investigator, wide receiver?" When he said it, he was smiling, and she could tell that he was by the inflection in his voice.

She smiled. "Just trying to help my quarterback, that's all."

He smiled too. "You are and thanks." He paused. "You mean Melissa's birthday would have been March 30."

DESCENT INTO HELL   121

"Yes, does it mean something?"

"It might. I'll get on this. See you tonight."

"Go get em, tiger."

Pickens hung up and sought out Billy who was still searching for posts from Nolan's sorority sisters.

"Billy, anything on social media from Nolan's sorority sisters?"

Billy turned and grinned. "Yes, there's one in particular from a Barbara Williams you may be interested in."

"Bring it up." He motioned to Amy. "Don't know if it means anything but Nolan's birthdate is the same as our homicide. That might explain what MB stands for, Melissa's birthday."

Amy's forehead furrowed. "Or it might mean something else."

"Or Malibu Barbie," quipped Billy. Everyone looked at him.

"Not funny, Billy."

"I'm serious, Sheriff. One of Nolan's sorority sisters lives in Malibu, California. Look at the pictures of her." All eyes turned to his computer. Barbara Williams had posted pictures of her in a skimpy bikini. The men's eyes lit up, and so did their faces. "She also didn't have nice things to say about Nolan."

Pickens scowled at the men. "Let's see what she said."

Billy pulled up her postings, and pushed his chair away from his computer so Pickens and Amy could read them. One in particular caught their attention.

Why's everyone care about Melissa Nolan? She was nothing but a slut. She couldn't wait to get in bed with that Tommy guy. She also slept with my boyfriend while I was in class. Screw her, that's what I say.

"Whoa, that girl had some serious issues with Nolan," remarked Zeke.

"Yeah, but not with Benson and Hicks. I'd rule her out as our killer," said Pickens. "Keep digging, Billy."

CHAPTER 20

It's finally over and done. She would be glad and appreciate what I did for her. Benson deserved it, and so did that bitch with him. I should have done it a long time ago, right after her death.

Maybe our children might have grown up together or maybe we would have gotten together. If it hadn't been for him, we might have had a chance for a life together.

I would have loved her child like it was my own. But we never got the opportunity to find out.

Thank goodness for Al. I couldn't have done it alone. What a rush when it was over. I never thought it would be so much fun. The look on his face when he saw the shotgun was priceless, as was hers. She wanted to say something, but I cut her off. Screw the bitch and him too.

CHAPTER 21

R etired Detective Frank Rinaldo was relaxing with a glass of iced tea at poolside of his home in Weston, Florida watching his grandchildren playing Marco Polo when his phone rang. He didn't recognize the number but knew the area code as being from Central Florida.

"Must be that sheriff Isabelle said was going to call me." He answered the call. "Rinaldo here, what can I do for you."

Pickens detected his Cuban accent.

"Detective Rinaldo, my name's JD Pickens. I'm the sheriff of—"

"I know who you are, Pickens. Dr. Montero said you might call." Rinaldo's tone changed. Although he expected the call, he didn't want to discuss the Nolan case. He was retired, it was a long time ago, he'd seen worse but Nolan's case still had a lasting effect on him.

Before he could cut him off, Pickens interjected. "Look, Frank. Mind if I call you by your first name? I know you're retired, and the last thing you want is some sheriff from Podunk bothering you about an old case. My name's JD, but I prefer Pickens."

"Podunk? Never heard of it, I thought you were from Florida." Pickens couldn't see Rinaldo smiling. "Yeah sure you can call me Frank, and I'll call you Pickens. What the hell does JD stand for?"

Pickens hesitated to respond as he didn't like using his given names but did it anyway.

"Joshua Daniel. My parents picked my name from the Bible, but I prefer JD."

Again, Rinaldo smiled. "I can see why. Hold on a sec." Rinaldo covered his phone with his hand and shouted, "Hey, cut that out you guys and go easy with Rita. Remember she's a girl."

His grandchildren had changed their game to Horse. They were going at it aggressively, especially his granddaughter.

"Grandpa, are you kidding?"

He hunched his shoulders and turned his palms up. "What can I say, *Hermosa Flor.*" Rita smiled.

"Beautiful flower, she's more like a stinkweed," yelled her brother and shoved her into the water.

"Hey, careful there," yelled Rinaldo.

Rita came up from under the water and started splashing her brother. Then they all started splashing each other. It was like a war zone with water flying everywhere.

Pickens waited for Rinaldo to come back on his phone.

Rinaldo got up and moved his chair away from the action and put the phone to his mouth.

"Teenagers. You got any kids, Pickens?"

Pickens smiled. "Yes, a daughter. She's eight years old."

"Cherish her, Pickens they grow up too fast." Rinaldo's attitude changed toward Pickens, and he considered being helpful. "So, what's an eleven-year-old suicide have to do with you?"

Pickens felt because of them both being parents he had made a connection with Rinaldo.

"Both victims were at Langston College the same time as your suicide was." He decided to add the info about Benson. "One of them had a fling with her."

Rinaldo sat up straight, and suddenly his interest piqued.

"Was his name Tommy?"

"Yeah, and his last name was Benson. Why'd you ask?"

Rinaldo took a sip of tea and rubbed his hand through his hair. *Mierda*, he said to himself, I had hoped that what happened to Melissa would never come up again. I might have to take a chance on this hick sheriff.

"Listen, Pickens, what happened occurred in the past. I don't want to dredge up old memories."

"Okay, I understand but I'm dealing with a double-murder, and it could help. Give me something, please."

Rinaldo bit his lip and said to himself, this guy's not gonna give up.

"If I tell you, will it stay between just you and me?"

"Absolutely."

"Okay, I'm gonna trust you. Melissa left a note for her parents before she took her life. She described how before she came home from school in 2004, she had an abortion. Best I can tell, she told a friend and the friend took her to a clinic for the procedure." Rinaldo rubbed the back of his head. "*Oh hombre*, when Mrs. Nolan read that part, she told me she almost fainted. Melissa's note said she couldn't face the shame for what she had done and the embarrassment she caused her family. She said the baby's father was a boy she met at school. I presume that was Benson.

"According to Mrs. Nolan, when Melissa came home she said she took some time before coming home to decide what she would do over the summer break. Mrs. Nolan asked Melissa about Tommy, the boy Melissa had told her that she was in love with. Melissa said it was over, and she didn't want to talk about it. You still there, Pickens?"

"I'm here."

"I thought maybe you hung up since you haven't said anything."

Pickens fumbled for a reply. "I was just listening, and I can tell how troublesome it must be for you. I emphasize with you. It must have been difficult listening to Mrs. Nolan. How come she shared so much with you?"

"After reading Melissa's note, she rushed to the barn hoping to prevent Mr. Nolan from discovering Melissa hanging from a rafter. She immediately called 911. Unfortunately, when she entered the barn, Mr. Nolan was on the ground with a heart attack and the site of both her husband and daughter caused her to faint.

"I was dispatched to the scene to investigate. The first thing I did was have the crime scene techs take Melissa's body down and then I looked for clues that might suggest something other than a suicide."

Rinaldo considered ending the conversation but reconsidered. He had already told Pickens more than he wanted to.

"What I'm gonna tell you next could cause trouble for me and my wife, Pickens. I've said too much already, but my wife thinks I can trust you. She trusted your wife."

Pickens smiled. "She has a way about her, and I'd trust her with my life, Rinaldo. Same as I'm sure you trust yours."

"*Si, compadre.* And Mrs. Nolan trusted me. She went with her husband to the hospital. I waited until I felt it was a respectable time and visited the hospital to talk to her. That's when she confided in me about the suicide note and its contents which I've already told you. She asked if I could keep the note and its contents from being made public and avoid a media circus. You know what that could be like, don't you, Pickens?"

"Yeah, I do. I'm trying to avoid one here with this case."

"*Exactamente*, Pickens. That's what I'm talking about."

"What did you do about the note, Rinaldo?"

"I've never told anyone this, Pickens and now it's our secret. I told Mrs. Nolan when she gets home to burn the note and don't tell anyone about it, and I wouldn't mention it in my report."

Pickens almost gasped. "You put your career at risk; you know that and possibly your retirement."

"Don't I know that. But I sympathized with the woman. After the ME had ruled that there was no suspicious cause of death, I closed my case as a suicide, and a nosey newspaper reporter accepted it. That's all I got, Pickens. Does that help?"

"Yes, thanks, Rinaldo. It's possible Melissa' suicide is somehow a motive for revenge by someone who knew her. I'll let you know when I know."

CHAPTER 22

"**D**amn it! Some PI named Bobby Ellison was nosing around in Al's old Tampa neighborhood. I need to tell her."

"I thought she had all bases covered."

"So did I. Now we have a new problem."

"What do you mean?"

"Just what I said, now I'll have to check out this Ellison and see if I can find out who hired him. Maybe it's that broad where she worked. She said she made sure there were no traces of her ever being there."

"Maybe it's nothing. Why not just leave it alone for now?"

"I can't, if she slipped and left some piece of evidence, I'll have to take matters into my hands—which I'd rather not."

"You're blowing this out of proportion. Leave it alone or you'll make matters worse."

"We'll see, but she left me no choice. If I have to do something, I will, and it will be fun. Oh, yeah, won't it."

"You're making a big mistake."

"Who the hell cares! "

CHAPTER 23

Irene Noristan hadn't heard from her investigator in over a week and was getting frustrated. Not only because he hadn't called her but because she wanted something else from him. She missed Benson who was great in bed and knew every way to please her—which was why she needed to see the investigator. She wasn't one to regret anything, but if she had hired Alice without a sufficient background check and she was involved in Benson's murder, she'd never forgive herself.

She looked up from her laptop and smiled when Bobby Ellison walked into her office.

"Where the hell have you been?"

He smiled, sat down in a chair in front of her desk and then turned and looked at where an assistant would have sat.

"Still haven't found a replacement for Parker? Is that why you're so bitchy?"

"Cut the crap, Ellison. For your information, I'm using a temp, she left fifteen minutes ago. Now, what have you found out?"

"Is that any way to greet a good man?" Ellison smiled. "It's great to see you too, Irene."

"Screw you! What have you found out?"

His eyes lit up. "Better, but much better if it was the other way around."

"Just give it to me, and I'm talking about your report."

He grinned. "Okay, here's what I got. Since your office wasn't a crime scene, I was able to do my investigation." He nodded toward her restroom. "You'd be surprised what evidence women can leave behind."

The space between her eyes narrowed. "What's that supposed to mean? I'm the only one who used that bathroom. Alice would have used the other one."

He pointed a finger in the air. "That may be what you thought, but seems Parker also used it." He tossed a plastic bag on her desk. "She used your lipstick, and I had those tested for fingerprints and DNA." He smiled. "She forgot to wipe them down."

"So that's where they went. You could have told me. I almost accused the cleaning service of stealing the lipstick." Her eyes narrowed. "So, where they helpful?"

He leaned on her desk. "I have a friend at a lab, and she ran the DNA and prints for me. You owe me two hundred bucks."

Her head snapped back. "Why, am I not paying you enough?"

"It's not for me; it's for my friend."

"Okay, I get it." She smiled. "You owe me one hundred dollars for the lipstick." Her palm turned up. "So, what did this friend of yours find out?"

He sat back in his chair. "My friend got a good DNA sample and fingerprints as well off the lipstick." Noristan sat up straight, suddenly her interest piqued. "The fingerprints were a match. Alice Parker wasn't your assistant's name. Her real name was Allyson Healey. She lived in Tampa, but not anymore." He checked his report. "I used my resources in law enforcement and contacted the Tampa Police Department. She went to Langston around the same time as Benson and Hicks. After graduation, she got in with a bad crowd and did some drugs, nothing serious, but enough to get her arrested twice."

"What about her parents? Do they know where she is?"

His palms turned up. "No, her mother said Allyson moved away months ago, and she hasn't heard from her since."

"What about other family members?"

He again checked his report. "None as far as my sources could tell." He closed the report folder. "So, we got a dead end. You gonna share this with the sheriff?"

Noristan leaned back in her chair and rubbed her chin. "I'll think about it. Leave the report on my desk and lock the front door."

He stood, turned and walked to the front door, locked it and turned the sign around, so it read *Closed*. Then he walked back to her office.

"What about this door?"

She got up from her desk, walked around it and sat on the edge. "Close it, and lock it too."

He did as told and walked toward her.

"This isn't payment in full, is it?"

"Shut up, Ellison, and get on with it. And here's your check."

CHAPTER 24

Getting info on that Ellison guy was easy. His PI website supplied enough—especially his address. He was so easy to follow just like Benson was. I was right; Al must have left some evidence of her behind. Why else would he be going to visit Noristan with a file under his arm?

They must be up to more than just discussing the contents of that file. Why else would Ellison have put the closed sign on the front door?

Al said that Noristan and Benson were getting it on. Maybe she's a player like Benson was and paying the PI in trade. Slut!

I'll wait until he leaves, then I'll approach her and see what's in that file.

When Ellison left, he turned the sign on the door back to open, smiled, and walked to his truck.

Noristan picked up the file from Ellison and read its contents.

"Shit! Alice or Allyson whatever the hell your name was if you had anything to do with Tommy's murder…" She slammed both hands on the desk. "I swear I'll wring your neck like a wet towel." She placed her hands on the back of her head, leaned back, and closed her eyes. Guilt consumed her like a raging inferno. She thought if only she had done the proper background check maybe Tommy would be alive. Again, she slammed both hands on the desk. Pickens wouldn't appreciate Irene hiring a PI to investigate Parker and might consider her an accessory. Irene picked up the file, tossed it in the wastebasket, reconsidered, grabbed it, set it back on her desk and then reached for the phone—but changed her mind.

Looking down at her desk, Irene remembered their first time. Tommy had come to collect the deposit on the contract, and she offered him a bonus—which he gladly accepted. There were numerous times at his place and hers. She glanced over at the couch, where they ravaged each other. It was also Ellison's favorite spot.

She was aware of the situation with Rhonda. It didn't matter because she was certain Tommy could never be in a monogamous relationship, and she was content remaining on the sidelines.

Somehow, Tommy had captured a place in her heart and her mind—something that had never happened before. She missed him not just for the sex—which was great—but what she felt when in his arms. No man had ever made her feel that way, and none would ever replace him.

Tommy changed her, and with him she no longer felt like the woman who enjoyed having flings with men and then discarding them like worn out shoes. The memory of him would always cling to her heart like a mother clinging to her child.

Longing for him caused tears to flow down her cheeks like a gushing waterfall.

Filled with guilt, sorrow, and rage, she placed her arms on the desk and lowered her head to them.

Okay, time to see what's in that file. First up, turn the sign back to closed. Well lucky me, your office door's closed. Next, out comes the super shorty shotgun from the briefcase and then close the door to conceal some of the noise.

Here we are or rather here we come, bitch!

So distraught about Tommy, Irene hadn't heard the office door open. She felt a presence, and the temperature in the room suddenly felt like it had dropped below zero. Something made her reconsider calling the sheriff and reached for the telephone. When she raised her head, the face of death grinned down at her, and she found herself staring into the barrel of a shotgun.

Panic engulfed her, she felt the rapid beat of her heart, worried she was about to have a heart attack, and grasped her chest. Perception told her that the end was near and wondered if it was true that your life flashed in front of you when you were about to die. Irene wasn't ready to join Tommy. She wanted to enjoy a longer life and have the pleasure of more men, like Ellison. Maybe another Tommy would come along, but she knew it wasn't about to happen.

With outstretched palms, she shouted, "Wait, don't, please! What do you want? I'll give you anything, but please don't kill me."

"Screw you, bitch! I want that file Ellison gave you."

Irene looked down at the file which held Ellison's report. She considered saying "screw you" but decided she best not. She could always get another one from Ellison.

"Either give it to me or I take it, your choice."

Irene didn't want to be a hero but felt if she didn't do something she'd end up like Tommy and Rhonda. The only way out of the room was through the office door but to get to it, she had to go around or over her desk. But the killer was still an obstacle to overcome.

"There's no way out if that's what you're thinking."

Irene looked left then right. She considered diving under the desk, getting her phone out of her purse and calling 911but reconsidered as she'd still have to get past the killer and the shotgun.

There was no way she was going to escape this dilemma since she could identify the killer—which meant she had to die.

She decided if she was going to die, she'd at least go on her terms and make Tommy proud.

She picked up the file and tossed it in the air. "Screw you, bitch..." It landed on the floor spilling the contents out. The killer looked down and watched it fall to the floor. Inadvertently, Irene knocked the bag of lipsticks off the desk. "That's for Tommy!"

"**Your mistake, you left me no choice.**"

Irene saw the shotgun pointed at her head, heard the blast, and felt it, but that was the last thing she ever saw. Her face popped like a balloon spewing blood, flesh, and bone everywhere. She slumped over her desk creating blood spatter on it.

"Whoops, guess I aimed too high. Oh well, at least you won't need makeup anymore. Damn, what a thrill. I could get used to this."

"Now you've done it. I have to put this file back in order. What's this? Is that Al? Shit. The stupid bitch, I told her to be careful. I may have to reconsider my plan. So long, bitch. To show how nice I am, I'll close the door and let you have some privacy, although you don't need it."

Where is everybody? Doesn't anybody keep decent work hours anymore? Lucky me, now I can remove these damn gloves and put them and the briefcase in the truck and t⌐ off.

What a fucking blast! Hell, yeah, I definitely coul used to this.

CHAPTER 25

When the office temp arrived at Noristan's office at nine-thirty, she saw the open sign and entered. She set her purse on her desk and made a pot of coffee. Next, she put her purse in the large drawer and then knocked on Irene's door.

"Ms. Noristan, it's me, your office temp. I made a fresh pot of coffee would you like a cup?" She knocked again. Since there was no answer, she decided to open the door. When she saw Noristan, she screamed. "Oh my God, no!" She stepped back and went immediately to the phone and dialed 911. She told the operator who she was and why she was calling.

"Ma'am, is there anyone else there besides you?"

"No, I'm by myself. Please send someone and hurry."

"Okay, ma'am, help is on the way. Wait outside the office so a ⌐eputy can readily find you."

The woman felt relieved that she didn't have to stay within ⌐ht of Noristan's body.

"Okay, but please hurry."

⌐y Amy Tucker took the 911 call from Liz Price and thanked ⌐ice had already called the EMT's and sent them to the scene. ⌐ was just arriving, and Amy waved him over.

Pickens could tell by Amy's expression that something was amiss. "What's up? I hope it's nothing serious." Amy pursed her lips and shook her head. "Shit, now what?" Pickens shouted.

"That was a 911 call. There was an incident at Noristan's office. When her office temp arrived, she found Noristan slumped over and bleeding on her desk."

He slammed his fist on the nearest desk. "Please don't say we got another shotgun shooting."

"Don't know if it was a shotgun, but my guess is we have another shooting."

"Has the medical examiner been notified?"

"I called her, and she's on her way."

He let out a deep breath. "Okay, let's go. We'll take my SUV. Zeke, you go too." The three then left for Noristan's office.

Noristan's office temp didn't have to wait long as a medical examiner's van and an ambulance pulled up followed shortly by two sheriff's vehicles.

When Pickens and Amy arrived, the medical examiner was already inside. The scene was marked off with yellow crime scene tape, and the EMTs waited while the medical examiner did her job.

Pickens approached the temp. "Are you the one who made the 911 call, ma'am?"

The woman removed her glasses and wiped the back of her hand across her eyes. "Yes, I'm...I was Ms. Noristan's office temp." Again, she wiped her eyes and then put her glasses back on. "I found her, but I didn't touch her."

Pickens felt sorry for her and didn't want to interrogate her, so he left it to his deputy.

"Amy, get her statement. Zeke, you come with me and put booties on." They put them on and latex gloves as well. Amy took her pad out, took the temp's statement, her contact information and then told her she could leave.

"Thank you, deputy. I've never seen a dead body before, and I hope I never see one again."

"I hope you don't either. Here, take my card." Amy handed her a card and then the temp left.

Pickens and Zeke cautiously entered Noristan's office. While the medical examiner was surveying the body, her team collected evidence. She paused and looked up.

"Morning, Sheriff. Morning, deputy." Zeke touched two fingers to his forehead.

"Good Morning, Marge. What's it look like?" Pickens asked.

She pointed to the body that they had raised up off the desk. "Another shotgun murder, and if it's the same killer you've got a serial killer on your hands."

Zeke shook his head and asked, "But why Noristan, Sheriff?"

Pickens rubbed the back of his head. "Beats me unless it's retaliation for Benson sleeping with her."

Marge chimed in with, "If it is, then there's a lot of women out there who could be next." She looked at the body. "It's possible your killer isn't male."

"What makes you say that?"

"Shotguns normally are a weapon of choice for males, but it could be a female. The reason I say that is because if this was all about Benson, then Rhonda was collateral damage. Think about it." Pickens' eyes narrowed. "If she was, then it was a jealous boyfriend or husband. But now with Noristan, it's possible the killer was seeking retribution for anyone who slept with Benson."

"That would explain why Parker's in the wind. Maybe she knew something or knew the killer." Pickens winked at her. "I'll consider it, thanks, Marge."

"Now what do we do, Sheriff?"

His forehead furrowed. "We have to find this Alice Parker and fast, Zeke. That's now the top priority." He looked at Marge. "Got a TOD yet?"

She thought about making a wisecrack but knew he was frustrated and decided not to. "Best guess, sometime yesterday afternoon."

"Thanks, we'll leave you to your business. Come on, Zeke; we gotta get Billy moving on this Parker." He smiled at Marge, and she smiled back. He and Zeke turned to leave.

"Wait, there's something you have to see."

He turned around and saw she was holding a small plastic bag. "What's in the bag?"

She grinned. "Lipsticks. The bag was on the floor. Somebody put them in there for a reason. Noristan's lipsticks are in her bathroom."

Pickens's eyes squinted. "Why would they do that? Unless she just bought them."

Marge smiled. "Women don't buy lipstick in a plastic bag like this. Someone definitely did it for a reason."

"She's right, Sheriff. I think there's more to the lipstick."

He turned, saw Amy standing in the doorway and waved her over. "You might be right, Amy. Marge, can you do a fingerprint test and a DNA test as well on them?"

"Looks like someone already had it done." She showed him the bag. "This is an evidence bag and the name of the lab is on it." She pointed to it.

He scratched his forehead. "Who'd do that?"

She put the bag in another evidence bag and tagged it. "Don't know, but my guess is someone was conducting their own investigation. I'll contact the lab and see what I can find out. You might get lucky, Sheriff." She winked. "I'll call you as soon as I have something."

"Thanks, Marge." He winked back and suddenly had a thought. "Any chance her phone or checkbook is available?"

"Phone's probably still in her purse. Don't know about her checkbook, why?"

"Maybe there's something worthwhile." He raised his palms. "I'm grasping at straws here, help me out."

"Since you're wearing gloves, you can check her purse. I'll check her desk drawer."

He grabbed the purse, reached in, and pulled out her phone. Marge checked the desk, but there was no checkbook. He walked over to the couch and raised the purse as though he was going to dump the contents out.

"JD, wait, don't—" She waved her hand for him to go ahead as she knew it was hopeless trying to stop him. When Pickens got something stuck in his craw, there was no telling what he'd do, and he was obviously frustrated with the case.

He dumped the contents of the purse on the couch. In addition to a number of female articles and other unmentionables, out fell the checkbook and Noristan's phone.

"Well, look what we have here." He picked it up and opened it to the last check written. It was dated yesterday for two hundred dollars. He smiled. "Ellison Investigations. Wonder what he was doing for her?"

"We can have Billy check for an address, phone number or maybe he has a website."

"Good idea, Amy." He turned back to Marge and handed her the phone. "Can you check her call log and let me know if anything interesting stands out?"

"If you want, I can record the phone as evidence and turn it over to you. You've already broken the chain of evidence any-way." She shook her head. "Here, maybe Billy can do it right away."

"Thanks, Marge, you're a sweetheart." He winked, and she winked back.

Amy shook her head. "You two need to get a motel room."

"Why? We have a house with our own bedroom. Don't you?' asked Marge.

Her witty remark made them all laugh including Pickens, after which he, Amy and Zeke left.

When they arrived at the sheriff's office, Pickens went right to Billy and found him on the computer doing research on Parker.

"Morning, Sheriff. I've been trying to find something on Parker but still no luck."

He placed a hand on Billy's shoulder. "Keep working, but I've got something for you to do first." Billy logged out of the site he was on for Parker. "See if you can find anything for Ellison Investigations, and here's Noristan's phone." He handed him the phone. "See if you can go through her call log and find her last month's calls."

Billy fired up his magic fingers and started with Ellison Investigations.

Pickens walked away and went into his office. Amy followed him. He sat behind his desk and looked up at her.

"What's up, Amy?"

She breathed in and said, "Maybe we should revisit Doris Young."

He slammed his hands on the desk. "Dammit, Amy, I told you she's not part of this investigation. What more do I have to say to get you to back off?"

Amy had to take a step back as she hadn't expected Pickens to get so angry.

"But…"

"Back off, Amy, and leave my office. Dammit, now you've given me a headache." She turned to leave. "And close the damn door."

She closed the door behind her and shook her head. Her face was the color of a fine Merlot, and she had clenched fists. For as long as she'd known Pickens, he'd never used that tone with her. If it weren't for the case, she might just leave and never come back. But as a trained counselor, Amy surmised that the case was frustrating him. Still, he had disrespected her.

When Amy stepped into the bullpen, the others—surprised by the confrontation—quickly feigned busy to avoid her wrath.

Pickens wasn't angry with Amy, it's just that he had received calls from county commissioners asking for status updates on the investigation—did he have a suspect, and would there be more murders. He gave them all a stock answer—he's pursuing several leads, one in particular, but that wasn't for public notification as Pickens didn't want the suspects to know he was on to them. He used them instead of him or her because he didn't know with whom he was pursuing.

When the mayor of Creek City asked if Pickens had considered getting help from outside sources and that the city would back him, Pickens replied that he already had and those sources told him he was doing everything by the book, and when it was time they'd get involved. Of course, he didn't reveal that those outside sources were his wife, his daughter, his dog and a retired detective. The answer managed to placate the mayor and the county commissioners.

Pickens felt like all athletes did when being harassed by angry fans and wanting to shout angry expletives. But he wasn't a player now; he was the coach and responsible for the entire team, so he swallowed his pride.

He could feel the fire burning in the pit of his stomach, picked up the stapler, and threw it against the wall.

"Shit, what the hell's a serial killer doing in my county?"

CHAPTER 26

Let's see what that damn PI's report says. Shit! What's this? Fingerprints, where did he get them? Al was supposed to be careful and wipe everything down. Are you serious, lipstick? Damn it, Al, how stupid could you be?

Ellison sure was thorough. I knew she'd had problems, but I didn't know about being arrested. Now he knows Al's real name and where she lived. Good thing she moved away in time. I told her she was making a mistake moving back home. She should have stayed in Orlando.

Next time she calls, I'll have to warn her. I may even have to take matters into my hands and make sure she can't give me away.

That sheriff doesn't have this report—at least not yet. He might not even know about Ellison. If he does, maybe I should silence him before the sheriff gets to him. Damn, there could be another shotgun funeral.

Okay, first up; make a new plan starting with what to do about Ellison and then Al. This was just supposed to be about revenge for Melissa. Now it's a real mess thanks to Al.

Maybe this is her calling. No, damn it, now what's she want?

"I told you not to call. I've got everything under control."

"I'm calling because you went too far." On the other end, the caller was breathing heavily. "You weren't supposed to kill Tommy. Just scare him."

"I meant to, but I lost control and screwed up."

"Why did you shoot his girlfriend? This was all about him." More heavy breathing and obvious annoyance.

"After I had shot Tommy, I had no other choice. What did you expect me to do? She saw me, and I couldn't let her describe me and possibly make a connection to you."

"Did you know she was pregnant?" The caller sounded exasperated.

"Shit, no I didn't. Now Tommy lost something just like Melissa did."

"Like we both did." The caller sounded woeful and then concerned. "Why did you kill Noristan? She's not part of this."

A hesitation before speaking.

"Because she hired a PI and he discovered who Al is and gave her a report. I had to get that report. She might have given it to the sheriff, and I couldn't let her identify me."

"The sheriff knows about the PI and is probably going to talk to him today. Does the report say where Al is?"

"No, just that she lived in Tampa but not anymore. It also says she was at Langston when we were there."

"Does it say she was in a sorority?"

"No, but I bet he could find out. If he does, he could link her to Melissa."

"And to us. How did Ellison find out about her?"

"He got DNA and fingerprints off lipstick of all places. Al screwed up. What do we do about her and the PI? If the sheriff locates her, we're both in deep shit."

"We can't let that happen and stay away from the PI. It's too dangerous going after him. Besides, the sheriff will find out about Al anyway. He has the lipstick. It was in a bag. You left it behind. It was in a bag on the floor. And he knows about the PI. He's probably contacting him as we speak."

"Damn, Noristan must have knocked it off her desk— which was why I didn't notice it. When Al calls, I'll find out where she is and decide what to do about her."

The comment surprised the caller. "Why?"

"Because I told you, she was unstable. She should never have gone back home."

"Well, it's too late now. Everything is all screwed up, and now we have to protect ourselves. I'll call again when I know more. You be careful and get rid of that damn shotgun. How did you get hold of it, anyway?"

"I'll be careful; you can bet on that. You be careful too. The shotgun stays. I like it. And as far as how I got it, sex and money will get you anything."

"You're unstable."

"We both are, but Melissa would have appreciated what we're doing for her."

"Talk to you soon." Both parties hung up. Now I'm worried that the PI might become the next dead body, the caller thought.

CHAPTER 27

At last, this must be Al calling. "Al is that you, where the hell have you been?"

The caller hesitated and then there was rapid breathing.

"Stop calling me Al, damn it! My name is Allyson."

"Okay, Allyson, I get it, but where have you been? That PI who investigated you discovered your real name."

"I know my mother told me." Allyson took a deep breath. "I heard about Noristan. Why the hell did you kill her? Are you out of your mind?"

"Calm down; I had no other choice. I wanted that PI's file, and she could eyewitness me."

"You didn't need the file. I could have told you what was in it. And so what if Noristan knew my real name. No one will find me."

"Well, I couldn't take the chance. She might have told that sheriff, and if he found you, it might lead to me. I should have gone after that PI and killed him."

"And make matters worse? You've done enough already."

"What did you expect me to do?"

"I expected you to do what you said you were planning. Not kill Benson, just scare him." Allyson let out a deep breath. "No one was supposed to get hurt, and now three people are dead. Why?"

"I meant to scare Benson, but things got out of control. I'm sorry. We need to meet and discuss this in person."

"Why, so you can kill me too because I know your identity? No way, you're crazy, and I want no part of this or you."

"You're a part of this no matter what happens. Please, let's meet."

"No, and don't try to contact me."

"I have your phone number and could track it, so could that sheriff. Don't think about calling the sheriff because he could track your phone."

"I'm not calling anyone, and I'm getting rid of this phone after I finish talking to you. Don't worry; I'm no longer in Florida, and no one will ever find me."

"You're not being rational, Allyson."

"Rational, that's a laugh. You're a fucking psychopath, and I wish I never met you. Goodbye, good riddance, and I hope you rot in hell."

"If I do, you'll be there with me... Don't you hang up on me... Damn bitch! I'll find you and kill you and your mother too just to get even."

After Allyson had hung up the phone, she removed the sim card, stepped on it and tossed the phone into a nearby canal.

CHAPTER 28

Pickens composed himself, opened the door and stepped out of his office. When the deputies saw him, they pretended to be busy not knowing what to expect. Amy went and poured a cup of coffee and then sat at her desk, picked up her phone, and acted like she was making a call. Pickens walked over to Billy.

"Billy, is there a word today that describes this case so far?"

Everyone focused on Billy waiting to see his response. Billy swiveled in his chair to face Pickens and inched his eyes up. "There sure is."

"Well let's have it."

"It's a quandary."

Pickens placed his hand on Billy's shoulder. "Well unquandary it, and give me something to work with."

Billy rotated his chair and faced his computer. "I found Ellison's website. His office is in Warfield, and his bio says he was a former Jacksonville police officer. He's licensed to do most anything. Private investigations, corporate espionage, security, plus others." Pickens eyed the screen and focused on Ellison's address and phone number. Billy copied them down for Pickens.

Ellison's website said that the firm had been in business since 2006 at the same location. Bobby Ellison was the principal licensed investigator. He was a retired Jacksonville, Florida police officer—before that he served in the military. The firm performed investigative services for attorneys and private individuals. Services included: catching cheating spouses, digital investigation, background checks and locating missing persons—to name a few. He showed the screen to Pickens.

"Want me to print the info?"

"Yeah, print it. Good job."

"Thanks."

"Amy." She looked up, and gritted her teeth in silent anger because of Pickens shouting at her.

"Now what?" she snapped.

He ignored her harsh reply. "We're going to Warfield to see this guy Ellison and what he has to say. Let's go."

She was about to protest his attitude but decided not to in front of the others.

"Whenever you're ready, Sheriff."

Pickens turned back to Billy. "Good work, now I have to talk to this Ellison."

Pickens felt he'd finally caught a break and possibly an honest to goodness lead. It was about time he scored a first down after gaining zero yardage. He was anxious to confront this hot shot PI Ellison and learn what his relationship was with Noristan. It was also possible Ellison was involved in her murder. Maybe payment for whatever service she paid him for wasn't enough, so he decided to extract a greater one using deadly force and things went sour. Or, maybe there was more to them, and she was foolish enough to try and blackmail him, and he wasn't going to let that happen.

He went to his office, unlocked the top desk drawer, and retrieved his gun and holster. He reconsidered the situation between Noristan and Ellison and decided she possibly had him do background work on a potential replacement for Alice Parker.

He stopped short when he left his office. "Shit!"

"What's up, Sheriff?" asked Billy. He knew when Pickens yelled his cryptic remark; that something was wrong.

"I was just thinking, what if Noristan decided to investigate Parker and hired this Ellison to do it for her?"

"I wouldn't put it past her," remarked Amy who had calmed down and understood that the case was more important than her ruffled feelings.

"Looks like you'll get a chance to ask him, Sheriff." Billy nodded toward the front entrance. Ellison had just entered and was being ushered by Price.

"This guy says he has business with you, Sheriff."

"Thanks, sweetheart, you're a gem," remarked Ellison.

Price excused herself but not before giving him a look that would freeze hell if it were possible. The way Ellison thanked her, she felt like he was undressing her and patting her ass. She abruptly left to go to the ladies' room.

Pickens and Amy put their hands on their weapons as a precaution.

"Whoa, Sheriff, I come in peace. I'm Bobby Ellison." Pickens and Amy removed their hands from their weapons. "Been out of town on a case and just got back. Saw the clip about Irene and thought I'd come see what you did about my report."

Pickens' forehead furrowed. "What report?"

Ellison's eyes narrowed. "What report? The one I left on Irene's desk. I thought for sure you would have it by now."

"Say that again, Ellison?"

"Are you serious, Sheriff? Irene paid me to do some investigating on Parker. I discovered her real name was Allyson Healey, and she was from Tampa. It's all in the report."

At least Ellison and Noristan weren't involved in something that went downhill, but Ellison kept referring to her as Irene so

there must have been a relationship between them—if necessary
he'd explore it later. What's in that report was more important.
    "We didn't find any report."
    "Are you serious?"
    "Yes. Do you have another copy?"
    "Sure, hold on, and I'll call my secretary and have her fax it.
Write your fax number down." Billy wrote the fax number on
a piece of paper and handed it to Ellison, who called his office.
"Roxanne, I need you to do something for me. No, not that."
Ellison cupped a hand over the phone. "She's been with me quite
a while and can be funny at times." Pickens and his deputies' eyes
narrowed. "Seriously, I need you to fax a copy of the Healey report
to this number. Thanks, sweetheart, I'll be back soon. Just take
messages." Ellison closed his phone. "It should be here any minute
but would you like me to tell you what it says?"
    'It would be helpful because we're in the dark here."
    Ellison grinned. "Then let me enlighten you." He told Pickens
how he got fingerprints and a DNA sample from the lipstick and
had a friend at a lab analyze then for him. After getting a match
for Healey, he contacted a buddy in Tampa and learned more about
Healey. "The report will tell you more, and you'll see."
    Pickens was pissed that Ellison had discovered evidence at
Noristan's office. He was annoyed because Noristan and Ellison had
jumped the gun and beat him to it. It made Pickens seem inept
at crime solving and evidence gathering. But neither he nor Amy
thought to look in Noristan's bathroom medicine cabinet—they
had no reason to and only searched Parker's desk.
    Ellison's report confirmed what Ellison had told them about who
Alice Parker really was, and now he could cross Parker's name off the
board and replace it with Allyson Healey. The report also revealed a
minor arrest record and a last known address in Tampa. What it didn't
show was a current address that would help Pickens find Healey.
    "What do you think, Sheriff, did I do a good job?"

Pickens wanted to say no just to piss Ellison off but decide not to. Instead said, "Not bad, and I may be able to use it."

Ellison's jaw dropped. "What? Are you serious?"

"Yep," Pickens replied with a grin.

"At least say thank you, Ellison."

"Okay, you just did."

CHAPTER 29

After Ellison had left, Pickens called a meeting of his deputies. He'd already had another setback when the lab reported that the fingerprints they found at Noristan's office—besides hers—belonged Ellison as did the DNA sample. Pickens was disappointed as he had hoped for a new suspect. Pickens stood in front of the murder board, pointed to Benson and Hicks, and took a deep breath.

"Look we're not getting anywhere, so we need to start a profile." He looked over at Sergeant Tucker. "Amy, you've got a background in counseling, maybe you could put it to use and come up with one." Pickens raised his palms. "What do you think? Can you do it?"

Amy started to say something, but Billy held up his hand and interrupted her.

"I may be able to help you, Amy." Pickens and Amy shot a glance at him. Billy ignored them and added, "I've been working on a timeline. It's not perfect, but it's a start."

"Well hell, show it to us, Billy," said Amy.

"Yeah, let's see it," said Pickens.

Billy turned the monitor so all could see, pressed several keys and up came a page. Across the top, it read BENSON AND HICKS TIMELINE. Beneath the title were dates, names, and occurrences starting with the suicide of Melissa Nolan.

Billy pointed to the monitor and articulated. "This is what I've put together. I chose the Nolan matter as the starting point because both Tommy and Rhonda were at Langston College the same time as her."

Amy interrupted him and stepped closer. "I think I get where you're going, Billy, and I can use this."

"You can?" he asked.

"Yes, because I believe you're on to something," she replied.

"Like what?" asked Pickens as he also moved closer but kept space between him and Amy.

Amy took her pen from her shirt pocket and pointed to the monitor. "I'll explain." She pointed to the next line that read Benson and Hicks murdered and the date. "We agree that Tommy and Nolan had a fling, and she was pregnant with their child and then took her life."

"Okay, I follow you, so far," said Pickens.

"I believe their death has to do with Nolan's suicide, and someone's seeking revenge for it."

"But why wait all this time?" asked Billy.

Pickens focused on the timeline and waited for Amy's reply.

"That's a great question. I think something may have happened recently that triggered Benson's murder, and Rhonda was in the wrong place at the wrong time."

"Okay, that works for me but why Noristan?" Pickens asked.

"That's easy because she had Ellison investigate Alice Parker or rather Allyson Healey." She pointed to the line with Ellison's name. "Billy has her missing before Noristan's murder, so she might be linked to Nolan or she's the shooter."

Billy enjoyed the interest his timeline generated, turned his head, smiled, tightened his fist, and muttered, "Yes."

Pickens scratched his chin and considered Amy's theory. "Okay, let's say you're right. What do we do with this?"

"I have an idea, Sheriff."

"Let's have it, Billy, so far you're on a roll."

Billy's face lit up with an alligator grin. "We could give Nosey the information, and have him do a news brief that Healey's a person of interest in a crime involving Tommy and Rhonda. That way he can't go off on a tangent and say we're about to solve the case. You know how he is. And Healey might go underground, and we'll never find her."

"Damn, that's an excellent idea, and you're right about Nosey."

"Thanks, Amy."

"I like it too, but I hate giving Nosey a scoop," commented Pickens.

"Think of it this way, it may be a scoop for him, but for us it's a way to get the public's help. We'll just have it say she's a person of interest in a crime involving Benson and leave Rhonda and Noristan's names out of it. Technically, they're all related through Benson, so that's all he needs."

"Okay, write it up, Amy, and let me look at it before we call Nosey."

CHAPTER 30

Pickens approved of the information for Noseby that Amy prepared and called him. When Noseby saw that Pickens was calling, he hoped the sheriff was finally going to give him something about the case that he could put in print.

Pickens thought of his father's advice and decided to follow it—one down at a time, see how many yards you gain and then call the next play. First down call was Nosey's scoop. After that, it depended on the outcome.

"Sheriff Pickens, you decided to tell me what's going on with these murders? I hope so because I need to give the public something to chew on."

Pickens smiled. "Today's your lucky day, Nosey, because that's why I'm calling you."

"Really, Sheriff, you're not joking with me?"

"Really, Nosey, come by the office and I'll give you the scoop of your life."

"I'll be there in ten; no make it five. Hell, I'm almost there."

Pickens looked at the receiver. "You are?"

"I'm walking in the door as we speak." Pickens glanced at the entrance. "I was on my cell when you called." Noseby waved the phone. "Now do you believe I'm a real reporter, not some high school news flash?"

Pickens hung up the phone, and everyone gave Noseby a round of applause, which caused his cheeks to turn red.

Noseby removed his hat and took a bow. "Thank you all, thank you so much. I'm honored to receive such a grand reception." The applause came to a sudden stop, everyone shook their head and waved their palms at him, but that didn't daunt Noseby from his grand acceptance. "Aw, you guys are too much."

"Sit down, Nosey, if you want that scoop."

"Sure thing, Sheriff."

"Amy, show Nosey what we have for him."

"Uh, Sheriff, my name's Noseby, not Nosey."

"Whatever. Shut up, and pay close attention to Amy."

Amy stepped in front of Pickens and placed the statement Pickens wanted Noseby to use.

"Just keep it simple and don't embellish it, and no mention of Hicks and Noristan."

Noseby's head slumped. "That's it; that's my scoop? Are you serious?"

"You want the scoop or not, Nosey?"

"But, Sheriff, this isn't a scoop. What can I do with this?" Noseby was hoping for something that would earn him a Pulitzer Prize in journalism, not a brief news flash.

"You can help us by putting it in the paper and getting it in other Florida papers; that's what you can do with it."

Noseby's brain started working at high speed. "Yeah, that's good. It'll be a news brief, and I can use my sources to get it in other papers around the state." His brain churned to a halt. "Wait, then I don't get credit for it. That's not fair, Sheriff."

"Last chance, Nosey, you want it or not? I've got other reporters chomping to get their hands on it." Pickens was fibbing, but he knew Noseby would take the bait.

"I'll take it, but you have to promise if anything comes from it you'll give me a real scoop."

"You have my word. Scouts honor." Pickens put a single finger up. He was never a scout and had no idea what their salute was like and was betting Noseby didn't either.

"Okay, I'll get it in this evening's paper, and it should be in several papers over the weekend, hopefully."

"Thanks, Nosey."

There was another big round of applause for Noseby and another blush.

"Aw, gee, thanks, guys," he said and left.

Noseby came through with the news brief. It appeared in the county paper and several newspapers over the weekend around the state. There was no headline; it appeared under the 'News Briefs' section as an also. Most importantly, it contained the telephone number Pickens wanted as an anonymous tip line.

CHAPTER 31

The telephone number that Noseby had listed in his article received many calls Monday morning. Most were from Tommy's stable of women inquiring of his demise and asking what they should do now that he was gone.

Liz Price answered the next call and handed the phone to Pickens. He signaled for Amy, wrote the caller's number on a pad and gave it to her. Amy gave it to Billy and told him to start a search. Billy promptly typed it on his laptop. Pickens gave him thumbs up.

Pickens waited two minutes and then pressed the speaker button.

"Sheriff Pickens, may I help you?"

There was ominous silence on the other end. Then a female voice spoke.

"I'm not sure. I saw an article in the local newspaper that said you were looking for someone."

Billy scribbled Jefferson County for the area code and number.

"I am, but mind if I ask your name?" The line suddenly went dead. Pickens glanced at the phone. "Shit, did the power just go out or did the county forget to pay the phone bill?"

Billy pointed to his computer screen; Amy grabbed the nearest phone.

"This line's working. Maybe you were disconnected. Be patient, she'll call back."

Pickens set the receiver down. "What makes you so sure, Amy?"

"You just have to trust me."

Pickens shook his head. "If you say so." Then he looked at Billy. "You get anything?"

He signaled a touchdown and said, "Got it. The call came from Monticello. The number's listed to Life's Little Treasures. Give me a minute, and I'll have more for you."

Jennifer Darling, co-owner of Life's Little Treasures, an upscale boutique on Jefferson Street in Monticello, Florida poured two cups of coffee and stood at the far end of the counter away from the cash register. Jennifer was an attractive thirty-four-year-old brunette with a slender figure. Annice Timmons, Jennifer's thirty-seven-year-old olive-skinned partner, had just finished helping a customer.

Annice waited until the bell jangled as the door closed, walked over near Jennifer and sat on a stool. Jennifer handed Annice a cup of coffee, glanced down to avoid eye contact and ran her finger around the rim of her cup—a nervous habit that had begun in her freshman year of college. Nearby was the Tallahassee newspaper opened to the page with the news brief that mentioned authorities in Central Florida were looking for information on one Allyson Healey, considered a person of interest in a crime involving a Tommy Benson. Annice glanced down at it.

"What did you tell him, Jen?"

Jennifer's lips tightened. "Nothing, I hung up."

Annice's eyebrows lifted. "Why? I thought we talked about it and decided you were doing the right thing."

"I know we did, but I can't believe one of my sorority sisters might have done something awful."

Annice reached out and touched Jennifer's arm. "You'll never know until you talk to that sheriff." She took a sip of coffee and then placed her hand on Jennifer's cheek. "I'll be right here beside you when you call."

Jennifer set her cup down and wrapped her arms around Annice. "God, I love you."

"Me too. Damn, I almost spilled my coffee, now make the call."

Pickens raised a finger when the phone rang again, signaling everyone to wait. The caller ID said it was the same number. Pickens hit speaker and answered.

"Sheriff Pickens speaking. I think we were accidently disconnected."

The caller waited and then said, "We weren't disconnected, Sheriff, I hung up on you." Amy grinned, Pickens waved a hand at her. "My name is Jennifer Darling. I own a boutique shop in Monticello." There was ominous silence before she continued. "I saw an article in the Tallahassee paper that you're looking for a sorority sister of mine. It said something about a person of interest in a crime."

Pickens' interest spiked. "What's your sorority sister's name?"

"Was it a serious crime, Sheriff?"

He signaled for Amy to get a pad and pen. "People died, Miss Darling."

Jennifer cupped her mouth. "Oh, God, no! Did she do it?"

Billy immediately typed in Jennifer Darling on his laptop. Pickens gave him another thumbs up.

"Look, Miss Darling, you called me. If you have information that can help, please, I'm asking you to help me."

While Pickens waited for an answer, Billy pointed to the monitor and the website for Life's Little Treasures. He pointed the cursor to "About Us." It listed the owners' names and a brief bio.

After graduating from college, Jennifer Darling managed several boutique stores before opening Life's Little Treasures with her partner Annice Timmons. Annice graduated from the University of North Florida and had previously owned an upscale boutique in Jacksonville.

Jennifer turned to Annice and mouthed, "What should I say?"

Annice mouthed, "Whatever you know."

"I'm waiting, Miss Darling," said Pickens.

"Give me a minute please, Sheriff."

Pickens looked to Amy for guidance. Amy raised her palm and mouthed, "Give her time, she'll open up."

"Whatever," Pickens mouthed back.

A minute turned to two then three. The wait was grueling like sitting outside the office while your parents conferred with the principal on what your punishment should be for getting caught smoking in the bathroom.

Three minutes became five then ten. Billy busied himself on the computer searching for Darling on Facebook and Linkedin. Amy made notes on a legal pad. Pickens kept running his hands through his hair. He'd wanted to call Darling, but Amy had said to give her time, and so he did. But waiting was worse than halftime in the locker room, his team down by two touchdowns, and waiting for the coach to launch into a tirade screaming how bad they were playing, and he could do better with the girls' soccer team—maybe even retire.

Finally, Jennifer shattered the silence when she mustered the courage to continue.

"She was one of six of us. We were all in the same sorority and attended Melissa Nolan's funeral."

Pickens interrupted her. "We know about Melissa and offer our condolences."

Jennifer wiped a tear. "Thank you. We were upset and in mourning over her death and made a childish pact to get even with Tommy for what he did to her."

"I can understand you were upset, but what was the pact, Miss Darling?"

Jennifer hesitated, glanced at Annice and whispered, "Should I tell him?"

"Yes, tell him," Annice replied.

"Miss Darling, who are you speaking to?" asked Pickens.

Annice waved for Jennifer to tell him. Jennifer rubbed her chest and replied, "First, can you stop calling me Miss Darling and call me Jennifer? Miss Darling just sounds so cold."

"Okay, Jennifer, but I'm still waiting."

"Thank you. I apologize for not telling you that my partner is listening. Annice gave me the courage to call you."

"Okay, at least I know who's with you. Please continue."

Amy bowed her head, extended a palm, and mouthed, "See, I told you so."

"Whatever," Pickens mouthed back.

"The six of us were going to put a scare into him. We didn't have a definite plan, but we'd make sure Tommy regretted what he did. After the funeral, we went our separate ways and not one of us ever mentioned the pact again. We graduated from college, and I thought that was the end of it."

"Maybe it wasn't for one of your sisters, Jennifer," said Pickens.

"Oh, God, I hope not."

Amy mouthed, "Get names."

"Right," he mouthed back. "Jennifer, can you give me the names of your sorority sisters?"

Pickens waited for her response, but there was nothing but silence on her end. He glanced at Amy and turned his palms up. Amy signaled for him to wait.

"Can I call you back, Sheriff?"

Amy nodded approval. "Sure, but don't keep us waiting long."

"I won't, I just need to compose myself," Jennifer replied and hung up.

"What do you think, Amy? You've dealt with grief; will she call back?"

Amy tilted her head. "I think she will. She's obviously in shock, but with her friend there to talk with she'll do the right thing."

"I hope you're right. This case has been like looking for a needle in a haystack, and we need a break." Pickens rubbed his chin.

"We may not have found the needle, but we found the haystack," replied Amy.

The room erupted in grins.

Annice reached out and held Jennifer in her arms comforting her. Jennifer wiped tears from her cheek.

"He may be right, Jen. Maybe one of your sisters decided to act on that pact."

"But it was just a silly thought at the time, and it was years ago. Why now?" The doorbell suddenly jangled.

"I don't know. Let me get this customer, and we'll talk more."

"Okay," Jennifer sniffled.

Annice greeted the customer but soon returned to Jennifer because their store didn't carry what the woman wanted.

"I know you think you owe your sisters loyalty, but this is beyond that. Call the sheriff back and give him their names and hopefully, you can file this in your forget drawer."

Jennifer could barely contain her grin. "Forget drawer? Where did that come from?"

"I don't know, but it means forget this whole thing." Annice placed a hand on Jennifer's. "That part of your life was a long time ago. Your life is here now with me."

Jennifer touched Annice's cheek. "You're right, as always. I'll call the sheriff."

Pickens paced the floor waiting for Jennifer's call. He was about
to give up and call her when the phone rang. He hit the speaker
button.

"Jennifer?"

"Yes, Sheriff, I have those names for you."

"Thanks, Jennifer, you're doing the right thing."

"I hope so. Are you ready?"

Amy grabbed a pen and pad.

"Yes, go ahead."

Jennifer breathed deeply and started.

"Allyson Healey, Barbara Williams, Myra Olson, Meghan
Bucknell, Brandi Gormley and, of course, me. That's all of them."

"Thank you, Jennifer."

"Can I get back to my life now, Sheriff? Or do you need more
from me?"

Amy wrote *no more* under the last name and put the pad in
front of Pickens. He nodded.

"No, Jennifer, that's all for now. If we need anything later, I'll
call you. Go ahead and get on with your life."

"Thank you," she replied and hung up.

"Feel better now, Jen?"

"Yes, thanks, Annice."

After the conversation had concluded, Pickens pressed the off
button on the phone and said, "Shit, more possible suspects and
motives to add to the murder board."

"Sheriff, watch your language there are ladies present," Amy
said.

No one noticed that Price had left the room.

"Sorry, but I could have said..."

Amy stopped him. "Never mind, shit's okay." Then she couldn't
resist saying. "Well, fuck!"

Pickens and everyone else's eyes hiked.

"Damn, Deputy Tucker, what got into you?" asked Billy.

Amy's smile was so broad she could feel her mouth stretching from it, and replied, "He's six feet, weighs 185 pounds, can run a mile in under six minutes, and…"

"Okay, we get it, that's enough for now and it's out of character for you," said Billy.

Amy's head bobbed back and forth. "So, arrest me."

Pickens shook his head. "Be right back, I have to make a call." He turned, walked into his office and closed the door.

CHAPTER 32

Pickens sat at his desk and dialed Detective Rinaldo in Broward County. While he waited for Rinaldo to answer, he wrote *Sisterhood* on his pad. Next to it, he wrote, *Retribution.*

Rinaldo grabbed his phone, checked the caller ID, saw it was Pickens, and answered. "Sheriff disc jockey, what the hell are you bothering me about now?"

Pickens grinned. "It's JD, not DJ. I need your help, *amigo.*"

"Sorry about that, JD. So, two phone calls and we're best friends already. You must be having serious problems, Pickens. Is this about the latest murder?" Rinaldo picked up his glass of lemonade and took a sip. "Hell, man, for a rinky-dink county you sure got a lot going on."

"No shit, Rinaldo, and I could use your help."

"Okay, whatcha need?"

"This mess is like looking for a needle in a haystack, and we just found the haystack but not the needle."

"And you want me to locate the needle? Are you loco, Pickens?"

"Something like that, but it won't be as difficult as you think. It has to do with Melissa Nolan again."

"Don't go there, Pickens. Those folks don't need any more heartache."

Pickens had already deliberated on the best approach to Rinaldo. If anyone was going to talk to the Nolans, it had to be him.

"I have no reason to bother them except I need any pictures they may have of Melissa's sorority sisters, especially those who attended her funeral." Pickens took a deep breath and continued. "Can you help me?"

Rinaldo rubbed his head and then his chin. "I remember those girls. They were awfully upset after the funeral. I saw them in a group arguing about something. You think one of them is involved in your murder?"

"Or all of them, except for one. I've already talked to her, and she gave me their names."

"And they're your haystack?"

"*Exacto*! So, will you help me?"

"Let me think about it and call you back."

"Thanks, *compadre*."

"Don't thank me yet, Pickens, and don't put Spanish down as your second language."

As Rinaldo debated whether he should help Pickens, Rosemary Nolan was at her home in Davie trying to decide what she should do. She had already shown her husband, Bill, the news brief in the Broward paper.

"It mentions Tommy Benson. Wasn't he the boy who broke up with Melissa?"

Mr. Nolan scratched his chin. "It was Tommy something, but that's all I remember. But if you're sure, maybe we should call Rinaldo and ask him."

Mrs. Nolan kissed him. "I'm going to call Rinaldo. Will you listen in?"

He grinned. "Of course, I will."

Rinaldo still hadn't decided if he should call the Nolans and needed some courage to help him. He kept a bottle of Jose Cuervo hidden in the pantry—at least he believed he did—retrieved it and a shot glass.

"Here's to courage," he said and downed the tequila. "Whoo, that went down smooth. Okay, I'm gonna do it, but oh, man, I hope I'm doing the right thing."

Rinaldo reached for the phone just as it rang. He recognized the number since he had recently called it and let the phone ring several times. Before the call went to voicemail, he answered.

"Mrs. Nolan, how are you?" He breathed slowly, hoping she wasn't calling because something had happened to Mr. Nolan.

"We're okay, and please call me Rosemary. We consider you part of our family, after everything you did for Melissa and us."

Rinaldo felt relief. "I just did my job, Rosemary."

"You did more than your job, Detective."

"I did what I believed was best for all and if I'm going to call you Rosemary, then you call me Frank. How's Bill?"

"He's okay and right beside me. Say hello both of you."

"Hey, Frank."

"Hey, Bill." Rinaldo was in no hurry to rush the Nolans, but he wanted their—rather needed their help—for Pickens. "So how come you folks are calling me?"

Mr. Nolan whispered to his wife, "You go."

"We saw a news brief in the paper about authorities looking for information on a woman in connection with Tommy Benson. Wasn't he the boy who broke up with Melissa?" Mr. Nolan reached for a hankie and wiped a tear from her eyes.

Rinaldo paced the living room, stopped to glance at the picture of his daughter and his grandchildren. He knew how fortunate he was to walk his daughter down the aisle and hold his grandkids in his arms when they were born. His grandkids could be a pain in the ass once in a while, and his daughter enjoyed teasing him. But

Rinaldo thanked God every day for his blessings. Unfortunately, the Nolans would never experience memories of their own. He went back into the kitchen and poured another shot of courage.

"You still there, Frank?"

Rinaldo inhaled. "Yes, Rosemary, I am. Benson was that boy." He ran his fingers through his thinning hair. "I have something to ask you."

"Okay, what is it?" Rosemary looked at Bill. He raised a palm.

"It's a rather delicate request." He downed another shot. "I got a call from a rural county sheriff. The person he's looking for was one of Melissa's sorority sisters." Rinaldo couldn't see Mrs. Nolan cup her mouth. "By any chance do you have pictures of Melissa's sorority sisters?" Another shot of courage as he waited.

"I'm not sure. Let me check, and I'll call you back."

"I hope I'm not upsetting you, Rosemary."

"It's okay, Frank. She went to check," replied Mr. Nolan. "We'll call you."

"Thanks..." But the call suddenly ended. "Pickens, you better hope I did the right thing and didn't cause those folks more grief."

Mrs. Nolan sat on Melissa's bed weeping. Mr. Nolan put an arm around her.

"You don't have to do this, honey. That boy deserved what he got."

"No, Bill, Melissa wouldn't agree. If one of her sisters extracted revenge for her, she'd be angry and would help that sheriff." She tapped him on his thigh. "I have to do this for Melissa."

"Okay, where do we look?"

She ran her fingertips over her clavicle. "Remember those sweet girls who came to the funeral."

"Oh, yes, they were her sisters. They gave us a picture of them."

"Right, I put it in the top dresser drawer." She got up and went to the dresser, opened the right-hand drawer, and rummaged through its contents. "Here it is. Look there were six of them. Maybe this will help Frank and that sheriff."

"Let's hope so." He held her hand. "And no more calls after this, sweetheart."

"I promise, but I'm glad we're doing something."

While Rinaldo waited for the Nolans to call back, he decided another shot of courage might be in order. If his wife knew what he was doing, he'd need more than courage to escape her wrath.

"Here's to big *cojones* because I'll need them." Down went the shot. "I hope Rosemary will forgive me for this." He picked up the bottle and considered another shot, but just then the phone rang. "Here goes nothing." He picked up the receiver. "Rosemary..."

Before Rinaldo could finish his sentence, Mrs. Nolan interrupted him. "Frank, I found a picture of those girls. What should I do with it?"

Relief but now what? Rinaldo contemplated his options. Should she mail it or fax it?

Mrs. Nolan resolved the situation for him. "I can fax it if you'd like?"

He exhaled. "Thanks, that would be a great help. My fax number is the same as my phone number."

"Okay, Frank, we'll fax it but no more after this. Let it rest," replied Mr. Nolan.

"I will, Bill, I promise." Rinaldo answered and waited for the fax.

CHAPTER 33

Pickens nervously paced the room ponderously awaiting Rinaldo's call. He knew his request was beyond a simple favor and could have a profound effect on both Rinaldo and the Nolans, but Pickens was desperate.

"Relax, he'll call. Give him some time." Amy remarked. "You asked him for a colossal favor."

Pickens rubbed the back of his head. "Easy for you to say, you've got more patience than any of us." He glanced at Billy busy working in the Nerve Center on his computer. "What do you think, Billy, will he call back?"

Billy clicked go in a search browser. "I think so, but Amy is right, just be patient a little longer."

"Shit, am I the only one who's anxious?"

"We all are, but it's out of our hands," Amy replied.

Just when Pickens' patience was about to boil over, the phone rang.

"Okay, let's see what Rinaldo decided." Pickens picked up the phone and answered. "Frank, I was about to give up on you."

"You should have because I was going to give up on you. I talked with the Nolans, and they remembered there were some of Melissa's sisters at the funeral. You hit a home run. Mrs. Nolan faxed me a picture of those girls taken at the funeral. I'm going to fax it to you, but don't call me for any more help. I did you a favor, but you have no idea how hard it was to bring up the past with the Nolans. Mr. Nolan doesn't want me to bother them anymore. Same goes for you."

"I hear ya, Frank, no more calls." Pickens breathed a sigh of relief. "I'm sorry for what you went through, and I appreciate your help."

"Yeah, well, that doesn't ease the pain for the Nolans or me. What's your fax number?"

Amy mouthed, "Leave it alone and move on."

"Okay, here's the number."

He gave Rinaldo the number and then both said goodbye.

When the fax arrived, Billy grabbed it, slapped his palms together, and exclaimed, "Damn!"

"You got something, Billy?" asked Amy.

"Yep, remember Malibu Barbie aka Barbara Williams." Billy's eyes lit up. "Maybe she should go back on the board."

"But she lives in California."

"Maybe so, but she could've been in Florida at the time of the murders."

Price retrieved the fax, gave it to Billy, and excused herself to take a call.

Billy handed Pickens the fax. "He's right, and now that we have Rinaldo's fax, we have a picture of Nolan's sorority sisters. Pin it on the board."

"We could throw a dart and whoever it lands on is our killer."

"That's a great idea, Amy," said Billy.

Pickens shook his head. "Glad you guys are in a good mood because we have a lot of work to do. Billy, do some more digging on the California chick and start on the others. Shit, it's time we got a break."

Pickens glanced at the murder board. "Hold on a sec; maybe a dart board isn't such a bad idea."

"Are you serious?"

"Hear me out, Amy. Not an actual dart board, but a new murder board." He picked up a piece of paper and a pen. "Call it new murder board or sisters in crime, whatever. On the left side, we list the victims starting with Benson and Hicks, then Noristan. List Nolan with a question mark because she's central to the case." He wrote the names on the paper. "Then we put the sister's names across the board and see if we can match the name with their picture. Billy, can you make individual pictures from what we have?"

"No problem, I'll scan and Photoshop."

"Good, after you do that, put a picture of each under the names we know, such as Darling, Healey, and Williams. The other four we'll just pick one and match it to a picture. Next, we'll list whatever we know about them, and as we discover more we'll list that info including any also known as. And if we get a photo of them, we'll match it to the correct name. How's that so far?"

"Damn, that's good, Sheriff," said Billy."

"Thanks, okay, team, let's get to it."

"JD!"

"Yes, Amy/?"

"You do realize today's Friday and it's almost five o'clock, don't you?"

Pickens checked his watch. "Shit, you're right, and it's rib night at Leroy's." His face lit up in a grin. "And I'm taking my two favorite girls there. Billy, is there anything I can do to help? I can come in tomorrow but not Sunday. Marge has me taking her and Sarah to Marge's parents. She'll kill me if I back out."

"We can't have that, JD. We already have three dead bodies," said Amy.

"Sheriff, there's nothing you can do right now unless you can do research. That I can take care of and besides you…"

"I'm not good with the computers. I get it, Belly."

"Take the weekend off, JD. I'll help Billy."

"Thanks, Amy. I could use the break."

Amy smiled and said, "Go on, get out of here before we change our minds."

"I can help too, Sheriff," said Price.

"But you've already put in a full week."

"I know, but I need the money." Price tilted her head. "My rent's not cheap."

"Okay then, if you all don't mind. I'll see you all Monday."

"And, JD, don't call us we'll call you," said Amy with a smile. Pickens shook his head, waved, and left.

Alone at home Saturday morning with Bailey, Pickens felt guilty that his team was working and he was watching television. Suddenly his phone rang.

"Shit," he said and answered the phone. "Madame Chairperson, how are you?"

"Cut the crap, JD, and call me Marilyn. We've known each other since high school and dated. You were my first..."

Pickens eyebrows raised. "Okay, Marilyn, why are you calling me? Remember we're both married." Pickens had an idea why she was calling—which caused a knot in his stomach.

"The mayor called about Nosbey's article. He wants me to make you call in the State or Feds. He doesn't think you're qualified to solve those murders. Can you help me out here, JD?"

Shit Pickens said to himself. Damn the mayor he's not my boss. "Hear me out, Marilyn. I've got a person of interest who could be or lead us to the killer. We're trying to find her. When we do, the case will be over. I don't need outside help." Pickens felt a little whit lie could help.

"How long before it's over, JD?"

Pickens took a deep breath and replied, "Less than a month."

"You've got two weeks, JD."

"Is that an ultimatum and a vote of no confidence?"

"Call it what you want, JD. I'm just trying to be helpful. Have a nice day."

"Yeah, you too." After hanging up, he yelled, "Son of a bitch!" Bailey walked over and sat in front of him, He stared into Pickens' eyes. "Sorry, Bailey." Pickens stroked the back of the dog's head. "You're gonna have to stay by yourself until momma comes home. I have to go into the office." Pickens retrieved his gun and holster and then left.

Amy and Billy were busy on their laptops attempting to find information on the sorority sisters when Pickens walked into the bullpen.

Amy looked up. "What are you doing here?" she asked.

Pickens glanced around and replied, "I couldn't just sit at home while you... Where's Price?"

"She left an hour ago. Got a call and said she had something important to take care," answered Billy. "Honestly, Sheriff, we don't need any more help. Ritchie came in and offered to replace Price." Billy held up a hand. "And before you ask, he's off the clock. So am I."

"Me too," added Amy. "Go home, JD, you'll just be in the way. And don't call us, we'll call you."

Pickens welcomed their enthusiasm and didn't want to spoil it, so he didn't tell them of the ultimatum.

"I have to do something," he said.

"You can go home and be with your family and let us do our job," Amy replied. "Look at it this way, JD. You're the coach, but this is a closed-door team meeting and you're not invited. When we have something, we'll let you know. Now go home and be a couch potato or whatever."

Reluctantly Pickens gave in, but he'd worry until he heard from his team, hopefully, a solution. He threw his hands up, turned, and left without saying another word.

CHAPTER 34

Despite his concerns about the case, Pickens made the two-hour drive via I-75 and I-90 to Live Oak on Sunday morning with his family to visit Marge's parents. They took Marge's SUV instead of JD's truck. Marjorie and Stephen Davids, retired physicians, lived in a retirement community on the west side of the city. The Davids owned a three-bedroom villa that backed up to the golf course. It had a large living room which they used for entertaining.

Both the Davids were in their late seventies. Stephen was an avid golfer and could be found on the golf course most mornings. Marion was an avid reader and belonged to a book club that focused on crime novels, both fiction and nonfiction, especially murder.

Pickens pulled into the driveway and parked. Sarah and Bailey got out and ran to greet her grandparents. Pickens and Marge shook their heads and then followed after them. Sarah leaped into her grandfather's arms while Marjorie ruffled Bailey's ears and let him kiss her.

"Gosh, Sarah, you're getting so big," said Mr. Davids.

"Nah, you're getting smaller, Grandpa."

Mr. Davids laughed. "Go say hello to your grandmother but don't jump on her." He put her down and called Bailey. "You come

give me a kiss too, Bailey." Mr. Davids bent down and let Bailey
lick his face.

Sarah snuggled against her grandmother. "Grandma, guess what?"
Mrs. Davids smiled. "Okay, what?"

"I'm gonna be a veterinarian like Great Grandma and Dr. Dee."
Sarah hadn't quite pronounced the word veterinarian correctly,
but Mrs. Davids understood. She glanced at Marge and Pickens. "Is
that so?" Marge tilted her head and grinned.

"Yep, I can talk to animals like Great Grandma did." Sarah put
a finger to her lips and looked at her mother. Mrs. Davids squinted
her eyes toward Marge. "Woops, I'm not supposed to tell anyone,
but it's okay to tell you, Grandma. Right, Mom?"

Marge mouthed, "I'll tell you later," to her mother and then
told Sarah, "Yes, but no one else."

Pickens and Mr. Davids shook hands and then he hugged his
mother-in-law. Marge hugged and kissed both her parents.

"Gosh, it's so good to see you, sweetheart," said Mrs. Davids as
she hugged Marge.

"You too, Mom." After hugging, they all went inside.

"So, JD how's the investigation going?" asked Mrs. Davids.
Pickens' eyebrows hiked. "We read the newspapers, especially the
one from your county."

"Don't let her start, JD, or she'll want enough to write a book
for her mystery book club," said Mr. Davids

"Hush, Stephen, I'm just curious."

"Yes, but they just got here. Let them relax and have coffee and
cake, for goodness sake."

Marjorie relented. "Okay, but after you and I are gonna talk, JD."
Pickens looked to Marge and her father for help.

"You're on your own, JD," said Marge.

After coffee and cake, Marjorie cleared the table and nodded
toward her husband.

"Stephen, why don't you and Marge take Sarah and Bailey up to the clubhouse and let her see the ducks."

Sarah's face lit up. "Can we, please, Mommy?"

Mr. Davids eyed his wife suspiciously.

"Okay, if Grandpa doesn't mind." Marge eyed her mother suspiciously.

"What about me? Aren't I invited?" asked Pickens.

"You and I are going to chat, JD," said Mrs. Davids. "Stephen, you go ahead and take the girls."

"Marjorie."

"Go on, now, do as I say, Stephen."

Pickens grinned. It was the same way his wife spoke when she insisted he do something.

"Let's go, Marge. There's no sense arguing with her."

Pickens mouthed. "Help," to Marge.

"Sorry, JD, you're on your own. Come on, Sarah. Let's go with Grandpa."

"Yippee," shouted Sarah and followed her mother and grandfather out the door.

Pickens poured a cup of coffee, sat, and rubbed his hand through his hair.

"Listen, Marjorie, I can't discuss the case with you and you know that."

Mrs. Davids smiled, placed her hands on her hips and gestured as though offering something forbidden between them. It was the same thing Marge did when she wanted something, and she always succeeded in getting her way.

"Come on, JD, give a girl a break," she said and winked. "I just want a little tidbit for my mystery club. Nothing that will compromise your case."

Why don't I believe you he thought to himself?

"You know I can't."

She pinched her thumb and forefinger. "Just a little something, that's all. Come on, you can trust me. I'm your wife's mother, doesn't that count?"

"That's not fair."

She winked again. "I'm also Sarah's grandmother. Whattaya say, JD?"

Pickens knew she was weakening him.

"Damn, you're good. So, that's where Marge gets it from. Does Stephen give in easy?"

"He doesn't think he's giving in. So, JD, you gonna share something?"

Pickens relented and gave her something she could share with her book club.

"We've got three bodies, no suspects, and a person of interest we're looking for."

Mrs. Davids shook her head. "Come on, get real. I know all that, I read what that Nosey fella wrote."

Pickens found it amusing that she left the 'b' out of Noseby's name and referred to him as the fella, not the reporter. When Noseby mentioned he was writing a full article about the killings, Pickens threw him some chum to make his article more newsworthy—nothing that would compromise the investigation. Noseby had asked Pickens if the three deaths were related and did that mean there was a serial killer loose in the county? Pickens response was "No comment." Noseby used that in his article.

Again, Mrs. Davids put her hands on her hips but not provocatively. It was the same posture that his mother and now Sarah struck when they scolded him.

"Give me something I don't know."

He knew she'd keep nagging him, so he decided to give a little more. "Okay, but this is confidential and you can't tell your book club."

She winked, smiled and crossed her heart. "You have my word, JD."

Again, he had his doubts but caved and told her about the group of sorority sisters, their pact, that one was a person of interest.

Mrs. Davids rubbed her hands together. "Oh, this is good, tell me more."

Pickens sipped his coffee and then threw a morsel and mentioned the suicide but not the abortion and no names.

"I may have a serial killer who's seeking revenge. That's it, Marjorie, I've already said too much."

But she wanted more and like her daughter; she could charm a man out of anything.

"JD, hear me out. I was a doctor and have medical training. Maybe I can help you."

"How?" Pickens was suddenly curious because he could use any help she could offer.

She poured herself a cup of coffee and sat with him.

"First, consider this, three bodies doesn't necessarily mean you have a serial killer. Three separate incidents, maybe. At our last book club meeting, we had an FBI behavioral analyst speak to us and that's what he said."

He considered her point.

"Two incidents could mean one of the victims was collateral damage." Pickens thought about it and agreed but didn't tell her. "He also said that serial killers or those that commit multiple murders might have experienced a psychotic break before committing their crime."

He nodded his head. "Sounds reasonable, the two female victims both had sex with the male victim. He also had a relationship with the woman that committed suicide—which is why we're pursuing the sorority sisters angle."

She rubbed her chin and contemplated his words.

"You know I'm an avid reader of mysteries so hear me out. Maybe you should consider widening your circle."

He tilted his head. "What do you mean widen it?"

"I'm sure there were more than five or so sisters in that sorority and most likely a house mother. Also, consider the person who committed the crimes could be someone outside of the sorority but related to someone inside, like a relative or friend."

"I didn't consider that angle, but now maybe I should."

"While you're at it consider the possibility that an event in that person's life may have triggered a psychotic break." Mrs. Davids turned and walked to the sink and placed her cup in it. "JD, in all my years as a physician I've come across a lot of things in medicine. I'm not a psychiatrist—and you may want to talk to one. There's a possibility you're dealing with a sociopath, or worse, a psychopath. I hope that helps."

Pickens smiled. "Damn, you're good. Maybe I should deputize you." When Mrs. Davids turned around, Pickens put his arms around her and squeezed her tight.

"Oh my," she said.

"JD, what are you doing with my mother," yelled Marge.

"I'm kissing her that's what I'm doing. She just gave me great advice to help solve my case." Both Pickens and Mrs. Davids laughed. "I'm thinking of whisking her off to a faraway island for a romantic weekend."

Mrs. Davids slapped him on the shoulder. "JD, I thought it was going to be for a whole year?"

"Mommy, you're not going to let Daddy take Grandma away, are you?" shouted Sarah.

"If he does, then I'm taking Sarah with me to a tropical island where she'll have lots of animals and creatures to talk to like she did with the ducks," said Mr. Davids as he came up behind Sarah and Marge.

Both Pickens and Mrs. Davids raised their eyebrows, and Pickens turned a palm up.

Marge tilted her head and mouthed, "Dad knows, he'll explain to Mom." Then she said, "What about me? Everyone is going off somewhere, and I suppose Bailey is going too."

"You can come, Marge. Sarah and I will need someone to cook and wash our clothes," replied Mr. Davids."

"Yeah, Mommy, you could," added Sarah.

"Thanks a lot. You all get to have fun, and I get to cook and wash dirty clothes." Marge shook her head. "Where's the fun in that?"

Mr. Davids evil-eyed his wife. "You took advantage of that young man, didn't you?"

She raised her chin. "I did no such thing." Then she ran her hands down her sides as if straightening her dress. "He asked me not to question him, and I honored his wishes." She looked at Pickens. "Didn't I, JD?"

Pickens turned his head and coughed, and she elbowed him in his side.

Sarah surprised them and called out, "Liar liar pants on fire!"

The adults couldn't resist laughing—which caused Mrs. Davids' crime to be forgotten.

"Tell you what, Marge, we'll all go out to lunch, and I'll treat," said Pickens. His offer caused everyone to place their palms against their cheeks in unison. "What, I've paid before," he said.

"Not since we've known you, JD," said Mr. Davids.

"You're right, Dad, he hasn't. Let's go before he changes his mind."

Pickens was dumbfounded but had no reply.

They all piled into Marjorie's SUV, and Mr. Davids drove to a restaurant that had outside seating so Bailey could join them. After lunch, they all went back to the Davids' residence, said goodbye, and then the Pickens family headed south on I75 for home.

For dinner that evening, Marge prepared a light dinner, and later the Pickens family relaxed watching television. Pickens tucked Sarah into bed and kissed her goodnight. Bailey kept her company.

"What did your dad say when he saw Sarah talking with the ducks?" he asked Marge.

"He wasn't surprised as he saw it happen with my grandmother. Said he was glad Sarah was going into the family business instead of law enforcement."

"Actually, so am I."

"That was sweet of you taking us to see Mom and Dad. I'll make it up to you later."

"Damn, wide receiver, your something else." He grabbed her hand. "Let's go make up."

CHAPTER 35

Amy had spent Monday morning working on the murder board. She labeled it 'Sisters in Crime' in red and laid it out as Pickens had suggested. Billy was able to obtain the women's names and had Photoshopped the individual pictures. Amy had placed them under their respective names. Down the side, she listed Benson, Hicks, Noristan, and Nolan in that order. She added what also knowns they had.

While Amy worked on the board, Billy searched the Internet for Barbara Williams aka Malibu Bobbie.

Pickens arrived earlier than usual because he worried that the weekend had proved fruitless since he hadn't received any calls from his team.

He walked into the office and called out. "Hold everything." Everyone froze and turned around. "New idea, don't do any more to the board. I'll show you what I have in mind."

He strolled over to the board as everyone's eyebrows lifted at the sight of the bounce in his step.

Amy mumbled, "Lucky guy." Pickens picked up a marker and was about write on the board. "JD, don't," she yelled.

He turned his palms up. "Why not?"

"That's a permanent marker, use the other one."

He switched markers, grabbed an eraser, wiped a clean area on the board, and drew a big circle. Next, he placed the pictures of the sisters around the inner edge.

"We just finished that, JD," said Amy.

Pickens realized what he'd done. "Sorry about that," he said, then continued and wrote Benson and Nolan in the center and double underlined their names. Then he drew a smaller circle outside the larger one and wrote Hicks and Noristan in it.

"Where's this going?" Amy asked.

Pickens held up a hand. "Just wait, and I'll explain." Next, he drew a line from the large circle to the small one and put a question mark underneath it. Then he turned, faced the deputies, and pointed to the question mark. "That's my new theory."

"A question mark?"

"Yes, Billy, a question mark. It represents someone outside the two circles." He pointed to the big circle. "This one represents the group that made the pact." He pointed to the small circle. "This one represents the two women that weren't part of it and may have been collateral damage, especially Hicks. Noristan's death may have been because she stuck her nose where she shouldn't have when she hired Ellison." Pickens paused for effect.

Amy walked over to the board, picked up a marker and drew a line from Allyson Healey to Noristan. "Maybe we have two shooters." Amy was still clinging to that possibility. "Healey may have been just trying to keep her identity concealed."

Pickens pointed a finger in the air. "That might be so, but she wasn't here just to enjoy the sights of our fine city; she was here for a purpose."

"Maybe," Amy replied.

Pickens again pointed his finger in the air. "And let's not forget that in both instances we have the same M.O."

"Okay, so where is this going?" asked Amy again.

DESCENT INTO HELL   187

"Let's assume whoever the killer was had a psychotic break occur in his or her life before going on a killing rampage." Pickens was reluctant to mention the words sociopath or psychopath for fear he might have to reveal his source.

"A psychotic break? Where did that come from?"

He wasn't about to reveal his source. It would be like the coach at halftime saying his revised game plan was from the cheerleaders' observations. He'd be laughed out of the locker room. "I did some research on my own about serial killers and it was a possible reason they start killing." Amy seemed to accept his explanation, so he continued. "Think about it, Amy. Benson and Nolan are the centerpieces, but Hicks and Noristan had no interaction with Nolan just Benson."

Amy sat on the edge of a nearby desk and ran her fingers through her hair. "Okay, so what you're thinking is that someone other than the sisters, who may have known Nolan but not Benson, may have killed him as revenge for her suicide?"

"Yes, and something happened to that person that caused him or her to snap."

"But why now, why not back then?"

"Because it may have happened recently, Billy." Pickens paused as he watched Price answer a call, wave Billy over, and hand him a slip of paper. Zeke waved to Pickens and walked out the door. Pickens nodded and was pleased that although the murder case was the top priority, his office was still functioning as it should. And with Sergeant Mia Dunne in charge of the Warfield satellite office and Ritchie Ortiz splitting shifts with Bobby Hawes, that office was also running as it should.

Pickens returned to the board and with a red marker, underlined Nolan, drew a line from her name to the circle with the question mark. "We have to consider that she may have known someone outside the pact. Any suggestions?"

"How about other sorority sisters?" asked Amy. "Maybe friends or relatives too."

Pickens erased the question mark and wrote other sisters and friends/relatives. "We'll include dropouts," he said and wrote it in the circle.

"Dropouts, what are they?" asked Amy.

"Girls who dropped out of the sorority. I dated a girl at FSU who said she was a dropout but still friends with her former sisters."

"I dated a few girls who were in a sorority and lived in the house. They said their house mother was worse than a drill sergeant," said Billy. "They called her a tyrant, but if you knew those girls you'd say they needed the discipline." Pickens high-fived Billy.

Amy shook her head and waved her palms at them. "You guys are real sexists, and that's demeaning."

"Sorry, I didn't mean to be demeaning," Pickens replied. Amy again nodded and waved her hand. Pickens raised a finger. "But Nolan may have confided in the house mother for support after Benson dumped her."

"So, you think the house mother might be our killer?"

He turned his palms up. "Maybe, Amy, so we add her to the list." He wrote 'H Mom' in the circle.

Amy fingered her cheek as she pondered his theory and the list. "That's a big list, where do we get names and we may need a bigger board."

Billy was on the computer researching Google, swiveled in his chair and remarked, "We could contact the Panhellenic Association at the college or the Sorority Chapter Association. Might be difficult getting any information, though."

"If we knew the house mother's name we could contact her or visit the sorority house and ask," added Amy. "For friends and relatives, maybe Nolan's parents could help."

Pickens thought of his last conversation with Rinaldo and ruled out Nolan's parents. "No, on the parents; we need another source." He looked up as though a light went on. "But we do have someone who could help." Amy and Billy's eyebrows furrowed. "Jennifer

Darling in Monticello, she may have a trove of information she can provide."

"But will she talk to us?" asked Amy.

"We can try. Billy, what's her number?" Billy checked his notes and handed Pickens the number. "Should I call or do you think it best if you did, Amy?"

"She talked to you before, so you call her. If she's reluctant, then I'll give it a try."

Pickens picked up the nearest phone, dialed Darling's number and then pressed the speaker button.

CHAPTER 36

Jennifer Darling and her partner Annice Timmons were rearranging several racks of clothing before considering closing the shop and taking a lunch break at Carley Jane's Eatery that offered a quiche and salad as one of its favorites. Jennifer and Annice were good friends with the owners.

The doorbell chimed as two middle-aged women entered the store, and each went to a different aisle. Jennifer and Annice greeted them separately. Just then the store phone rang.

Jennifer told her customer that she'd be right with her and walked around to the counter. She recognized the number on caller ID and decided to let the call go to voicemail. Then she pressed the mute button that allowed the store to prevent customers hearing messages. It was one of the unique features they purchased from their provider. She went back to her customer and apologized for the interruption.

When Pickens heard the voicemail message, Amy told him to say his name but leave off sheriff in the event Darling and her partner were with customers. "Ms. Darling, this is JD Pickens I need to speak to you..."

Amy mouthed, "You'll call back."

Pickens raised a finger. "If I don't hear from you, I'll call back shortly; it's important that we talk."

"They're probably with customers."

"Maybe, or the store is closed. We'll wait thirty minutes. That should be enough time if they're with customers."

Annice rang up her customer and then the woman left. She looked at the flashing red light on the phone and asked, "Who called?"

Jennifer clenched her jaw. "That sheriff."

Annice lightly stroked Jennifer's forearm, pressed the 'play' button, and they listened to Pickens message.

Jennifer stepped back and bit her lip. "What should I do?"

"We could ignore his call," Annice replied.

"But what if he calls back?"

Annice scratched her chin. "Let it go to voicemail. He'll think we're with customers or closed."

"Okay, but he'll just keep calling and might come here. He's not that far from Monticello."

Annice considered their options. "Okay, we don't know what he wants. Maybe he just has more questions about your sorority sisters." She rubbed the back of Jennifer's hand. "Wait until he calls back and see what he wants. We'll deal with it then."

"I'm not comfortable talking about those girls and Melissa. It took a while to forget what happened."

"I know, sweetheart," Annice said and held Jennifer's arm. "But he did say people died, and you saw what that article in the newspaper said. Maybe you can help him find who he's looking for."

"I guess you're right."

Pickens paced the floor waiting for Darling to call. Amy made notes about what was on the board, and Billy researched the sorority's website hoping to get a house mother's name. Unfortunately, the website didn't mention the name of the house mother, only that it had one and none of the members were listed.

"How long has it been since I called?" asked Pickens.

"Fifteen minutes," replied Amy. "Give her the other fifteen and then call."

Pickens picked up the receiver, pressed speaker and dialed Darling's store number. "Let's hope she answers or her partner does; if not I'll keep trying."

"The store could be closed, Sheriff."

"It wasn't the last time we talked to her and that was also on a Monday, Billy." Pickens picked up a paperclip, mangled it, and threw it in the wastebasket. Darling's phone rang and was answered, but there was silence. "Are you there, Ms. Darling? It's Sheriff Pickens."

Jennifer covered the receiver with her hand. "What should I say?"

"Wait, don't say anything." Jennifer grimaced as Annice went to the door, turned the open sign to closed, and locked the door. "Put it on speaker."

"Ms. Darling, I know you're there," said Pickens.

Annice extended a palm and mouthed, "Okay."

Jennifer took a deep breath and answered. "Yes, Sheriff, I'm here, sorry it took so long to answer."

Amy raised her hand and mouthed, "She's scared or nervous, be patient."

Pickens nodded. "That's okay, Ms. Darling. Look, I just have a few questions to ask you."

Annice lowered her palms, raised them and mouthed, "Stay calm and listen to him."

Again, Jennifer took a deep breath. "Okay, but please call me Jennifer." Annice smiled. "How can I help you?"

Pickens followed Amy's advice and calmly replied, "Okay, Jennifer, and please call me JD."

Amy mouthed, "Good thinking." Next, she gave him her notes. While they were waiting to call Jennifer, Amy had compiled a list of questions for Pickens to ask her based on his theory. Using her training as a counselor, she prioritized them to make Jennifer comfortable in responding and not repulse her.

He reviewed the list and mouthed, "Good."

"Seems a bit informal to call you JD," Jennifer replied. "But since you asked."

Pickens glanced over Amy's list and was about to ask Jennifer the first question when Amy pressed the mute button.

His jaw dropped. "What, why?"

"Listen to me; you don't want to frighten her." Pickens grimaced. "Yes, that's what you do. Take your time, give her a chance to answer, ask her if she needs time to consider her answer, and it wouldn't hurt to ask if she'd like to call you back before answering." Amy looked him directly in his eyes. "Trust me on this."

"Okay, you're the counselor. Slow and relaxed and give her time to think or call back." Amy nodded. "Got it, let's do this." Amy pressed the mute button.

"Are you still there, Sheriff, I mean, JD?"

"I'm here, Jennifer. Can you tell me how many active sorority sisters there were during the year when Melissa Nolan last attended?"

Jennifer thought back to her time at Langston College and the sorority house.

"Yes, there were only thirty," replied Jennifer. "Langston is a small college, so we were limited in the number of members. Only eighteen lived in the house, the rest lived in a dormitory or rented an apartment."

Pickens checked the next question since Jennifer answered it. "Was there a house mother?"

Jennifer grinned. "You mean a house director, JD. Yes, and she lived in the house on the first floor where the senior class members did. Anything else?"

Pickens changed the order of his questions and asked, "Can you tell me the house director's name?"

Seconds went by and Jennifer hadn't responded, so Amy mouthed, "Let her call back if she wants to."

"Jennifer, if you need time to recall her name, you can call me back or I can go on to my next question."

"Are there many more, JD?"

"Yes, there are."

"Please, go to your next question then."

Pickens surmised the last question might have been difficult for her to answer, so he moved down the list.

"Are there any pictures available of the members from the year you and Melissa were sisters?" He decided to bundle that question with the next on the list. "Also, is it possible to get a list of those members?" Jennifer's silence this time was longer. Pickens waited and waited. "You still there, Jennifer?"

Amy pressed mute. "Give her time."

After several minutes of silence, someone responded, but it wasn't Jennifer. "Sheriff, this is Annice Timmons, Jennifer's partner. Your questions have dredged up old memories, and she needs to compose herself. It may take several minutes, but I promise she'll call back. I hope that's okay with you."

Pickens rubbed his chin. "That's fine, Ms. Timmons. Let her take all the time she needs. We'll be here."

"Thank you and call me Annice." The line went dead.

"Dredged up old memories, sounds like someone might have had a psychotic break or is still experiencing one. If Amy's theory of two killers is correct, those two may be them."

"I was thinking the same thing, Billy," said Pickens.

Amy abruptly stood up. "You're both wrong. And stop jumping to conclusions. Didn't you hear the crack in Jennifer's voice when you asked those questions?" Amy's eyes narrowed. "In my years of counseling, when someone's voice starts to crack, it's generally because they're under stress from reliving something in their past. Trust me on this."

Pickens slumped into a nearby chair. "You're right; it's just that I'm anxious for answers and something we can use to solve this damn case."

CHAPTER 37

Damn that Allyson, if I find her, she'll never breathe again after I finish with her. Who's calling now? Damn it, where the hell did I leave my phone? Shit, in my purse.

"What's up, why are you calling?"

"Have you heard from Allyson?"

"Yes, the bitch said she's going into hiding, and no one will ever find her. I've tried her phone numerous times but get nothing. I told you she was unstable."

"Maybe it's because of Noristan. Benson and that whore of his were mistakes, but Noristan was crazy."

"Don't say that. I told you I don't like it. I did it to conceal Allyson's identity and ours."

"And now that's started a firestorm. The sheriff is asking a lot of questions and digging into the past. You may want to consider disappearing like Allyson did."

"What about you, what are you going to do?"

"I'm considering it. It may not be long before the sheriff discovers who we are. Think about disappearing before it's too late.

"I'll think about it."

CHAPTER 38

Annice hung up the phone, wiped Jennifer's eyes and then squeezed her hands. Jennifer's body trembled, so Annice pulled Jennifer into her arms and held her tightly.

"I can't go through this again. I was the last of our sorority sisters to see Melissa alive, and I'm responsible for getting her the abortion," Jennifer whimpered. "She stayed at my apartment, and I took her to the clinic for the procedure. I knew she was depressed, and I should have called her parents."

Annice stroked her back. "I understand, and you don't have to do this. I'll call the sheriff and tell him you don't want to answer any more questions. But you're not responsible for Melissa's decision. It was her choice."

Jennifer looked into Annice's eyes with a pained stare. "Maybe, but that doesn't change the fact that after Melissa had the abortion, I let her go home and then..."

"Stop it!" Annice snapped. Jennifer's head jerked back. "You're just beating up on yourself for no reason other than you feel guilty. There was nothing you could do once Melissa went home. Only her parents could have stopped her." She squeezed Jennifer's arms. "You've got to stop blaming yourself."

Jennifer's head shook. "But…"

"No, but, you have to stop."

Jennifer broke into sobs. "Okay, I'll try, but you have to forgive me."

"Forgive you for what? You haven't done anything. Look, you've already answered some of the sheriff questions, you can do this."

Jennifer held her chin high. "Okay, let's call him."

An hour had passed, and still Jennifer hadn't called. Pickens was beginning to think that she wouldn't. Liz Price said she was going out to lunch and asked if she could get them anything. Price made a list of their orders and left. Forty-five minutes later, Price returned with their sandwiches and the waiting continued.

Pickens breathed a sigh of relief when the telephone rang. He pressed the speaker button.

"Am I speaking to Ms. Darling or Ms. Timmons?"

"It's Jennifer, JD."

Pickens pumped a fist, satisfied they were back on first name basis.

"Should I repeat the last question, Jennifer?"

"No, as for a list of names and pictures, in my senior year I was an officer, and I know for certain it's against the bylaws to give you one. You can try the Chapter, but you'll probably need a subpoena." Jennifer paused to get her point across. "I'm also not comfortable revealing the house director's name; she deserves her privacy."

Pickens collapsed into a chair. "Okay, Jennifer, I understand, I just hoped…"

"Sorry, JD, please don't be disappointed with me. I'm still a member even though I'm no longer at Langston."

"I'm not disappointed with you; you've been very helpful. I have one more question and then I won't bother you anymore."

"That's what you said last time." Jennifer and Annice grinned.

Amy mouthed, "She gotcha."

Pickens smiled. "Did Melissa have any friends outside the circle? Like a former roommate or a dropout?"

"Dropout? You're astute when it comes to sororities. Did you date one?"

Amy glared at him, but he ignored her.

"Yes, and she said she was still friends with her sisters. Did Melissa have one?"

Jennifer contemplated the question. "Come to think of it; there was one. She was M..." Jennifer couldn't say the word. "They were freshman roommates and rushed together. She wouldn't have got in if it wasn't for..."

Amy gave Pickens a thumbs-up.

"Do you remember her name by any chance? If it's confidential I'll understand, but we're at wit's end here, Jennifer."

Annice mouthed, "Tell him."

"If I could remember her name, I'd tell you. She dropped out after... But Allyson Healey would know. Allyson moved out of the house, and they became roommates. Sorry."

"Thanks, anyway, and I promise I won't bother you again unless you remember that girl's name."

"If I do, I'll call."

Pickens breathed a heavy sigh after the call ended. "Shit, I thought we had a break. We gotta find Allyson Healey." He checked his watch. "Damn, I'm on carpool duty today. Billy, you keep digging on the names we have so far and try and find Healey. We'll continue this tomorrow."

"JD."

"What, Amy? I gotta go."

Amy had a gleam in her eye. "You did the right thing today, and I'm proud of you."

"Thanks. It wasn't easy with Jennifer. It was difficult, really difficult."

Jennifer breathed a sigh of relief after ending the call, but her hands were still trembling. Annice grabbed hold of them, steadied her and then brushed a hand over Jennifer's cheek.

"Feel better now?"

"Yes, but that was worse than taking the SATs. I haven't been this nervous since then." She covered Annice's hand. "I'm glad you were with me. I don't think I could have got through it without you."

Annice smiled. "Yes, you could have, but I'm glad I was here. I'll always be here for you." Annice glanced at the clock. "Let's close up. I've had enough for today." Annice grabbed Jennifer's wrists, leaned in and kissed her softly. "Then let's..."

"Wait," Jennifer abruptly said.

"What?"

"I just remembered that girl's name. We have to call JD."

"Okay." Annice dialed the number and pressed speaker.

Amy was considering leaving because she had a group session for veterans and their spouses at the hospital when the tip line rang.

Price answered and handed the phone to Amy.

"Sergeant Amy Tucker speaking..."

"Is JD there? It's Jennifer Darling, Deputy Tucker."

"Sorry, Jennifer, he left for the day. Can I help you?"

Annice mouthed, "Tell her."

"I remember that girl's name. She went by the name..." Amy wrote down Lizzy. "I'm sorry, Sergeant, I don't remember her last name, but it sounded like it was German."

"That's okay, you've been a tremendous help. And, Jennifer, don't beat yourself up over what happened to Melissa. It wasn't your fault."

Jennifer gasped. "What makes you think I am?"

"I'm also a licensed family counselor, and I can tell when someone is blaming themselves for past happenings. You're lucky you have your partner to lean on. Thanks for this information."

Jennifer pressed the off button. "Am I that much of an open book?"

Annice smiled. "Yes, you are."

Jennifer wrapped her arms around Annice and kissed her tenderly. "Now, let's…"

Later that evening, after tucking Sarah in bed, Marge poured a glass of wine, got a beer for Pickens, joined him on the couch, and asked if there was anything new with his case.

"Remember that woman, Jennifer Darling, I told you about who was a sorority sister of Melissa Nolan? Well, I called her and got some interesting information."

"Was it helpful?"

He took a sip of beer. "Oh yeah, she said there was a girl Nolan knew as did that girl Healey. She dropped out of the sorority after Nolan's death, and she and Healey became roommates. Jennifer couldn't remember her name but will call if she does." He took another sip of beer. "At least we have something that might help us, and if Jennifer remembers that girl's name, we'll have another person of interest."

Marge sipped her wine. "Jennifer, huh? You're on a first-name basis with a young woman you've never met?"

Pickens bit his lip. "Oh, come on, Marge, it's how she wanted me to call her."

"Just don't call her if it has nothing to do with the case."

"Come on, Marge; you know better."

Marge wiggled her eyebrows and checked her watch. "Bedtime. Let's go, quarterback. And I don't want to hear you call out Jennifer's name when we…"

CHAPTER 39

Pickens had no idea where he was or how he got there but was certain that he wasn't in his house or any structure for that matter. He had already felt his way around for something—anything—but there was nothing but space. Pickens desperately wanted to know where he was, so he followed his Father's advice and what he'd learned in training. When you find yourself lost or in unfamiliar territory, stop and ask the important question—no, not where are you—but what do you see? Sadly, all Pickens saw was nothing. It was dark, and the blackness was so thick he would need a chainsaw to cut through it.

"Anyone there," he yelled. "Mom, Dad, Marge? Are you there?" Nothing, not even an echo. "Shit!"

He started to panic and considered that he was in a cavernous cave, deep within the earth, lost and alone without a cell phone—and no one would ever find him. Then Pickens remembered a trick his father taught him the night of a summer storm when the electricity went out. His father learned it in the army while serving in Vietnam. Close your eyes for a moment to adjust your night vision, visualize your surroundings—a fruitless endeavor since he had no idea what they were—then open your eyes and expect to see something, anything. Unfortunately, when Pickens tried it, all he saw was that same blackness. Of course, the trick worked the night of the storm because a fragment of light filtered through the windows, but where he was, there were no windows. He tried it again, but this time kept his eyes closed a while longer. When he opened his eyes, the blackness was gone replaced by a crimson color all around him, so he gave up on the eye thing.

He had no idea what to do next and there was nothing his parents, his wife or his old football coach could do to help with his situation.

Time to take control, it's the fourth quarter, time's running out and the ball's in your hands. Do you pass or run?

Suddenly someone shouted, "Go for it, Pickens!"

He threw caution to the wind and took a step forward, stumbled, almost fell, reached out and braced his hands against the cave's walls to steady himself. He quickly jerked his hands back when they touched a slimy substance. Next, he attempted to wipe his hands on his shirt; unfortunately, his chest was bare.

"Now what?" he shouted as if someone could hear him.

Pickens was beginning to experience that feeling of hopelessness when all seemed lost and considered his life may be over, and he wasn't in a cave but his grave. Maybe the answer was that he was already dead and experiencing an out-of-body experience. If so, then his last ray of hope had steadily diminished like the wick of a candle as it reaches its end, and he had to confine himself to the reality that he already died.

Suddenly, his body started shaking like he was experiencing a seizure and his heartbeat quickened. He thought he was going to have a heart attack. Then just as quickly as his body shook, it abruptly stopped, and he felt something soft touch his cheek. He heard a sound—it was barely audible—like a voice calling him.

"Come on, Pickens, wake up."

Just when he thought the end had come, he felt wetness on his cheek. Was it an omen of things to come or was his casket filling up with water—what an awful way to perish alone. His fear worsened, but he heard the voice again.

"Is someone there?" he called out, but again nothing and no echo.

He heard it again and was positive it was a female's voice, but he could barely make out what it was saying. There it was again—soft and tender—and calling his name.

"JD."

Was it possible the voice was calling him or was it just his imagination playing tricks on him? Something touched his cheek—soft, gentle and reassuring. Another brush against his lips caused warmth throughout his entire being.

"Come on, Pickens; time to wake up, sleepyhead." The voice sounded familiar. "You have only a few minutes to shower and dress before breakfast." Was it possible he was only dreaming? "Sheriff Pickens, you have to get up. We're running late." Someone yanked his arm. "Up you go, JD."

Pickens managed to open his eyes, and the darkness was gone replaced by barn wood gray on the walls, a trio of windows looking out into backyard gardens, and sunlight radiating on a divine presence—who was none other than his lovely wife, Marge. The only red in the room was an accent pillow on the floor that was part of the comforter set.

"It's about time," his wife said. "You were out like a light, and you're all sweaty. I hope whatever you were dreaming about included me." Her lips formed a radiant smile. "Get moving. I'll see you downstairs for breakfast. And hurry because I have a lot of work at the office and want to leave early."

As he carefully observed his lovely wife walk away, he suddenly felt a weird feeling in his stomach and worried that maybe his nightmare was a harbinger of things to come.

CHAPTER 40

After dropping Sarah off at school, Pickens arrived at the office later than expected. When he entered, Amy and Billy were waiting impatiently.

"I hope those expressions on your faces mean you have something important for me," Pickens asked.

"Oh, man do we," replied Billy.

"Okay, lay it on me."

"Go ahead, Billy you go first since you were here late last night, and you were here early this morning."

The corners of Billy's mouth turned up in an alligator grin. "Thanks, Amy. I got some info on those four other sorority sisters of Jennifer. Barbara William lives in Malibu; she's an actress." He smiled. "Well, a hopeful one. Myra Olson is a CPA in Jacksonville, Meghan Bucknell is an attorney in Atlanta, and Brandi Gormley is a teacher in Miami. I have addresses and telephone numbers for all of them, and I made a list."

Pickens gave him a thumbs-up. "Great job, but where'd you get that info from?"

Billy's grin conveyed he had secret knowledge. "I Googled the names and found a wealth of women with similar names. I also took a chance on Facebook and was lucky to find women who were from Florida. I narrowed my search parameters to them and focused on those who went to Langston." He watched Pickens and Amy to see their reactions. "The rest was easy. All I needed were those that were there the same time as Darling. I couldn't get home phone numbers, but I got their place of business numbers." He hunched his shoulders. "Sorry, it's the best I could do."

"Don't apologize; you did way more than I expected. Good job." Billy held his chin high. "We'll use that list to contact them and see if it helps." Pickens turned to Amy. "Okay, what's your information?"

"Jennifer called after you left yesterday."

"Really? Did she remember that girl's name?"

Amy nodded. "Yes, but only her first name. It's Lizzy, and she thinks her last name is German." She glanced at her notes. "I'm thinking maybe one of those girls Billy got info on might know her last name."

"It's worth trying. Who should we call first?"

"Let's start with Bucknell in Atlanta. Since she's an attorney, you should call her."

Pickens bit his lip. "Thanks, I get the difficult one. You think she's gonna talk to me because I'm the sheriff?"

"Better you than me," Amy replied as she casually anchored a hand on her hip.

"Then you get Olson the CPA," Pickens retorted with narrowed eyes. "And, Billy, you call Gormley, the teacher."

Billy looked at the clock on the wall. "She'll be in school now. I'll call her after three."

"Better if you call her before lunch. You'll have to leave a message anyway. Hopefully, she'll call back," said Pickens and checked his watch. "What the hell, I'm gonna try the attorney." He looked at Amy. "You might as well call that CPA."

Pickens suddenly did a double take when he saw Matt Riley in the crisis center on the phone.

"Billy, what's Riley doing here, where's Price?"

Billy rubbed his chin. "She called and said she had a family emergency and will be gone the rest of the week. Matt agreed to stay until noon."

"But he's been here since midnight, which means he'll be working twelve hours. That's too long and who takes over at noon?"

"I got it covered," answered Amy. "I called Chief Watson at the fire station, and he's sending one of his dispatchers to help us out until we get someone to fill in for Price."

"Shit, that means I'll owe him. He'll probably want me to buy a table at the Firemen's Ball."

Amy grinned. "That's what he said when he agreed."

"Damn it; I was hoping to avoid him." He scratched his chin. "What about Stacey Morgan?"

"What about her?" answered Billy.

"Maybe she's willing to come in for a few days. Call her and ask."

"I already did, but she can't come in until tomorrow and can only work from nine to five. It's the best she can do since she has to take her daughter to her mom's house."

"I can work until nine if you need me to," said Matt.

Billy breathed deeply. "Great, thanks, Matt. Are you sure?"

"It's only three days."

"I know, but you have classes, and it's a long drive to school."

"Not this week, it's spring break. You know, maybe Stacey would be willing to come in. You could ask her again."

Pickens rubbed the back of his neck. "Well, it'll have to do for now until Billy can talk to Stacy. Thanks for your help, Matt." Matt waved his hand. "I'm gonna call that attorney from my office after lunch."

Pickens emerged from his office looking like he had been run over by a steamroller. He glanced at Amy who had just hung up the phone from her call to the CPA. Billy was shaking his head as though he was disappointed with the results of his call to the teacher.

"How did your call to the attorney go?" Amy asked.

Pickens breathed a heavy sigh. "Shit, not good. She played the confidentiality and subpoena card."

Amy winced. "Did you use the one officer of the law to another card?"

He curled his lip. "Yeah, and in a few short words all but told me to go to hell. How did you do with the CPA?"

Amy nodded. "Just about the same. She said it's tax season and didn't have time to talk and then hung up on me." Amy rubbed her forehead. "Think maybe Healey got to them?"

"I wouldn't be surprised if she did. At least we know Jennifer didn't." Pickens turned to Billy. "How did it go with the teacher?"

"Not much better. I called the school. They said Gormley was on maternity leave and wouldn't divulge her phone number."

"Shit," Pickens said and scratched his forehead. "Maternity leave, huh. That would give her a chance to come here and do the shootings."

"I don't think so. What reason would she have? Think about it; she's a teacher and pregnant or just had a baby. Where's the psychotic break in her life?" remarked Amy.

"Okay, but it's something to consider." Pickens collapsed into a nearby chair. "It's like we're some big city cops trying to conduct an investigation and no one wants to cooperate."

"Yeah, and now we know how they feel," Amy added.

Pickens slammed his fist on a nearby desk. Amy and Billy's heads snapped back. "Damn it, every time we think we have a break we end up with shit." He ran his fingers through his hair. "Maybe we should call for outside help."

"You're not considering the...?"

"Yes, Amy, the FBI. Maybe they can get the answers we can't."

"Don't be hasty; wait until Friday or Monday and if we don't come up with something, then call the Feds."

Pickens waved a dismissive hand. "Okay, I'll think about it. But if anyone else gets hurt because I held onto this case, I might have to resign as sheriff." Amy's mouth fell open. "That's right you heard me. You and Billy keep trying to come up with something." He turned to Billy. "You keep doing what you do and see if you can somehow get something on this Lizzy woman." He looked at the wall clock. "I have a meeting at the high school. Spring football practice starts in two weeks, and the coach wants to go over scheduling."

Even with all the chaos surrounding the case, Pickens knew to keep a sense of priority. His father had instilled in him that when things were out of your control, reach back to family and friends. They'll remind you of who you are, where you came from, and you would eventually realize that you can get through whatever life throws at you. His dad said it helped a number of times in Vietnam during harsh conditions.

"After, I'm picking up Sarah. It's my last day of carpooling. Have something tomorrow or I may call the Feds. I might even call Ellison. Why not? He did get info on Healey."

Amy and Billy raised their eyebrows with looks of bewilderment. They'd never considered that Pickens might consider resigning.

"Amy, we better find something on Lizzy and quick," said Billy.

After Pickens' meeting at the high school, he picked up Sarah and Annie and then dropped Annie off at her house and drove home.

As he and Sarah were about to enter the front door, Pickens noticed a note taped to it that read—GOODBYE SHERIFF BOOM.

He instinctively surveyed the neighborhood, unhooked his holster and then ripped the note off before Sarah could see it.

"Stay behind me, Sarah."

Inside, Bailey barked incessantly, so Pickens stuffed the note in his pocket, unlocked the door, and carefully entered with Sarah behind him. Bailey jumped up on him—something he rarely did unless something was amiss. Bailey was breathing heavy, and his tail wagged a mile a minute. Pickens rubbed Bailey's head.

"What's up, boy? Something wrong?"

Bailey ran to the front window stood on his hind legs with his paws on the sill, looked out the window and barked several times. Pickens walked over and looked out at the street.

"Sarah, you wait by the door with Bailey." She stood by the door and looked around the room. "Bailey, make sure she stays there." Bailey positioned himself in front of Sarah so she was sandwiched between him and the door.

Pickens wished he hadn't left his radio in the SUV or had a shoulder radio. He removed his weapon, and before searching the house he contemplated two scenarios. If someone was still in the house, Bailey would have the intruder pinned against the wall. The second scenario was the possibility of a bomb but then that meant someone had to enter the house. And as in the first scenario, Bailey would have attacked that person. Just to be safe, Pickens decided to call for backup and reached for his phone.

"Daddy," said Sarah.

Pickens raised his hand. "Not now, Sarah."

"Daddy," Sarah said again only more forceful. "Daddy, there's no one in the house."

Pickens turned around. "How do you know?"

Bailey stood next to Sarah with his tail wagging and barked. Sarah tilted her head toward the dog.

"Oh," he said. "You talked to him." Pickens holstered his weapon.

Sarah grinned. "Yes, Bailey said a woman tried to get in the house, but he growled. Then he went to the window and barked repeatedly. She left in a hurry and climbed into a truck like yours." Bailey barked again. "That's all he said."

Pickens bent down and rubbed the dog's head. "Good job, Bailey. I might make you a deputy." Bailey wagged his tail and barked. "Sarah, I'm gonna call for backup." Pickens dialed Amy.

Amy and Billy were deciding whether they should contact Ellison or wait until tomorrow for Pickens to decide. When she saw that it was Pickens calling, she answered, but before she could speak Pickens interrupted her.

"Get a deputy to my house immediately and send one to Marge's office."

Amy's neck stiffened. "I'll send Zeke to Marge's office, and I'll come to your house myself. What's wrong?"

He lowered his voice so Sarah couldn't hear. "Someone was here and left a note on my front door. I think it was the killer. I want a car parked out front. Better yet, I want you inside the house and someone on the street."

"I'm on my way, and I'll call Sergeant Dunne and get her to send someone."

After speaking to Amy, Pickens made several calls. The first was to Marge.

He didn't wait for Marge to acknowledge his call, he immediately launched into the reason he was calling.

"Marge, there's a deputy on his way there. Don't leave until he gets there. I haven't got time to explain, but trust me."

Marge wrinkled her brow. Pickens had never sounded so concerned when he called her, and she wasn't about to question his motive.

"Okay, JD, I'll wait. Are you and Sarah all right?"

"Yes, and so is Bailey. I'll explain when you get here." He abruptly ended the call and made another one.

Amy pulled up to Pickens' house and soon after Zeke also arrived behind Marge as she pulled into the driveway.

"Zeke, you wait here I'm going inside with Ms. Davids." Amy followed Marge into the house.

Pickens had just finished his last call when they entered. Sarah was in the kitchen with Bailey.

Marge grabbed hold of Pickens. "What happened? Where is Sarah?"

He hugged her. "I'll tell you later, but everything is fine. Sarah is in the kitchen with Bailey. Go talk to her."

"You sure?"

"Yes, now go, I have to talk to Amy." He nodded for Amy to step aside. Marge went to the kitchen.

"What happened?" Amy asked.

He reached into his pocket. "The killer left this on the front door." Pickens shook his head. "She must be losing it."

Amy's eyebrows hiked. "Shit, we gotta get you and your family out of the house and quickly."

"Relax, she just tried the doorknob and left."

"How can you be sure it was a woman and that she's gone?"

Pickens nodded toward the kitchen. "Bailey told Sarah." He raised his hand. "I know, it sounds crazy, but it's true. He said she drove a dark pickup like mine."

Amy didn't question Pickens; she went along with his comment about Bailey and Sarah.

"She, damn. JD, if she's the killer, we may be dealing with a sociopath or worse, a psychopath." Pickens' eyes bulged. "If we assume it was either Healey or the Lizzy woman, we need to take extra precautions. What do you want to do, JD?"

"Have Zeke canvass the neighborhood. Maybe one of my neighbors saw her or the truck."

Amy stepped outside and told Zeke to canvas the neighborhood, but be discreet. Then she closed the door and waited for Pickens to say what the next step was.

"I called Ellison and filled him in on what happened." Amy's mouth fell open. "I had to do something, Amy. Besides, he has all the info on Healey, and I gave him Lizzy's name since she roomed with her. He can probably get answers we can't."

Amy nodded agreement. "Billy and I were debating calling him when you called."

"Good, we're on the same page. And tomorrow I may call the FBI."

Amy frowned. "Do you think they'll help? We don't necessarily have a serial killer on the loose."

"With what happened here, I'm not taking any chances and could use all the help I can get." Pickens thought of his mother-in-law's comment about a sociopath or psychopath. "Besides, I know someone who knows someone."

Amy gave him an incredulous look. "It's an inside thing, Amy." She was still confused. "And I gave Nosey another scoop. A real one this time."

Amy tentatively smiled. "I bet he was thrilled. So, what else do we do?"

"I want a car out front all night, and I'd like you to spend the night in here. Marge would sleep better knowing you're here."

"I'm happy too, but I'll have to get someone to relieve Zeke. He's been on all day."

Pickens grabbed Amy's arm and asked, "You really think it's possible we might have a sociopath or psychopath on our hands?"

"Yes, it's possible. I'll do some research on the topics and see what I learn," Amy replied.

Sergeant Mia Dunne arrived and walked up to the front door, tapped on it and then entered.

"Sergeant Dunne, what are you doing here, I thought you were sending a deputy?"

"I was going to, Sergeant Tucker, but when you said our sheriff and his family needed help, I wasn't about to send anyone but myself. He's my sheriff, too."

Sergeant Mia Dunne was a former Army MP who had served two tours in Iraq, held an Associate's Degree in Criminal Justice, and wore her uniform as though she was still in the service. Her white blouse highlighted her caramel colored skin. Dunne stood on ceremony and always addressed Pickens as Sheriff Pickens, and her deputies addressed her as Sergeant Dunne as did Pickens and Amy.

"And my sheriff also," said Zeke as he stepped into the house. "Hello, Sergeant Dunne." Dunne put two fingers to her forehead.

"Sheriff, I talked to your neighbors. No one saw anything except the neighbor three houses over."

"That would be Mrs. Wigelworth; she's the Neighborhood Watch," said Pickens.

"Yes, it was. Mrs. Wigelworth told me she was about to leave for the grocery store when she saw a dark truck go past. She couldn't see the driver because the windows were tinted, but the truck had a Florida tag."

"Good job, Zeke."

"Um, Sheriff, I think you might want to talk to your neighbors." Zeke went to the window. "You've got a small crowd of concerned neighbors on the street."

Pickens looked out the window. "Shit." Marge and Sarah walked into the room as he made his comment. The ladies and Sarah had their hands on their hips and were frowning. "What, it's a guy thing."

"Oh, thanks for mansplaining," said Marge and started counting. "One, two, three, four sheriff's cars out front. The neighbors must love that." She went to the window. "Oh, yeah, and you've got an audience waiting for reassurance, Sheriff." She pointed her thumb at the door. "You best go take care of it."

"I was just about to do it. Come on, Zeke. Let's go do some reassuring." Pickens and Zeke left the house.

"So, ladies, which one did he appoint to spend the night here to make sure Sarah and I feel protected and can sleep well tonight?"

"Both of us," answered Dunne.

"Sergeant Dunne, you don't have to," Amy said. "The sheriff has already asked me to."

"I told you he's my sheriff too, and I'm not going anywhere as long as there's some whacko out there. I already called my husband, and he's picking up the girls and will be fine at home with them so I'm staying." Dunne's husband was the principal of Warfield Middle School and a veteran of Afghanistan.

"Okay, ladies, Sarah and I would feel better having you both here and besides I want to see how Pickens handles four females under the same roof for the night."

The four laughed but when Pickens and Zeke returned they acted seriously.

"I spoke to our neighbors and assured them it was nothing serious just a precaution because of the case. They felt better knowing Zeke would be out front during the night."

"Good, then Sarah and I are going to fix dinner for all of you, including Deputy Jackson. Hamburgers will have to do." She waved the back of her hand. "Since this is going to be your command center for the night, you all go and strategize or whatever you do when you're together."

"I think they sit around and drink beer, Mommy."

Sarah's remark brought laughter and lightened the mood. While Marge fixed dinner, Pickens and his sergeants talked about the case. He brought Dunne up to speed on what steps he had taken so far. They all agreed that he shouldn't contact the FBI just yet. They'd wait until Ellison got back with his investigation and to see if Noseby's article produced any results. Also, Zeke was to go home after dinner.

During dinner, Zeke said he wasn't going home. He'd clock out and keep watch on his own time. He wasn't about to abandon his sheriff. After further discussion, Zeke agreed to go home at midnight after a check of the neighborhood. The front porch light was to be left on as would the screen porch light. Motion-sensor floodlights covered the perimeter.

Later, Marge and Sarah went to bed. Pickens tucked Sarah in and left Bailey to guard her.

"You watch over her, Bailey." Bailey thumped his tail twice and nestled against Sarah. Pickens kissed her and said goodnight. Then he went to Marge's bedroom. She was just about to climb into bed when he pulled her into his arms.

"I love you, wide receiver."

"I know you do, quarterback, and we'll get through this. Sarah told me what happened." She kissed him softly on his mouth. "Don't worry; we'll sleep better knowing all that firepower is watching over us."

He pulled her to him and held her tightly. "No whack a doodle's going to harm my family." Marge smiled. "It's Billy's term for whoever left the note. Goodnight, wide receiver."

"Goodnight, quarterback. When this is over, I'll make you forget that there ever was a case." Marge winked and nodded toward the bed. He grinned and left.

Pickens stayed in the living room with his sergeants. Amy and Sergeant Dunne split two-hour shifts and alternated sleeping on the couch, and Pickens sat in his favorite chair. He later decided that when and if they found Healey and the Lizzy woman, Dunne would be in charge of tactical command since she had experience as an MP. And although they would try to capture the killer or killers, the use of deadly force would not be ruled out.

At midnight, Zeke made a final check of the neighborhood and then went home.

CHAPTER 41

Sarah woke before her mother to let Bailey out and do his business. To get to the screened porch, she had to go through the kitchen. She walked past Sergeant Dunne who was wearing a long apron over her uniform and preparing breakfast.

"Good morning, Sergeant Mia."

Sergeant Dunne smiled. "Good morning, Sarah. Did you sleep well?" After last night's dinner, Sergeant Dunne had bonded with Sarah and asked her to call her Mia, but Sarah chose to call her Sergeant Mia.

"I sure did, with Bailey, you, and Sergeant Amy protecting me." She glanced into the living room. "I guess Daddy slept well too." Pickens was in his chair cutting wood.

Dunne chuckled. "He had a long night. Breakfast will be ready soon." Sarah grinned and went to let Bailey out.

Marge had already showered and dressed for work before she came out of the bedroom. When she saw Sergeant Dunne preparing breakfast, her eyes sparkled.

"Sergeant Dunne, I could have done that. You should have waited; you've been up most of the night."

Dunne waved her off, removed four pancakes from the griddle, put them on the plate with others and covered it.

"It's nothing, Ms. Davids; I'm used to doing it for my family." She smiled." They like a big breakfast in the morning whenever I'm home. And please, call me Mia. Since I spent the night with you and your family, I feel like I'm part of yours, especially with Sarah and Bailey." Dunne picked up the bowl she had put several eggs in and began beating them.

Marge's eyes twinkled. "Yes, they do get to you. If I'm to call you Mia, then you have to call me Marge. I insist."

Dunne tossed her a two-fingered salute. "Okay, Marge."

"Where's Amy?"

"She went out to get the newspaper and reassure your neighbors we're still on guard."

Marge heard a snort and blinked. "What's that sound?"

Dunne pointed to the living room.

Just then, Amy came through the front entrance holding the newspaper, set it on a nearby table, and glanced at Pickens. "Is he still at it? He sounds worse than a sputtering old lawn mower on its last legs."

Marge grabbed a strip of uncooked bacon just before Dunne could put the rest in the microwave. She walked over to Pickens chair and dangled the bacon strip over his nose and mouth.

He swatted the strip and mumbled, "Phwt." Then he opened his eyes and frowned when he saw Marge. "Don't anyone dare say I was snoring."

"Yes, you was," shouted the women.

"You was, Daddy," added Sarah as she and Bailey walked into the living room. Bailey barked to echo Sarah.

Everyone burst into laughter. The morning at the Pickens' household was getting off to a good start.

When the coffee pot beeped, Pickens sat up. "Dang, is that fresh coffee I smell?"

Sergeant Dunne nodded to the pot. "And I have pancakes, scrambled eggs and bacon coming up. I couldn't make biscuits, so I toasted English muffins."

Pickens smiled. "You sure know the way to a man's heart, Sergeant Dunne."

Dunne grinned. "That's why I have two daughters and a hunk of a man at my house." Again, everyone broke out in laughter.

"You know what, Sheriff? I could get used to this," said Marge.

Pickens raised a hand. "Well, don't, Marge. I have a feeling we won't be needing the cavalry tonight." He didn't mention that while he snored, he had a dream about an old cabin and a body and considered it might be a premonition just like that nightmare the previous night.

"So, what's the game plan for today?" asked Amy.

"First order of business is breakfast 'cause I'm starved. That's what, Amy." More laughter.

Sergeant Dunne put the food on platters and set them on the counter so everyone could serve themselves buffet style. As they ate breakfast, Pickens read Noseby's article containing the information that he supplied Noseby. The gist of it was that his office was asking for information that would help locate Allyson Healy and the woman known as Lizzy. Noseby mentioned that both attended Langston College and were sorority sisters and roommates. They were persons of interest in three homicides. Noseby provided a tip line like the last time.

"Nosey nailed it with this article," Pickens remarked. "We should get some feedback and soon."

"I wonder if Ellison saw the article?" asked Amy. "Maybe it will help with his investigation."

"Let's hope so," he replied. "Okay, this is the plan for today. Marge, you take Sarah with you. She can miss school for today." Marge nodded agreement. "Sergeant Dunne you follow Marge to her office and then you go home."

"No way, sorry, but I'm sticking around. If I need to, I'll go home and change clothes and then come to your office."

Amy put her fork down. "But, Mia, you've already put in a twenty-four-hour day."

"So what, Amy," Dunne replied. "It's not the first time. In Iraq, it was almost routine. No one's taking me off this case."

Pickens knew it wasn't worth arguing with Sergeant Dunne, especially when she was so determined. "Okay, go home and change, check on things at your office and then meet us at mine. Amy, you can take the day off."

"No way, if Mia's not taking the day off then neither am I, and don't try to talk me out of it."

"Looks like you haven't got a say in this, JD. These are two stubborn women, and you're outnumbered. What would Quarterback Pickens do? Would he take the sack or throw the ball away?" asked Marge.

"I hate throwing the ball away. Okay, you win." He placed a hand on his heart and shook his head. "Thanks, I'm glad you have my back. Amy, at least go home and freshen up."

"I've already done that here, and I have a change of uniform at the office."

"Damn, you two are something else. Okay, so I'll take Bailey with me in my truck." Bailey barked and wagged his tail. "He wouldn't let me leave him here anyway. I'll leave my vehicle in the driveway as a diversionary tactic in case anyone gets the idea to come back. But I don't believe that's gonna happen. If everyone is ready, let's saddle up and get going."

CHAPTER 42

While Pickens and his sergeants were executing his plan, Billy was at the office researching names of female truck owners with the first name of Lizzy also Lizabeth and Elizabeth—in the event Lizzy was a nickname—on the motor vehicle database and the Langston College site for graduates the same year as Darling and Nolan. So far, he hadn't been successful.

At 8:45, Stacey Morgan arrived to relieve Matt Riley. As she walked up to him, she smiled and asked, "Hey, Matt, how's your sister enjoying school at Langston and sorority life?"

"She loves it, Stacey."

When Billy heard Morgan's question and Riley's reply, he nearly fell backward in his chair. He leaped up and shouted, "Hey Matt, your sister's at Langston College, really?"

Stacey took a step back, and Matt gave Billy an incredulous stare.

"Yeah, why?"

Thinking Billy wanted to interrogate Matt, Stacey placed a hand on his arm and said, "I better go clock in, I'll catch you later." Stacey glanced at Billy's desk and saw the open box and the half-eaten pizza. "Has he been here all night?"

"He was here when I came on duty. He's been at the computer but dozed off several times." Matt raised his palm. "I better go."

Stacey turned and started for the time clock. Just then, Pickens walked in and greeted Stacey. She stopped and turned abruptly. Pickens walked up to her, wrapped his arms around her and cradled her against his chest. Stacey's cheeks turned red.

"Stacey." Pickens looked down. "This is my new deputy. Say hello to Stacey Morgan, Deputy Bailey." Stacey reached down and took Bailey's paw. "Stacey, we need some help. If you think you're up to it, we could use you permanently. Amy will coordinate it with you and Billy."

"My husband read this morning's paper and we discussed my working full time. So, yes, I'm up to it."

"Good."

Matt anxiously waited while Pickens and Stacey had their conversation.

"Morning, Sheriff."

"Morning, Matt, thanks for staying on until Stacey arrived."

"No problem, I don't have class today." He glanced toward Billy. "Billy wants to speak with me, so if you'll excuse me."

Pickens looked at Billy's desk and saw the pizza box. "Did he have pizza for breakfast?"

"It was here when I arrived, and he never left during my shift but did take a few naps."

Pickens shook his head. "Well, let's go see what he wants."

Billy waited anxiously to talk to Matt.

"Good morning, Sheriff, is everything okay at home?" asked Billy.

"Yes, thanks."

"Whoever the person was is a real meshuggener."

Amy arrived and overheard Billy. "Meshuggener, is that your word for the day? I thought you gave that up."

Billy shrugged. "What can I say; I have to improve my vocabulary."

Matt rocked in place. "I don't mean to be rude, Billy, but you wanted to talk to me about my sister."

Pickens and Amy crossed their arms. Billy held his hand up for them to disregard their implication.

"It's about this case we're working on, Matt," answered Billy. Pickens and Amy stood at ease.

"What's my sister have to do with your case?"

"I heard you say she goes to Langston College and is in a sorority." He pointed to one of his monitors. "By any chance is this the one?"

Matt glanced at the screen. "Yeah, it is. My girlfriend was in it, and that's how Janet got in. Why?"

Pickens edged closer. Amy waved to Stacey and was about to walk over and talk to her, but she was also curious and also edged closer.

"Because..."

Pickens interrupted Billy. If Matt's sister could offer help that would lead to the identity of the killer or one of the killers, Pickens would have to take command of the situation. He was the sheriff and the quarterback. It was his responsibility to guide his team to the end zone. He'd been in situations like this before, and he knew the playbook, had the players, knew his team, so he was the man to do the job. He couldn't delegate his role to someone else. He had to take charge and now.

"Matt, we're up to our asses in shit with this case and need a break," interrupted Pickens and pointed his index finger at the screen. "There's a woman who was in the sorority in 2004, and she may be the killer or one of the killers."

Amy raised an eyebrow and shot Pickens a *See?* look. Meaning both Pickens and Billy had come around to the possibility there were two killers.

"If so, your sister could help identify her and help prevent any more killings."

Matt glanced at the three of them. He was uncertain and concerned about involving his sister in a homicide investigation and the possibility of breaking her sorority vows.

"Come on, Matt, do the right thing," said Billy. "We need you, man."

Matt took a long exhale and answered. "Okay, but if it will get her in trouble or possibly kicked out of her sorority, then all bets are off." Matt addressed Pickens. "I'm serious."

Pickens extended his hand. "You have my word, Matt." Both shook hands.

"Okay, what do you want me to do?"

"If your sister could check member names from 2004 and their pictures, it would help identify one of the killers." Pickens breathed a heavy sigh. "All we have is the name, Lizzy. If she can't, at least it was worth a try."

Matt rubbed the back of his neck. "Tell you what, let me call my girlfriend and see if she can help. She still has a connection at the sorority and if she can get the info, then my sister doesn't have to compromise her vows. Will that work?"

Pickens laid a hand on Matt's shoulder. "It's worth trying. Thanks, Matt."

Matt checked his watch. "I'll call her at lunchtime because she's in class now. She's a math teacher at the middle school. That's the best I can do. Besides, Janet's on spring break and won't return until Friday."

Pickens raised his palms. "That's good, Matt, and thanks again. Call me when you have an answer." Pickens considered that if Matt could get some names and pictures, he'd at last have more tangible evidence as to the identity of Lizzy.

While Pickens and his team waited for Matt to call, Ellison was in Tampa doing further investigation on Allyson Healey. After speaking with Allyson's mother and advising her that Allyson was wanted for murder, Mrs. Healey told Ellison that Allyson had called her. What Mrs. Healey said to him, Ellison believed and called Pickens.

When Pickens saw that Ellison was calling, he pressed speaker so Amy and Billy could hear him.

"I hope you have something good for me, Ellison, because I need a break."

On the other end, Ellison was smiling. "This may be your lucky day, Pickens. I spoke with Healey's mother. She was forthcoming and said Healey recently contacted her."

"Damn, Ellison, that sounds good. What did she say?"

"Healey's not your killer, and she's left the state. Mrs. Healey doesn't know where to, but she gave me an address where Allyson stayed when in Creek City." Ellison reeled off the address.

"I know that address," interjected Billy. "That's Mrs. Gronfein's address. She's an elderly widow, but why would Healey use that address?"

"Who knows," responded Ellison. "But she wasn't alone when she stayed there. She had a roommate."

"We know about Lizzy, Ellison," interrupted Pickens. "But we can't find anything about her. Billy searched the Internet for a registration for her but got zilch."

"How're you spelling Lissie?"

"Lizzy, with two z's," answered Billy. "I figured it was a nickname for Elizabeth or Lizabeth."

"Well, you figured wrong. It's Lissie, with a double s and ie on the end."

"Damn, I'm sorry, Billy. I should have asked Darling how to spell it," said Amy.

"Don't beat yourself up over it. I spelled it the same way until Healey's mother corrected me," remarked Ellison.

Pickens and Billy shook their heads. "Okay, we'll do another search. And we may have a lead at the sorority. Won't know for sure until after lunch."

"You let me know, and if I have to go to Langston, I can do it today. One more thing, Lissie was Healey's roommate at Langston."

"That much we know, which is why we need more on her. I'll call you when I have more. Thanks, Ellison."

"Hey, wait, Pickens. Healey told her mother that you'd be surprised when you learn who Lissie is. That's all she said."

Pickens' head jerked back. "What the hell does that mean?" Unfortunately, Ellison had ended the call.

"Billy, try and find anything on this Lissie woman now that we know how to spell her name." He rubbed his hand through his hair. "I'm taking Bailey for a walk and then going to the county attorney to get a search warrant for Gronfein's property." Pickens pointed to Amy. "You call Sergeant Dunne and tell her if she wants to be tactical command to get her ass up here and quick."

"Say, if you're planning on descending on Mrs. Gronfein's house with a slew of sheriff's vehicles, you'll frighten her and she's liable to have a heart attack."

"Okay, Billy, what do you suggest I do?"

"Let me call her first. She knows me from when I was in high school. She was my English teacher, and I used to mow her lawn. If anyone's there, I'll calmly ask her and tell her to leave if they are."

"Call her, but we're going there regardless." Bailey was sitting at Pickens' feet. "Okay, Bailey let's go."

As Pickens left, Billy glanced at Amy. "He's not a happy camper."

"Can you blame him after last night? You'd better come up with something on Lissie and something from your phone call."

Billy dialed the Gronfein residence, but the call went to voicemail. Fearing he might alarm her, he decided not to leave a message.

"She might be at the Senior Center. It's where she goes most mornings." He paused a moment and scratched his forehead. "Come to think of it, I haven't seen her there in months."

"Or she could be another victim," said Amy and both looked at each other with incredulous stares.

"Damn, I hope not."

CHAPTER 43

After taking Bailey for a walk, Pickens decided to change course and drive by the Gronfein residence.

"Okay, Bailey let's see for ourselves if anyone is home. If there's a car in the driveway, I'll call Billy and let him know Mrs. Gronfein is there. I'd ring the bell, but I don't want to frighten her."

When he reached Mrs. Gronfein's street, he slowed. The neighborhood was one of the older subdivisions with property sizes a half acre or quarter of an acre. Mrs. Gronfein's was the latter. Trees and dense shrubbery surrounded the property affording privacy from the neighbors. The driveway was visible from the street but not the garage entrance.

"Hard to say if she's there. She could be out shopping. Might as well wait until Billy calls her." He reached across and patted Bailey's head. "No one's going to hurt our girls, right, boy?" Bailey barked. "Now, let's go get that subpoena."

Billy tried Mrs. Gronfein again only this time he used his personal phone and was grateful that she answered.

"Billy Thompson, is that you calling me? I knew I recognized the number." Her voice had changed slightly and her

inflection was indicative of her old age, but there was no shortage
or loss of memory. "You haven't called me in a long time. Say,
did you call earlier? The phone rang, but I couldn't get to it on
time and there was no message." She hesitated. "Is there something you need at the house? I hope not because I'm visiting my
daughter and the grandkids. I had my phone calls transferred
to her home." Both Billy and Amy were relieved that she wasn't
another victim. "I hope you're not calling to tell me my house
burnt down."

"No, ma'am, nothing like that." He closed his eyes and took a
deep breath. "It's about someone who may have used your address
for identification purposes. Does the name Allyson Healey sound
familiar?" Billy pressed speaker so Amy could hear.

"Allyson, hmm, oh yes. She was one of those lovely young
women who are renting my house while I'm away. I'll be back next
month. Is there a problem?"

Pickens and Bailey walked into the office just as Billy was
about to respond to Mrs. Gronfein's question. Pickens held up the
subpoena. Billy waived Pickens over.

"Can you hold on a second, Mrs. Gronfein, and I'll answer your
question?"

She nervously replied, "What's wrong, Billy?"

Pickens lowered the subpoena, raised his eyebrows, walked over
and whispered, "What's up?"

Billy placed his hand on the receiver and whispered, "Mrs.
Gronfein." Pickens nodded.

"Billy, are you still there?"

"Yes, ma'am, I'm here. By any chance was the other woman's
name Lissie?"

They could tell by her silence that Mrs. Gronfein was contem-
plating it.

"No, I don't think it was Lizzy. But it was something similar."
More silence as she pondered her memory. "Wait a minute. Now

I remember Allyson said the young woman worked for Sheriff Pickens."

Amy and Billy gasped. Pickens went rigid.

"Could you repeat that Mrs. Gronfein, I'm not sure I heard you correctly?" asked Billy.

"Allyson said the other young lady worked for Sheriff Pickens. You probably know her."

Pickens looked around the room and paused at Stacey. He shook his head no and rubbed his chin.

Amy hunched her shoulders and said, "Price? Can't be."

"Mrs. Gronfein, this is Sheriff Pickens."

"Well, hello, Sheriff. How's that beautiful daughter of yours?"

"She's fine, ma'am. Forgive me for interrupting, but by any chance was the other woman's name Liz?"

"Now that I think about it, yes it was. Is there something wrong? The only reason I rented my house to them was that she worked for you. I verified it with one of your deputies."

Pickens was about to reply when Sergeant Dunne came in and wandered over to listen in on the conversation. Pickens acknowledged her presence by waving.

Amy shook her head and mouthed, *not me,* as did Sergeant Dunne.

"Sheriff, is there some reason why you're asking all these questions? Do I need to come home?"

Amy wrote a note on her pad and showed it to him. It read, *Don't alarm her.* Pickens held up his palm.

"No, ma'am, there's no need for you to be alarmed. We're just following procedure. I'm sure there's nothing wrong, and you can continue to enjoy your grandkids."

"Thank you. Is Billy still there?"

"Yes, ma'am, I am."

"Good, are you still doing that word a day thing I taught you?"

He nodded his head. "Yes, ma'am, I am."

"Good boy. The word for today is befuddled, which is what I am right now. So much so that I'm going to have a highball. You know that saying, it's four o'clock someplace?" Pickens and his deputies grinned. "Well, as far as I'm concerned, it is here. If there's nothing more you need, then you all have a nice day."

"Thank you and you too," replied Billy.

"Wait...wait...Sheriff Pickens, would you go by my house and check on those young ladies, please?"

"I already did, Mrs. Gronfein, and there was no one home. I'll go by again later."

"Thank you." And the call ended.

Pickens deputies' mouths fell open, and they were flabbergasted. Billy slammed his fist on his desk. "Damn, I can't believe it's Liz. She was one of us."

"Worse than that, Billy," said Amy. "The bitch not only betrayed our trust but was on to us. That's why she told you she had a family emergency. And now she's probably on the run."

"And I believed her."

"Hold on," interrupted Pickens. "We all believed her. Let's not go there. Right now, we have to focus on finding her. We'll start with the Gronfein residence. She's probably not there, but we have to check just in case. Now that I have a subpoena, we can search the house for any clues or evidence."

"You think it's worth going there, JD? She's seen our murder board and overheard some of our conversation."

"And most likely has anticipated what steps we'd take," added Billy.

"I don't care. When someone threatens my family, I'll do whatever it takes to find them." He put his hand on his holster.

When Pickens had approached the county attorney for the subpoena, she was reluctant to issue one for a person of interest and an unknown assailant. He told her about the note, and the attorney relented and issued the subpoena. But, she made Pickens swear not to take justice into his hands and let the legal system resolve the matter.

Pickens looked up at the wall clock. "It's twelve-twenty. Has Matt called?"

Just then, Billy's desk phone rang. "This could be him now." He answered the phone, and as he listened his shoulders slumped. "Okay, Matt, thanks. I'll tell the sheriff."

"So, good news or bad news?"

Billy slowly shook his head. "Bad news, sorry. His girlfriend's contact is away on spring break and won't be back in her office until Monday, but she's willing to help."

"Shit, that won't help us. Amy, pull Price's employment file. Let's see if there's anything useful in it."

While Amy went to get Price's file, Billy tried calling her.

"There's no answer, and the number doesn't even go to voice-mail. Should I try tracking her phone? If it's on, I may be able to locate her." Pickens nodded yes, and Billy attempted to track Price's phone. "Nothing, she either has it off or is out of range."

"Try searching for a truck registration for her."

Billy's eyebrows spiked up. "You don't think she's..."

"After yesterday, anything's possible," said Sergeant Dunne.

As Billy searched motor vehicle records, Amy walked over with Price's file.

"Damn, she listed a temporary address at the motel. It's my fault; I should have followed up after she came on board."

"Is there a previous address?" asked Pickens.

"Yeah, in Sanford. Billy, try this address for Price."

Billy searched the name Price and the address for a truck registration.

"Got a Malcolm Price in Sanford with two vehicle registrations. One's a truck, and the color is black. Hold on, and I'll see if he has a phone number." He pumped his fist. "Got it!"

"Give me the number and I'll call him," said Dunne.

"Later, Sergeant, I may want to call the Sanford police and have them go by his residence and see if she's there."

"Won't that alert her," asked Dunne.

"Possibly. Wait until I get back. Right now, the four of us..." Pickens pointed to Bailey. "Are going to the Gronfein residence." He turned to Dunne. "Forget about tactics; we'll worry about them when we get there. Bailey and I will go in my truck. You two take whatever vehicle you want and make sure to wear your vests. Let's go."

CHAPTER 44

Pickens drove past the Gronfein property and parked beyond the house out of sight under the shade of a live oak tree.

Sergeant Dunne parked by the bushes near the driveway so she also couldn't be seen from the house. The four slowly approached the house on foot—keeping enough distance between them so they weren't a soft target and had their radios on and guns unholstered.

Pickens signaled for Amy and Dunne to check the garage and the rear. He and Bailey approached the front entrance and waited to hear from his sergeants.

"Can you see through those windows on the door?" asked Dunne.

Amy rose on her tippy toes and peered in. "Just barely, but there's a dark truck in there. Better let Pickens know someone might be home."

"And might be waiting for us. I'll call him." Dunne called Pickens on the radio.

"What's the verdict? Anything in the garage?"

"The truck's in there. What do you want us to do?"

He considered the possibility of an ambush. Bailey nudged against him as though saying *caution*.

"Tell Amy to unlock the back door if she can. I'll wait until you say it's done and then I'll go in the front door. You two let me know that you're going in quietly and on the count of three, Bailey and I will go in." Bailey nudged him again. "And be careful. We know they have at least a shotgun but could have more firepower."

"We're ready, Amy's working on the lock," replied Dunne. "She's got it."

"Okay, on my count, ready, one, two, three, go." Pickens kicked the door in, crouched low and entered with Bailey crawling behind him. "This is Sheriff Pickens. We know you're in there, and we have a subpoena. We're coming in. We can do this peacefully or not." Hearing no reply or a gunshot, Pickens carefully began his search.

Sergeants Tucker and Dunne entered prepared to fire at will. They carefully searched every room, but there was no one in residence.

"It appears they only used the spare bedroom and the one bed," remarked Dunne. "My guess is the bedsheets and pillows haven't been changed in weeks. And whoever slept in that bed had some restless nights." Pickens and Amy raised their eyebrows. "What? A mother notices these things. Those women were slobs as far as I'm concerned."

After Dunne's comments, Pickens surveyed the kitchen. It was a mess. Dishes were piled in the sink, and empty food cartons were on the counter.

"Somebody was upset," said Pickens. "I'd say whoever it was threw the chairs at the wall."

Pausing to examine the room, Amy replied, "Sure looks like it."

Sergeant Dunne raised her eyebrows. "Maybe we should check the garage and the truck."

She and Amy went into the garage. Dunne put the garage door up and then she and Amy inspected the truck. Seeing it empty, Dunne put the door down, and they went back into the house.

"They could have another vehicle and could be anywhere around town," said Amy. "But the garbage hasn't been put to the street for some time according to the stench, so my guess is they left town."

Before Pickens could respond, they heard a vehicle pull into the driveway.

"That could be them now," said Pickens. "Check the windows, but don't let them know we're here."

They each peered out the windows careful not to move the curtains. A maroon Camry parked in the driveway and two people got out of the car—a man and a woman. The two walked up to the front door.

"What the hell, Florence, I thought Maureen said nice young ladies were renting her house."

Pickens stepped into the entryway, pointed his gun and said, "Who are you people?"

The man raised his hands and stepped back. The women clutched her chest.

"Don't shoot... please... don't shoot..." the man shouted.

Seeing they were unarmed, Pickens lowered his weapon but was prepared to shoot if necessary.

"Who are you?" he asked again.

The man took several deep breaths to calm himself before replying.

"We're the Bushnells. We live two houses down. Mrs. Gronfein called us and asked that we check her house. We have a key that she left with us for emergencies. Who are you?"

"Sheriff Pickens. My deputies and I have a subpoena to search the house. We received a call that suspicious people were living in it."

"You don't mean those two sweet girls that Maureen rented the house to, do you?" asked Mrs. Bushnell.

"I'm not sure, but we had to check it out. There's a truck in the garage that we've been looking for." Pickens holstered his weapon. "You can put your hands down, Mr. Bushnell."

He lowered his hands then wiped his brow. "Thanks, Sheriff. We saw the sheriff's car parked alongside the road and worried something might have happened, so we came to check on the tenants. As for the truck, we saw it pull into the driveway yesterday and later saw a gray car leave. Don't know if it came back. We turn in early so it could have."

"I didn't see it leave this morning when we left for the Senior Center," said Mrs. Bushnell.

"Okay, thanks, and I'm sorry if we frightened you." Pickens reached into his pocket. "Here's my card if that car comes back or if you see it again, call me." He looked at the door casing. "I'll send someone to fix that. Don't be alarmed when you see a forensic vehicle later." He waved his palm. "There hasn't been a crime, but we have to fingerprint the house, garage and the truck."

"Thanks for telling us. Maybe we should call Maureen."

"No need, ma'am. We've already spoken to her. You don't want to alarm her."

"Okay, we'll be on our way now. Come on, Florence, let's go home."

"Wait," said Pickens. "Those women left the house a mess. You could do Mrs. Gronfein a favor and have it cleaned after the Forensic team is finished. And the garbage needs to be put to the street."

"Oh my," replied Mrs. Bushnell. "We'll have our cleaning service take care of it. Maureen will appreciate it."

Pickens watched as they left and then addressed Amy and Dunne.

"I'll call Marge and tell her to get a team out here, and I have to call Mrs. Wigelworth and ask if she's seen any suspicious vehicles in my neighborhood. I'll call her when we get back to the office." He looked around the house and rubbed his hand down the back of his head. "Shit, I hoped we were on to something here."

"Hopefully we'll get some prints and DNA, and we'll know more about the killers," said Amy.

"Yeah, hopefully."

"JD, are you okay? You almost shot those people. It's not like to you to react that way." Amy ran a hand through her hair. "You seemed too eager to get payback for yesterday."

Sergeant Dunne also recognized his actions as symptomatic of what she'd seen in Iraq when soldiers returned from a mission and had suffered casualties. They were eager to get back out and exact revenge. She broke from her usual decorum and reached out and placed a hand on Pickens' shoulder.

"We'll find them, JD, and bring them to justice. I promise you."

Pickens felt like he did in high school after throwing an interception. He was so mad he just wanted to get back on the field, but his coach put an arm around him and told him to forget it, take a seat, and prepare for the next offensive series. On those occasions, Leroy had sat next to him and put an arm on his shoulder and offered his comfort and support. His two sergeants weren't football players, but at that moment they seemed like sisters offering support and understanding.

He clenched his jaw. "Yeah, I guess I was a bit anxious and a little eager to get even with her for going after my family." His eyes went soft. "Thanks for your understanding." Then with a gleam in his eye, he said, "I knew I made the right decision when I hired you two. But if either of you asks for a group hug, I'll bust you both down to recruits." The sergeants grinned, and Bailey raised a paw. "That goes for you too." All three chuckled, and Bailey barked. "Now I have to call Marge."

When Marge saw it was Pickens calling, she hoped he had good news.

"JD, can we finally go home? Sarah's enjoying herself touring the lab, and my staff adores her. But she misses Bailey and her friends at school."

"You didn't let her see the autopsy room, did you?"

"Absolutely not, although she wanted to see a dead body. But I refused."

"Good. The reason I'm calling is that I'm at 9020 Mallard Road…"

"That address sounds familiar. Is it the Gronfein residence?"

"Yes, how did you know?" He rubbed the back of his head.

"I've occasionally picked her up and taken her to the Senior Center when I brought desserts for their social hour." Marge ran her hand through her hair. "Why, has something happened to her?"

"No, we discovered that the person who put the note on the door was renting the house from her. Her truck is still in the garage, but there's no sign of her. We searched every room, and all we found were Mrs. Gronfein's belongings. And you're not going to believe this, but we think the killer was Liz Price who worked for me. Damn it; she was right under my nose."

"Don't beat yourself up over it. You couldn't have known."

"Yeah, I guess you're right. Anyway, I need you to send someone here to gather evidence."

"I'll send someone right away. Any chance Sarah and I can go home?"

Pickens rubbed his chin. "I'll send a deputy to follow you, and he'll stay until I get home. First, I'm gonna call Mrs. Wigelworth and ask if she's seen any suspicious vehicles. Sergeants Tucker and Dunne are with me. We'll wait for the tech and then go back to the office." He glanced at his sergeants and winked. "I love you, wide receiver."

"Love you, too."

He closed his phone, smiled at his sergeants and they smiled back.

"Change of plans. You two go back to the office, and I'll wait for the evidence tech. See if Billy was able to contact Price and have him do a complete background check on him and Liz or whatever her name is."

"We can wait with you; we don't mind."

"No, Amy, you two have a job to do at the office. I'll be okay. Have Billy send a deputy to relieve me and have him arrange for McCann's to take the truck to impound. Also, get someone out here to fix the door." He waved his hand at them. "Just go now."

Amy and Dunne left and later Deputy Jackson arrived.

"Zeke, McCann's should be here shortly to take the truck from the garage, and someone is coming to fix the front door. Once the evidence tech is finished, I'm leaving. You stay parked in the driveway and stay alert in case the two women come back. I'll make sure Billy sends a relief for you. Any questions?"

"Nope, I'm all set.

After the tech had finished gathering evidence, Pickens left.

When Pickens walked into the sheriff's office, Stacey was answering a call on the tip line. She pressed hold, held her hand up and called to him.

"Sheriff Pickens, there's a Malcolm Price on the tip line. He wants to speak with you and no one else. What should I do?"

Pickens stopped in mid stride and replied, "Transfer it to my line. Give me a minute to get to my office." Amy and Billy had dazed looks, but not Dunne. She cocked her head and raised her eyes. "You three come into my office."

Stacey waited and then transferred the call.

Pickens wrinkled his brow and picked up the receiver. "Sheriff Pickens, how can I help you, Mr. Price?"

Price cleared his throat before responding. "I believe you may be looking for my ex-wife..." There was heavy breathing and then, "I saw the newspaper article and recognized the Healey woman..." A long pause then, "My ex and her were roommates in college."

"We know that Mr. Price, and she was working for me up until a few days ago."

"I didn't know that. We were divorced two years ago, but the last time I spoke to Lissie she was going to hook up with Healey..." Another long pause. "They were more than just roommates, but I didn't mind. When Allyson was with Lissie, my wife was a different person altogether."

Pickens scribbled—*Price and Healey lovers.* The deputies' eyebrows shot upward.

Price continued. "Three years ago, my wife lost our child during birth and later suffered postpartum psychosis. She was treated by her doctor, prescribed medication but after a while refused to take it. I pleaded with her to follow her doctor's orders, but she refused. Her condition worsened, and she became prone to violent outbursts."

Pickens interrupted. "Did she hurt herself or anyone else, Mr. Price?" He pressed the speaker button so the deputies could listen in. "Mr. Price, did she hurt herself or anyone else?"

"I heard you, Sheriff... The answer is yes, but never seriously and it was mostly me. It happened around the time of the anniversary of our little girl's death in March. I finally had to divorce her. Seven months ago, she asked if she could borrow my truck as her car broke down and she needed it for a new job. I said yes and then she left town with it. I didn't mind because I wanted to help her. Last I heard she was with Healey..." Price took several deep breaths and then asked, "Did she hurt someone?"

While Pickens talked with Price, Amy Googled postpartum psychosis and learned that recovery generally took six months to a year. In Price's case, there may be something else in her background that caused it to last longer—or maybe it wasn't psychosis but a psychotic break due to something in her past. Before Pickens could respond, she wrote, *Don't answer that, ask about her family history.* He nodded agreement.

"Does she have any siblings, Mr. Price?"

"No siblings..." They heard deep breathing and then, "Her parents divorced while Lissie was in college. It was a rocky marriage for a long time. After the divorce, Mrs. Strauss..." He paused. "Strauss was Lissie's maiden name. Mrs. Strauss started drinking and became an alcoholic. When Lissie graduated, she tried to get her mother into rehab but it didn't help. Mrs. Strauss ended up committing suicide...excuse me a moment, please."

"Take your time, sir." Amy scribbled, *The divorce and the suicide may have been the initial triggers.*

"Sorry, it was a difficult time for Lissie, but I was there to comfort her. In fact, I was there during high school for her after she confided in me about her parents' marriage. I guess the best thing for Lissie was agreeing to marry me and then getting pregnant. She was so happy for the first time in her life..." He hesitated. "I guess I failed her like her parents did."

"You did your best, sir. It sounds to me like Lissie failed herself."

Amy waived her palms and scribbled, *Don't say anymore, you've already said too much.*

"Maybe, but you didn't answer my question, Sheriff. Did Lissie hurt someone?"

Pickens raised his eyebrows at Amy. She nodded no.

"Mr. Price, do you know where her father lives?"

"No, and I don't think Lissie does either. After the divorce, he had no contact with her, and she wasn't interested in ever seeing him again. Sheriff, are you going to answer my question or not?"

Amy mouthed, "Go ahead, but say a person of interest."

"Mr. Price, I'll be honest with you, we're looking at her as a person of interest in a homicide as well as Allyson Healey. If you have any information that could help us find them, we'd appreciate knowing it."

"I'm sorry, but I can't help you. I thought Lissie was in Tampa where Allyson's mother lives. That's all I can tell you. If you don't mind, I need to go to a meeting at church, and I have to leave now. I'm sorry..." He paused and then said, "I was going to renew the insurance and registration next month on the truck, but maybe I'll just let both expire."

"You may want to wait. The truck is here in Creek City in impound. You can get it after we're finished with it. We'll call when we can release it. Also, if we have any further questions, may we call you?"

"Sure, but I don't know what else I can tell you."

"You've been helpful so far, and I appreciate that you called me." The line went dead. "Well, that was an interesting conversation. Any comments, Amy?"

Amy was suddenly still as she contemplated a response.

"Now we know what triggered Liz's psychosis, but what about Allyson?" Amy paused to examine her question. "Maybe the combination of the anniversary of Tommy's breakup with Melissa, Liz's loss, the proximity to the anniversary of Melissa's suicide, and possibly Liz's mother's were too overwhelming." She raised a palm. "That's my best guess. But, I want to do more research on sociopaths and psychopaths."

"That's a pretty good guess as far as I'm concerned," said Pickens. "Sergeant Dunne, what's your assessment?"

"I agree; however, we still don't know where the two women are."

"I'll try Googling the Strausses and see if there's anything for the father or Lissie Strauss," said Billy. "Geez, I wondered why she was taking so much time away from her duties. I should have questioned her, but I thought maybe it was a family matter. Shows what I know."

"Same goes for me, Billy," remarked Amy.

Pickens threw his hands up. "Shit, I was hoping for a promising lead. It is what it is, so we'll go with what we have. Hopefully, you'll find something, Billy." He shook his head. "I feel like I should say class dismissed, but I won't. Instead, I'm going to call Marge. Sergeant Dunne, would you follow her home and wait until I get there?"

"Sure, I can hang around longer if you want me to."

"No, after I get there, you can go home. You put in a long day, and you need to be with your family. I don't think anyone is going to try anything while I'm home and my sheriff's vehicle is in the driveway. Amy, you go home too. After you've exhausted your searches, Billy, you also go home. We'll continue this tomorrow, and maybe we'll get a break."

After his deputies had left his office, Pickens called Marge.

"JD, can Sarah and I go home now?"

"Wait until Sergeant Dunne gets there. She'll follow you and wait until I get there. She's leaving now. I've got a few things to wrap up here and then I'll leave. I love you, wide receiver."

"I love you too, quarterback. Oh, wait, I have the preliminary report from Mrs. Gronfein's house. The place was pretty much wiped down. Someone didn't want to leave evidence they were there. There were no latent prints from the truck in the garage. We did get some prints in the house, but I'd bet they're Mrs. Gronfein's since most of them were in her bedroom and bathroom. In one of the other bedrooms, the team found an empty pill dispenser for an expired prescription."

"That must be for Price's postpartum psychosis."

"No, this prescription is for something more serious, and it's not for Price. I'm not familiar with it, and I don't know what treatment its's for. It's not in my field of medicine, so I won't comment. But, I can say, it's for a Liesel Strauss, and her doctor is in Sanford. I suggest you contact him. It's in the report. I'll fax it to Billy. Sorry, JD."

"No problem and thanks."

When he arrived at his house, Pickens sent Dunne home and then parked his truck in the driveway as an added precaution. He had already called Mrs. Wigelworth, and she assured him that she hadn't seen any suspicious vehicles in the neighborhood. Marge was preparing dinner when he and Bailey entered the house.

"Something smells good."

"Daddy, you're home." Sarah ran to greet him and Bailey. He lifted her in his arms and kissed her. "So, you missed me?"

"I did, Daddy, and Bailey." He put her down, and she hugged Bailey as he licked her face. "I missed you so much, Bailey."

"I'm going to say hello to Mom." He walked into the kitchen and wrapped his arms around Marge. "Damn, you feel good, wide receiver."

"So do you. Are we safe now?"

"Almost, but I want you to take Sarah with you tomorrow, and I'll take Bailey again." She gave him a pained gaze. "Just as a precaution, that's all. Price and Healey have probably left town, but just in case."

She shook her head. "Okay, but I'll be glad when this is over."

"Me too. What's for dinner?"

Marge smiled. "Tripe stew," she replied. He dropped his arms to his sides. "Gotcha. We're having chili the way you like it."

"Whew, you had me there." He grinned. "I'll get even tonight."

"I hope so. Go freshen up, and we'll all have dinner together."

Later after dinner and television, Pickens tucked Sarah in bed and left Bailey to watch over her. Then he and Marge retired to their bedroom.

"Is this how you get even, quarterback?"

"Yes, but what difference does it make? I'm making love to the most wonderful woman on this planet."

"Oh, I like that."

CHAPTER 45

"**A**re you sure you did the right thing by leaving that note? Someone could have seen you."

"Yes, and no one saw me except that yappy dog. Who's it gonna tell? If it weren't for that damn dog, I would have left the note inside his house. Now that would have been something."

"You're crazy. You know that?"

Don't call me crazy, you know I hate that word, and I'm not crazy. If it weren't for me, your plan would have failed."

"It did fail. No one was supposed to die. I told you I just wanted to scare Benson. Hicks and Noristan weren't in my plan. You made them your plan. It was stupid."

"You're really starting to piss me off as Allyson did."

"And what, are you going to kill me too?"

"Who knows, I just might, if you don't quit whining. I did what I had to do."

"You don't get it, do you? If someone saw you and that truck, the sheriff could find us."

"Relax, no one saw us and, besides, we got rid of the truck."

"How did you know there would be a car in the garage?"

"Simple, Allyson and I parked it there when we rented the house. No one will guess we did. See how simple my plan is."

"Okay, but what if they locate the house and find evidence that leads them to us?"

"You're not too bright, are you? The only way they'll find the house is if they know who owns it. Old lady Gronfein owns it, and she's not telling anyone. She had a for rent sign in the yard, and we snatched it right up. She was happy to rent the house to two beautiful young ladies. We'll be gone a long time before they realize we were there. That's if they find out Allyson and I were there."

"I hate to admit it, but you're plan worked so far. Where are we going from here?"

"A place up North I know of and far away from Florida. Don't worry; they'll never find us. Toss your phone out the window I already threw mine. We'll use pre-paid phones, and I have enough money stashed at the place to last us for months."

"I hope you're right. I don't want to go to jail."

"You worry too much. It's not going to happen."

CHAPTER 46

Billy had arrived earlier than usual to continue his Internet search on Price, Strauss, and Allyson Healey. Although not officially Price's supervisor, Billy was responsible for scheduling the three crisis center personnel. Since he had worked closely with Price, he felt responsible for not recognizing anything strange in her character and wanted to find her in the worst way to prove himself to Pickens and Amy.

As he walked into the office, Billy waved to Matt Riley.

"Say, Billy," Matt called out. "Does the sheriff still want my girlfriend's help?"

"It's not necessary. We got what we needed. Thanks anyway."

"Okay, just trying to help."

After pouring himself a cup of coffee, Billy went right to his computers.

Stacey Morgan arrived to relieve Matt and Amy was right behind her.

After pleasantries, Amy got a cup of coffee and went right to work on her computer finishing her research that she had started at home. She had narrowed her focus on antisocial personality disorders and concentrated on sociopaths and psychopaths and printed out information from several websites. Amy had already Googled the drug Price was taking.

From her research, Amy couldn't be certain what the medication was for and thought it best that she call the physician whose name appeared on the pill dispenser and not jump to conclusions. As for Healey, Amy knew little of her background and why she too was involved in the murders.

"I got it," Billy yelled.

Stacey and Matt were having a conversation, but when they heard Billy their mouths fell open. Amy gasped, got up, and walked to his side.

"Got what? Amy asked. "Is it relevant to Price or Healey?"

Pickens had just entered the office and called out, "What's relevant?"

Billy turned his monitor so Pickens could see the screen. "Info on the physician's name on the pill dispenser. He's a psychiatrist in Sanford." He rubbed both hands on the back of his head. "Oh man, I had no clue while she worked here." He drew back in his chair. "Sorry, Sheriff, it's all my fault."

"Bullshit, it's my fault," said Amy.

"When you two finish shitting on each other, look this way." Pickens pointed his index fingers at his chest. "It's my fault. I'm the sheriff, and I'm responsible for what happens in this office. None of us could have seen this coming."

"All three of you are full of shit!" yelled Ellison. "It's none of your faults. It's all on Price."

Everyone turned when they saw Ellison walking toward them.

"What are you doing here?"

"You could at least say nice to see you, Ellison, but I guess you're too busy shitting on yourself too, Pickens." Ellison waved a hand. "Healey's mother called me. Yeah, can you believe it? I bonded with her."

The blaming of each other over Price suddenly stopped as all were interested in what Ellison had to say.

"Allyson called her after she saw the newspaper article. She didn't say where she was but wanted to assure her mother that she was all right but couldn't come home. Mrs. Healey asked her if she did something awful. Allyson said no she didn't. It was all Price." Ellison took a moment to let the information register with Pickens and his deputies.

"Allyson said they only planned on scaring Benson, but Price went too far and took matters into her hands without consulting Allyson. She left town and stayed away from Price. After Price had killed Irene…" Ellison paused a moment to control his emotions. "Allyson called Price and told her she wanted nothing to do with her and was going into hiding."

"Why didn't Mrs. Healey tell her to turn herself in? There might be mitigating circumstances."

"She did, Pickens, but Allyson said she was afraid of Price and didn't want her to go after her mother. She all but told her mother that Price is coocoo." Ellison shook his head. "She seemed a bit strange to me, and I only saw her that one time when I told you about that report for Noristan. So, stop blaming yourselves and find the crazy bitch."

Amy glared at Ellison. Because of her background and experience as a counselor, she considered mental illness a serious disease and took umbrage with Ellison's comments. Although she wanted to say something, she had to admit that Ellison was right about one thing; they had to find Price before she harmed someone else. For that reason, she remained silent.

With all the chaos, Pickens forgot that he brought Bailey with him. He looked around and didn't see him, so he walked into his office and saw Bailey's torso under his desk. Bailey had the common sense to remove himself from the scene and find serenity under the desk.

Pickens rubbed his chin and came to the conclusion that the situation required a calm and confident leader, and he steeled himself to be the one. He stepped out from his office to address his deputies and Ellison.

"Okay, everyone, this is no time to panic. Ellison is right, we have to find Price and we need a game plan." Ellison grinned, but Pickens ignored him. "You're up first, Amy. Call that doctor and use your background to get him to say when he last saw Price and renewed her prescription." He pointed to Billy. "You're our command center. All communications go through you, and you give a periodic briefing. Also, see if there's a driver's license or vehicle registration for Price."

"I already did that." Billy handed Pickens two sheets of paper. "I did it last..." He hesitated when he saw Pickens scowl. "I did yesterday afternoon. They're both in the name of Liesel Strauss with the Sanford address. She owns a 2007 four-door gray Toyota Camry."

"Good, put a BOLO out on the vehicle."

"Hold on a minute," interrupted Ellison. "Why not add the picture and do a BOLO that she's wanted for three homicides? It will cover the whole state, and you might get lucky."

"Okay, we'll do that, but first I'm going to get an arrest warrant out for both women."

"Hold off on Healey for now. Just say she's a person of interest. If Billy can find a vehicle registration you add that along with her driver's license photo."

"All right, that's what we'll do. And while we're at it Billy, change Price's case file to Price-Strauss. Oh, on the BOLO, add that Price-Strauss may be traveling with a companion."

"Smart move, Pickens. Anything else I can do?" asked Ellison.

"Yeah, if you have any contacts with the Feds or anyone in Georgia and Alabama, contact them for help. Those women may be smart enough to have left Florida already."

"Sounds like a good plan, Pickens."

"Yeah, we may be a tiny rural county law enforcement agency with limited resources and only a half dozen of us, but we're a great team." Amy and Billy smiled.

"I'll second that. I've been around much larger organizations than yours, but I'd gladly work with you folks, anytime."

"Thanks, Ellison. You know, you're not such a bad guy for a PI." Ellison grinned. Pickens turned and addressed Morgan. "Stacey, you answer every call that comes in on the tip line. Get a name, number and address of anyone who calls. You can funnel the calls through Billy, but use your discretion as to what ones are relevant. I'm going to give Nosey another exclusive, and when he runs Price's picture I bet we get a lot of calls from the locals who saw her in their shop or restaurant. So expect that."

"Will do, Sheriff."

"Do me a favor, Pickens. Don't put Healey's picture in the paper. In the BOLO yes, but if you don't put it in the paper, maybe she'll consider turning herself in or at least call you. You may need her testimony when you have Price in custody. What do you say?"

Pickens considered Ellison's request. "Okay, but if we don't hear from her within the week, I may give Nosey another scoop."

"Thanks," replied Ellison and left to make some calls

"All right, everyone has their mission. We're on offense now, and we're not quitting until we catch those women." Pickens looked around and saw four faces with astonishing looks staring at him. "Well, let's get to it. Bailey and I are going to the county attorney's office to get that warrant." He whistled. "Come on Bailey." Bailey scampered out of the office and followed Pickens out of the building.

Amy called Strauss' doctor. He was reluctant to offer any information on Strauss, but Amy played the murder card and he relented. Strauss had called him last week and asked for an emergency meeting because she was out of pills and having anxiety attacks. Dr. Camuso scheduled a Saturday morning appointment in Sanford. After speaking with her, he became concerned about Strauss' condition and gave her a sample pack that he kept locked in his office and wrote a ninety-day prescription so she could fill it locally.

"What were you treating her for?" asked Amy.

"I'd rather not say," Camuso replied.

Amy wondered if the physician had mistakenly misdiagnosed Price and was protecting himself.

"Have you heard from her since?" asked Amy.

"No, I haven't. If I had known what Strauss did, I would have had her taken into custody. Given what you've told me, I'm afraid she may be dangerous to herself or the public. Please find her, Sergeant."

Ya think, Amy said to herself. "We're doing the best we can. Thank you, Doctor." His last comment wasn't what Amy wanted to hear, and she understood why Healey was afraid of Strauss.

CHAPTER 47

J ennifer Darling and her partner, Annice, were preparing to open their shop in Monticello. Jennifer was adding the cash, checks, and credit card receipts from yesterday's sales and preparing the morning bank deposit. Annice started for the door.

"Jen, I'm going to get coffee and fresh muffins at the restaurant. I'll be back soon and then we can walk to the bank together to make the deposit. I won't be long."

Jennifer smiled and waved. "Okay. Wait, make my muffin a blueberry one." Her eyes were wide and glowing. "Wow, what a day we had yesterday."

Annice offered a satisfied smile and responded. "We sure did, see you in a bit." She left the store, closed the door but inadvertently forgot to lock it.

When Jennifer finished adding the receipts, she started preparing the bank deposit when the bell on the door jangled.

"You're back already? That was quick. Did you get my blueberry muffin?"

"Hello, Jennifer."

Jennifer gasped and dropped the deposit bag. "What are you doing here?"

"You know why. You couldn't keep your mouth shut, could you?" Jennifer's hands and fingers trembled. "I'm the one who kept your promise regarding Benson. I did what was necessary."

Jennifer backed away from the counter. "There never was a promise to kill him, and you know that. It was just a silly pact."

"Not for me, and you should have kept your mouth shut. Talking to that sheriff was a mistake."

Jennifer glanced at the door hoping Annice would come back. "I did what I felt was the right thing." When she saw the shotgun aimed at her, Jennifer immediately recalled what she'd learned in her self-defense classes. Unlike Irene Marsden, she knew what to do.

Just before the blast, Jennifer dived onto the floor. The shot missed her, shattering the glass accessory shelves on the wall.

Annice walked past the bookstore just as the owner was putting a rack of used books out front when she heard the gunshot.

The owner heard it also and said, "That sounded like a car backfiring, didn't it?"

Annice froze. "Or a gunshot. Call 911." She turned immediately, and instinct told her to go to the shop.

Jennifer crawled underneath the counter and pressed the alarm just as the second shot was fired hitting other shelves on the wall behind the counter and missing Jennifer.

"You can't hide, bitch. I'll get you."

Another shot, but this time at the wooden front of the counter hopefully protecting Jennifer. Just before firing another shot, police sirens sounded.

"You got lucky this time, but I might be back. Count on it."

The shooter bolted out of the store and ran to the waiting car—which drove off just as Annice was approaching the store. When she saw the shooter, she feared for the worse and entered the store.

Not seeing her partner, she called out. "Jennifer, where are you? Are you all right?"

Jennifer stood and stared at the front door with fear in her eyes. "Is she gone?"

Annice walked around the counter. "Yes, she is. Are you okay?"

"Yes, she missed me. I did what we learned in class and dropped behind the counter. Luckily before the first shot." Suddenly realizing how close she came to death; Jennifer's body shook, and she collapsed into Annice's arms just as a Monticello police officer entered with her weapon raised.

Seeing the two women, the officer holstered her weapon. She surveyed the damaged counter top, shelves and the front of the counter with pellets lodged in the thick wood. She rubbed her chin and wondered how anybody could have survived the horrible scene.

"Anybody hurt? I received the 911 call and came as soon as I could." Officer Sandra Schuler had been a friend of both women since they originally opened the store. She was their first customer, and her husband had done the remodeling of the interior. Officer Shuler was the first to respond when she saw the location.

"We're fine, Sandra, luckily the shooter missed," replied Annice.

"Do you know who it was, Jennifer?"

"Yes, her name's Lissy Strauss…She…she was a former sorority sister, and I'm sure the sheriff in Creek City is looking for her. His name is JD Pickens." Annice brushed some bits of broken glass from Jennifer's hair and debris from the shelves off her back and shoulders. "Oh, God, she just wanted to kill me." Jennifer clutched her heart suddenly aware of how close to death she had been. "I'll never forget that horrible expression on her face and the evil in her eyes. She was like a rabid dog." She turned and put a hand on Annice's cheek. "All I could think of was that I'd never see you again and that stupid argument we had about opening later this morning." Annice brushed a tear from Jennifer's cheek.

"Maybe none of this would have happened." Annice wrapped her arms around Jennifer. "Hold me tight and don't let go. I love you so much."

"I love you, too, and forget about that silly disagreement."

"I don't think it would have made a difference when you opened," said Officer Schuler. "The person who did this had a lot of anger and could have done it any day. Today just wasn't your lucky day."

"She's right, Jen."

"I guess so." Jennifer took a deep breath and composed herself. "Sandra, would you call Sheriff Pickens and let him know?"

"I'll take care of it." Officer Schuler scratched the back of her head. "I've got to call this in, and this is a crime scene so don't plan on opening today."

"We don't plan on it," replied Annice. "In fact, we're taking a week off and going to the coast for some sun." She affectionately stroked Jennifer's arm. "Right, Jen?" Jennifer gave her a silly grin and nodded agreement.

"Sounds like a good plan," said Officer Schuler and glanced at the damage. "I'll have Dillon make the place look like nothing happened. I'm going to stick around, and when you're ready to go home I'll follow you and stay there too."

Annice touched Jennifer's arm. "Thanks, Sandra, but what about Joey?"

Officer Schuler grinned. "Dillon and Joey will be fine. It will be a night of bonding playing video games. They won't mind."

Jennifer and Annice smiled.

When the police department finished with the scene, Jennifer and Annice closed the store and went home. Officer Shuler followed them and cleared the house.

Earlier that morning, Billy arrived at his usual time, waved to Matt and then went to the breakroom and made a fresh pot of coffee.

After pouring a cup, he walked over to his desk, sat back and relaxed as his computers came alive. He had a good night's sleep and felt fresh and comfortable at last.

Amy strolled into the building with Stacey beside her. Amy glowed from a fantastic night at home, and she too was ready to get to work. Stacey punched in and relieved Matt.

Pickens and Bailey came in next. Pickens had a little bounce in his step as he, too, had a wonderful evening at home. Bailey pranced over to Stacey, and they swapped kisses. Next, the dog walked over to Amy and Billy for belly rubs and then went into Pickens' office. He found a corner, circled a few times, plopped down on his stomach and took a nap.

Ellison was the last to arrive with fresh doughnuts.

"Damn, those look good," said Billy.

"Have at 'em," Ellison replied. "I knew you folks liked them. I'm not hanging around to enjoy them. I just wanted to report that I made some contacts with law enforcement agencies here in Florida, Georgia and Alabama. If Healey or Price are spotted, you'll know pretty quickly, Pickens."

"Thanks, Ellison. I got an arrest warrant for Price-Strauss but not for Healey. The county attorney said I didn't have enough evidence to prove she was complicit in the murders, so she's still a person of interest."

"Good enough. I got to go now; I have a cheating spouse in Gainesville that I have to check on." With that, he left.

Pickens gave Billy the warrant, and he issued the BOLO.

The atmosphere in the office was much calmer than yesterday since they now knew Price was the killer and with the BOLO, a massive manhunt would take place. Pickens, was confident that he'd get no more calls from the mayor or county chairperson. But he'd be happier if Price was in custody. In appreciation for his team's hard work, Pickens bought everyone lunch.

After lunch, Stacy answered the phone, stood, and called out to Pickens. "Sheriff, it's a call from the Monticello Police Department. They asked for you specifically."

Pickens raised his eyebrows. "Okay, transfer it." Amy and Billy were curious about the call.

Pickens listened as the chief of police told him about the morning's events and Strauss' last remark. "Thanks, Chief, I appreciate the call." Pickens put the phone down, breathed a heavy sigh, and stepped out of his office. "Strauss was in Monticello this morning and attacked Darling."

Amy flinched, dreading the worse. "Is she?"

"No, she was lucky, but Price implied she might return. She got into a gray Camry and left." Pickens kicked the wastebasket. "Damn it; she's still two steps ahead of us."

Later, Pickens calmed down, and he and his deputies discussed the situation. They cleared the murder board and decided there was nothing they could do but wait to see if the BOLO provides anything helpful—like where Price-Strauss was.

Stacey answered a call on the tip line. She put the caller on hold and called out to Billy.

"I've got a woman who says she has information on Price but will only speak with you, Billy."

Pickens bolted out of his seat as soon as he heard Stacey. Amy stood, walked over to Billy and mouthed, "Speaker."

Billy razed a finger, pressed the speaker button and then signaled for Stacey to transfer the call.

"Deputy Thompson, to whom am I speaking?" He hunched his shoulders and razed his palms indicating it was the best he knew to say. Pickens waved him off.

"This is Allyson Healey, Deputy. I know you're looking for me." Billy looked at the caller ID display and immediately typed in Healey's phone number on his computer. "I asked for you because Liz said you were her supervisor. I had nothing to do with those murders. That was all Liz. I wasn't even with her, and I had no idea she owned a shotgun..." Healey hesitated.

"Our plan was to scare Tommy when the time was right, but she didn't wait and went too far. I think there's something wrong with her, and she takes these pills." Pickens glanced at Amy. "I also believe she has someone else because occasionally I've overheard her on the phone. I don't know if it was a man or a woman, and I've never met the person..." Another hesitation. "Besides her truck, she kept a car in the garage. She said she didn't want her exhusband to know she had it or he'd want the truck back. Deputy..."

"Yes, Allyson."

"Would you tell that private investigator to look out for my mom?"

"I will..." The line suddenly went dead. "Sorry, Sheriff, she wasn't on the line long enough to track, and the number probably belonged to a prepaid phone."

"Shit," Pickens said and turned to Amy. "Do you believe her?"

"Yes," she replied. "She's frightened. All the more reason we have to find Price."

"I agree, but all we can do is wait and see what happens with the BOLO. You think Allyson is still in Florida?"

"No, and I don't think Price is either."

"Probably so, and until we hear something there's not much we can do except wait and rely on other law enforcement agencies to hopefully find Price." Pickens turned and walked toward Stacey. "Stacey, if you want this job full time, it's yours. But you'll have to start at eight-thirty. It's the best I can do because of Matt's situation, and Billy will have to arrange the shifts with the three of you. You want it?"

Stacey's blues eyes glowed, and her face lit up with a huge smile. "You bet I do. I already discussed it with my husband and my mom. They both said yes, and if it gets to be too much for my mom, there's always daycare."

"Then it's yours. Welcome back."

"Way to go, Stacey," yelled Billy. Amy smiled.

Pickens enjoyed the camaraderie amongst his team, but until Price was in custody the knot in his stomach would persist.

CHAPTER 48

Pickens took Marge and Sarah to Leroy's Friday evening for rib night. After greetings, Pickens called Leroy aside.

"You okay with fishing Sunday with my dad and me?"

"Sounds good to me. Is he gonna fish or just shoot the breeze?"

"Probably do both." They both laughed, and Pickens joined his girls while Leroy went into the kitchen.

After a rib dinner, Pickens and his family went home for a good evening of television followed by a good night's sleep.

Sunday morning, Pickens, his dad, and Leroy went fishing. Marge, Sarah, and Bailey visited Pickens' mother.

Two weeks passed since the BOLO and nothing had happened as of yet, and the case was going cold. Business at the Sheriff's Office was back to usual with no surprises. Sarah was back to going to school, Marge had her office back, but Pickens continued taking Bailey to work with him.

Pickens and Amy were in his office discussing the case.

"Think we could have done things differently, Amy? Like maybe I could have called for outside help sooner?"

"Maybe," Amy replied. "But considering that Price was right under our noses and knew almost everything we were doing, she would have bolted sooner. Don't second guess yourself, JD. We did our best, and it was what it was."

Pickens grinned. "Yeah, you're right, it was what it was."

The bodies of Tommy Benson and Rhonda Hicks were released to Rhonda's parents so they could have a proper burial. Eddie Hicks attended with his mother out of respect for his wife and best friend.

Ellison retrieved the remains of Irene Noristan, had her cremated and buried her ashes in his backyard garden where he could see her grave marker from his screened-in porch. Malcolm Price retrieved his truck from the impound and brought it home.

By the end of May, still nothing had been heard about Price-Strauss and Healey, so their files were marked as cold cases. Spring football, the high school prom, and graduation all went by without any glitches. Mrs. Gronfein returned home, and at the suggestion of Pickens she changed all the locks to her house. Pickens assigned a deputy to drive by her house once a day. Billy made a special trip on his way home in the evenings. Three nights during the week he had dinner with Mrs. Gronfein and surprised her on Memorial Day with a three-year-old Beagle adopted from the animal shelter. Ironically the dog's name was Lester, the same as her late husband.

Life was slowly getting back to normal in Creek City.

On the second Saturday in June, Pickens was dressing for the Growers' Festival. Marge was baking cupcakes for Sarah and Annie's birthday party the next day. Sarah and Bailey were in the backyard playing. When he walked into the kitchen, Marge's back was to him. She wore tight fitting jeans and a halter top that exposed her back and had on spiked heels. When she bent over to take the cupcakes out of the oven, Pickens had to take a step back and his eyeballs almost fell out of their sockets.

"Damn, wide receiver; you're gonna make a parade of men jealous today and some women angry because their husbands will be gawking you."

She straightened up and smiled. "That's my intent. Besides, I'll have the sheriff to protect me." She winked. "You'll protect me, won't you, Sheriff?" He glanced at the cupcakes cooling on the stove. She stepped in front of him to block his view. "Won't you, Sheriff," she repeated.

He nodded his head. "Absolutely, and I'll be the proudest fella in that parade."

Seven weeks earlier, after selling her car in Georgia to a sleazy used car lot owner for cash, Allyson Healey, with nothing but a mini-backpack, walked to the highway to thumb a ride. It wasn't long before a blue pickup truck slowed to a stop. The driver, Marti Kelsey, a woman in her early fifties with bright red hair and a pierced nostril, signaled for Ally to get in.

Allyson climbed into the truck and said, "Thanks for stopping."

"No problem," Marti replied. "I'm on my way up North, but I'm stopping at a restaurant in town for lunch. Care to join me?"

"Sure, why not."

Marti parked in front of Gwen's Diner, known for its Southern homestyle cooking. Lunchtime was over, the crowd had dispersed, and Marti and Ally were the only customers.

"Have a seat wherever you like, ladies, and I'll be right with you," said the waitress.

Allyson sat at a table by the window, and Marti sat across from her. When the waitress came over, Allyson ordered coffee and a house salad.

"That's it? You sure you don't want something more substantial?"

"No thanks."

"I'll have the same as she's having," said Marti.

"Suit yourself," replied the waitress and walked away.

The waitress brought their orders, set them down and walked away. Allyson took a sip of coffee and ate some salad. She rotated her cup in her hands and looked forlorn out the window.

Watching Allyson, Marti suspected that she was troubled.

"So, what should I call you?" Marti asked.

Allyson hesitated then replied, "Ally...Ally Grealey."

Marti figured that really wasn't her name but let it go without questioning it. "Where ya headed, Ally?"

"Nowhere," Ally replied without even glancing at Marti.

"So, where ya from?"

Ally continued staring out the window and responded with, "Nowhere."

Marti reached out and placed her hand on Ally's. "Okay, Ally Grealey, how about a ride to nowhere?"

Ally looked down at Marti's hand. "Sure, why the hell not."

They got up, Marti paid both checks, and they left.

During the drive, Ally was silent and continually stared out the window with despairing eyes fixed on nothing.

Marti glanced in the rearview mirror and then said, "I own a ten-room motel and a restaurant about two hours' drive from here. It ain't much, but I need a waitress and housekeeper. Breakfast and lunch are busy, but we don't serve dinner. Can't pay much, but you get free meals and a bed with company. If you're interested, job's yours, no questions asked." She waited for a reply then asked, "Interested?"

"Let me think about it."

CHAPTER 49

When Jerrold and Marion Brug returned from a five-month long vacation of traveling across the country in a rented motor home—with no access to television or newspapers—to celebrate their retirement, they decided to use the Labor Day weekend to air out their rustic lakeside log cabin in Central Alabama. They drove up on Friday and planned on spending time on the lake bass fishing and evenings on the porch relaxing and tossing back a couple of Kentucky Mules.

The quarter-mile dirt road through dense shrubbery and loblolly pines afforded privacy from the highway.

As they drove up to the cabin, Mrs. Brug noticed a gray car parked in front of the cabin.

"What's that car doing here? You didn't hire someone to clean the cabin did you, Jerry?"

"No, I have no idea who it belongs to."

"I told you we should have locked the cabin."

"Why, what's there to steal? Besides, if someone wanted to get in, they'd find a way." He pointed at the dashboard. "My pistol's in the glove compartment. Get it out just in case."

Mrs. Brug retrieved the gun. Mr. Brug parked, and both carefully approached the cabin with the pistol in his hand.

"Is that a Florida license plate?"

"Yeah, let's be careful." They carefully approached the door, turned the knob and the door opened.

"What's that smell?"

"Don't know but you best get behind me." He steadied his weapon and entered the cabin. "Damn, it's worse in here, and it looks like someone trashed the place."

Mrs. Brug yelled, "Don't go any farther, Jerry." She pointed. "Look up."

He saw the body dangling from the loft railing.

"Outside quick. We have to call 911." He dialed 911 and gave their location. "Go sit in the car and open a bottle of water. I don't want you to have to see that again and have to explain it to the authorities when they arrive. I'll handle it."

Within minutes, three Alabama State Troopers arrived, an ambulance and a crime scene investigation vehicle. The troopers took a statement from Mr. Brug and then searched the Camry. In the glove compartment was the registration, and when they opened the trunk they found the shotgun and boxes of shells.

The body was carefully lowered from the railing and searched for identification, but there was none. On the floor was an empty pill dispenser with the name Liesel Strauss on it—which matched the name on the registration. In a corner under an empty pizza box, they found a purse with Price's driver's license inside.

After questioning Mrs. Brug, the trooper learned that she was Strauss' aunt and the sister of Strauss' father. Liesel knew about the cabin because her parents took her there when she was a youngster.

One of the troopers went back to his vehicle and put Strauss and Price's names in his laptop. When he saw the BOLO for Price-Strauss, he radioed headquarters.

Pickens was in his office finalizing plans for the weekend. First up, was the high school football team's home opener, and he would be on the sidelines as an assistant coach. Saturday, the Pickens family would drive to Lake Grove to spend the day at Marge's parents, Sunday morning fishing with his dad and Leroy, then a fish fry for all three families at Leroy's home. Sleep late Sunday before setting up the tents and grills for the neighborhood block party. All he needed was for all forms of crime to take the weekend off.

His plans were abruptly interrupted when he received the call from the Alabama authorities that they had found his wanted person. According to the authorities, the only latent prints discovered in the car belonged to Price-Strauss, and the shotgun and its case were wiped clean. The same applied to the cabin except for those that belonged to the Brugs. It appeared that Price-Strauss subsisted on frozen pizzas, can goods, dried cereals and other products easily purchased at a convenience store. If she had a companion, there were no signs of another person. He was also told of the connection with Mrs. Brug.

Pickens called the mayor and advised him that the case was solved and the killer dead. Next, he called the county chairperson and told her the same. Then Pickens sat back in his chair with his feet propped up on his desk and breathed a sigh of relief. He kept only two major case files on his desk and grabbed the one marked Price-Strauss. With force as powerful as a gandy dancer driving a spike into a rail, he stamped it, 'Case Closed.' As to Healey's file— Pickens wrote 'Inactive' on it and tossed it in his out tray.

Pickens last call was to the reporter, Noseby, to give him a heads-up on the story.

Next, he got up and walked into the bullpen to address Amy and Billy.

"Tonight's the first home game if either of you are going, your welcome to join my girls and me for ribs after at Leroy's." He smiled. "Win or lose; I'm buying." His generosity caused puzzled expressions. "Price-Strauss is dead. She hung herself in Alabama."

Amy, Billy, and everyone else in the office raised their hands and shouted, "Touchdown." Pickens grinned.

After a victory celebration at Leroy's Bar-B-Que Pit, Pickens took his ladies home. He tucked Sarah in and then joined Marge to watch television before both retired to their bedroom.

"Ready for some wild sex, wide receiver?"

"Um, no."

He couldn't believe what she'd said. Was he having another nightmare or did she really refuse sex?

"You're not serious, are you?"

She pointed toward the doorway. "Yes, unless you want to corrupt Bailey's morals."

Pickens sat up straight. "It's okay, deputy, you're off duty. You can go relax in Sarah's room." Bailey barked twice meaning no. Pickens collapsed on the pillow. "Shit!"

"Watch your language, young man."

EPILOGUE

A week later, Ally Grealey stood behind the counter taking a break with a cup of coffee, puffing on a Virginia Slim, and reading the newspaper. Her hair was dyed bright red; she wore blue glasses and had both a pierced lower lip and a nostril.

A Georgia trooper walked in and sat down at the counter.

"I'll have a cup of coffee and some of that peach cobbler," he said.

"Sure thing, be right with you." Ally set her cigarette on the ash tray, got his coffee and peach cobbler and set them in front of the trooper.

"Anything else?"

He glanced at the page she was reading, and the article by a Florida reporter. "Hell, of a thing, that woman murdered four people in Florida, attempted to kill another, and then hung herself in Alabama." He ate some cobbler, took a sip of coffee and followed with, "What kind of person does that?"

"A psychopath," Ally responded without looking up.

He raised his cup. "Here's to her descent into hell."

"Where I hope she rots," Ally said and picked up her cigarette.

The trooper glanced at it. "You should give those things up."

Ally took a long drag, inhaled, crushed the butt in the ashtray, looked up and exhaled. "Maybe now I can."

AUTHOR'S COMMENTS

The events that took place in this book weren't part of an actual criminal case. They were derived from my imagination. Any resemblance to actual events, locales, or persons, living or dead is entirely coincidental.

I'm grateful for the numerous websites that gave me an enormous wealth of information making it easier to do research.

My thanks to those who anonymously provided information relevant to the sequence of events portrayed in this book.

A special thanks to Heather for taking me to task and making me a better writer.

Thank you for reading my book. I hope you enjoyed it and will recommend it to family and friends. If you feel like it, I'd appreciate a review on Amazon or a post on my website www.georgeencizo.com.

Made in the USA
Columbia, SC
25 September 2018